THE WITCHES OF AUBURN

BOOK TWO

The Sins of Our Fathers

HAZEL BLACK

Also by Hazel Black

THE WITCHES OF AUBURN SERIES

The Gifts of Our Mothers (Witches of Auburn, Book 1)

Gisel (Witches of Auburn 1.5) A Novella

THE WITCHES OF AUBURN
BOOK TWO

The Sins of Our Fathers

Brunswick House
New York

The Sins of Our Fathers
Copyright © 2017 by Hazel Black

Edited by:
Rhonda Helms

Copyediting by:
Ashley Williams, AW Editing

Interior Design & Formatting by:
Christine Borgford, Type A Formatting

Cover Design by:
Cover Design by James, GoOnWrite.com

Brunswick House Publishing
244 Madison Avenue
New York, NY 10016

First Brunswick House ebook and print on demand edition: October 2017

The Brunswick House name and logo are trademarks of Brunswick House Publishing, LLC.

The publisher is not responsible for websites (or their content) that are not owned by the publisher.

Manufactured in the United States of America

ISBN 978–1-943622–14–6 (ebook edition)

ISBN 978–1-943622–15–3 (print on demand edition)

To Vivian,
Carry on.

Prologue

THERE WAS NOTHING STRANGE ABOUT that late afternoon in May. No signs that would hint at the coming chaos. The skies over Southern New Jersey were bright and sunny. The gentle breeze carried a handful of clouds across the light blue canvas. It was why, when a tornado touched down, it took everyone by surprise. Tornadoes were rare in the area, as in there might have been one in the last sixty years.

The National Weather Center would later launch several investigations into what occurred that day. Rutgers University created a semester-long class to study the phenomenon that still cannot be completely explained. There are theories, of course. Well-thought-out explanations that, in part, addressed what happened in the county of Salem, but much of the results of the storm could not be explained because they were not initially associated with the path of destruction. The following are only a few of those that remain a mystery.

A field alive with a dense mix of wild flowers in Upper Pittsgrove Township turned gray and died within the first few hours following the storm. The blooms fell over. Long wilted stems littered the ground.

If people were able to remember, they would have expected a would-be-senior at Woodstown High School named Chrissy to arrive the first day of school, prepared to take on her role as captain of the cheerleading squad, but Chrissy didn't come to school ever again. It was as if she had never been there.

The entire left side of Borough Hall, which was built in 1928 near the center of Woodstown, crumbled. Reports indicated the collapse was due to a crack in the building's foundation, but the lack of damage to the rest of the structure was still unexplained.

If there'd been anyone immune to the craft, they would have remembered the original facts of the thirty-year old bus accident that broke the hearts of the nation. They would recognize the sudden discrepancies in the news reports, archived newspapers, and people's memories compared to the original facts of the horrific incident on I-95 in Maryland. The seven person death toll suddenly had an eighth casualty. The bus passengers were fourth grade students on their way home from a field trip to Gettysburg. Hector Villafane's name was added to the list of the deceased.

The day after the storm, Hector's mother was found dead of a broken heart.

The witches remembered. It was all a part of their storied past. Born to each coven were the only ones who would never forget a spell or the condition of the world before it was cast. Their recollection would persist with the beautiful magic in their blood.

WRATH

Ever

I FLEW HIGH OVER THE railroad tracks and Alloway Lake. Ike and I spent the last day before he left for school canoeing the lake. We'd laughed at how good it felt to be out in the sunlight, together, and not have to hide our relationship. We didn't speak of the curse that caused our parents' history, or the fact that he wouldn't be at Woodstown High School when my senior year began in a few weeks.

I turned west toward Cumberland County and dipped down closer to the woods on the other side of Upper Pittsgrove. The Dead Field was right below me. I banked left and flew in a large circle, taking in the area from above. I was sure it was the barren field below, but the patch of land beneath me was in ruins. I landed and grabbed a handful of soil, letting it trickle through my fingers. Remnants of stems and stalks covered the ground, but their dull gray color melded into the diseased land beneath them.

I need to see you. Ike's voice warmed me. I wasn't sure "need" described how I felt about him. It was scarily close to an obsession.

You just saw me last night.

Can you come back tonight?

I'd already spent too much time at Rowan University. Ike was exhausted from football and the heat. He fell asleep every time I was there, which I didn't mind, but he needed a good night's rest more than he needed to see me.

Why are you not answering yes?

I knew he was laughing at me.

The wind swirled around low to the ground, and I tilted my head, listening. Murmured chatter slipped on the tips of the breeze as it blew toward me from the other side of the field.

Shh. Someone is coming. I needed him to be quiet so I could concentrate and listen.

Who? Where are you?

I'm at the Dead Field thinking of you.

"I don't know what happened." The voice was across the field in front of me. I stayed safely invisible in my spot.

"It's finally displaying why it's called dead field. The arsenic caught up to the flowers."

The woman's short curly hair barely moved as she shook her head in dismay. She put her hands on her stout hips and stared at the ground. "That makes no sense. The tests said the soil make-up is the same. Why would things start dying now?"

"I don't know," the man said. "But the way it looks makes more sense than all those flowers blooming. It used to make me crazy. We couldn't build on the land or farm it, but those flowers taunted me every season."

"Only you could be taunted by a field full of wildflowers." The man took a step closer to the woman and kissed her neck. They were old enough to be my grandparents.

"You better behave."

Are they gone? I wish I could read your mind.

I rolled my eyes at Ike's impatience.

Just hold on a minute.

"Or what?"

"Or those flowers won't be the only thing taunting you," she teased and walked back the way she came with the man following close behind.

I stayed silent and invisible, still concentrating on the tainted soil that had somehow found a way to defeat the warrior flowers. The hair on my arms stood, my ears strained to pick up any miniscule sound, and a chill slipped across my chest. I wasn't alone, but this was Upper Pittsgrove. I shouldn't have had to worry.

Air whooshed by me, moving in the same direction the couple had gone.

Ruby. Where are you?

Why? Even though she answered, it was pretty clear she wasn't interested in talking.

I need your help in Upper Pittsgrove. I tried to sound nonchalant. No one even knew I was there, but the sense that something was about to happen crawled down the back of my throat and formed a lump that lodged there.

Are you okay? Because I kind of can't ask Sam to take his hand off my boob, tell him I'm a witch, and disappear to come find you . . . but I will if you need me to.

I'm fine. Not sure I can say the same for this couple that is with me.

Call Gwen. She's in Alloway helping her mother move their stuff to our house.

I followed the breeze past an ancient farmhouse abandoned in favor of a dated colonial on the edge of the property and then stopped and listened.

"What should we do to them? Electrocution? We haven't done that in a while." I could barely hear the voices and wasn't sure I was correctly making out what was being said. Electrocution? I moved again, slowly and barely impacting the air as I stayed focused on the voices around me.

"I can't find the peanut butter," the man inside the kitchen said.

"We are definitely not out of peanut butter," his wife answered from the bedroom. She was folding his undershirts with the windows opened wide.

"Well, I can't find it," he practically mumbled under his breath.

"Robbery? Double suicide?" The whispers came again. The cold, business-like way they discussed their afternoon activities in the presence of the victims was scarier than the ideas of what they might do. I was reminded of the cruel attack on my dog and the destroyed dress in my bedroom, which was child's play compared to what they were contemplating. The Virago didn't seek entertainment from the arts. They created havoc to combat their boredom.

"You are an idiot," the elderly woman called out to her husband. She dropped the shirt she had been folding onto her bed.

My heart raced in my chest. If she made it to the kitchen, I thought they'd both be killed. For what or in what way, I couldn't tell, but something dreadful was about to happen. I could feel it in my bones.

"Robbery. I'll go cut the phone line. We might be here for a while."

My spine straightened at the detached tone in the invisible voice. I crouched behind the corner of the house and waited for the air to divulge the witch's departure. The screen fell out of the bedroom window as the other one entered the house.

I followed the breeze to the pole by the street and circled around to the box.

"Who's there?" she said. There was no whispering this high in the air. "What do you want?"

"I could ask you the same?" I said over the pounding of my heart in my ears.

Ever, came Ike's voice in my head.

Not now.

I kept moving. Dodging what I assumed were her movements to determine exactly where I was located.

"Just enjoying the lovely afternoon. It's a shame you aren't going to be able to say the same." The air swept by a second before her arm was around my neck. "Your shadow betrays you." Her breath rushed across my ear as she said, "You're strong. Young." She twisted until the two of us were above the road.

"Stronger than you," I said and pried her arm off me. I held her wrist between both hands and used her as a counter weight as I swung us in the air. Like a figure skating pair, we soared in a circle with me leaning back, her arm firmly in my grasp. An eighteen-wheeler approached. I calculated the time until its arrival and on our last rotation, I released her and launched myself high into the air. She appeared, hit the truck between its headlights, and was thrown into the ditch on the side of the road.

The witch lay in the dirt, moaning, but she was alive. Her left leg was mangled. She grasped it before disappearing again. The tractor trailer pulled to the side of the road, and I flew back to the house and into the open window.

"What was that?" the woman yelled from the kitchen. She wasn't talking about the collision out front, though. The dresser drawers in her bedroom were being searched and slammed shut one by one.

I landed next to the dresser and closed the drawer that had just opened.

"What the—"

"Your friend needs you," I whispered to the invisible evil beside me. Her breath caught in jagged shock. "You'd better hurry. She ran into something trying to cut the phone line."

"Why, what is going on in here?" The woman surveyed her ransacked bedroom. I followed the breeze out the window and waited outside. "Dear Lord. Stanley, get in here. Someone tried to rob us."

"Maybe they took the peanut butter," he said, but as he came to a stop in the doorway, his mouth hung open at the sight of his bedroom. "Call 9–1-1."

"I was just in here," she said and dialed the phone next to their bed.

Ever!

I'm sorry. There's a lot going on here. There's been a robbery.

At your house?

No. I'm still in Upper Pittsgrove. The truck driver was searching the ditch and the fields on both sides of the street. He'd felt the impact but never saw what he'd hit. He turned back, inspected the front of his truck, climbed back into the cab, and drove off a moment before the police cruiser arrived at the couple's house.

I waited near the pole by the road, still invisible, and listened to the witches beside me.

"I think my leg is broken."

"How did you get hit by a truck?"

"I didn't get hit by it, some crazy witch threw me into it."

"Who was she?"

They couldn't feel me and had no idea I was there.

"Who knows? This whole area has been a yawn since that Auburn crew came back. It's like they're starting a movement or something."

"We have to get you out of here."

"I can't fly."

"Stay here. I'll fly home and get the car."

"Pathetic," she whispered under her breath.

I waited until she was loaded into the car and driven away. The couple thanked the trooper for coming and walked him outside. They discussed deadbolts and window locks and the alarm system they were going to have installed. Once I was sure the couple was safe, I flew home to find my mother and Ike waiting for me in the kitchen.

"I'm okay," I responded to both their aggressive stances and wide-eyed glares. "I swear. It was just a little issue."

"What happened? Exactly?" my mother asked. Ike seemed happy to let her be the interrogator.

"I was out flying and looking around. I landed in a field by this older couple's house."

"What older couple?"

"I have no idea who they are." My mother exhaled her frustration with the situation. "I was about to leave, but then felt two witches pass me, so I followed them. When I heard what they were planning to do, I had to step in."

"How did you know they were witches?"

"They were invisible. I knew they were evil by the things they were saying."

"Like what?"

I hesitated to weigh my possible answers. The situation had to have been significant enough to warrant me ignoring Ike's calls in my head but not dangerous to me personally, or else they'd both drive me crazy. Together and individually. "I thought they were going to rob them." My mother's head tilted to the side as if she didn't believe me. "Or maybe worse."

"Ever!" they both yelled at the same time.

"What did you want me to do? They seemed like a sweet old couple! I wasn't going to let something happen to them."

"Call me. Always, first, before you do anything else, call your mother."

I exhaled loudly, letting them both witness my depleting patience with this conversation. I may not have called my mom, but I called Ruby, which had to count for something. I wasn't about to bring her into this, though.

"I will. Next time. I promise."

"Where were you?"

"In Upper Pittsgrove. Right next to the field they call Dead Field."

My mother was lost in thought as she placed the location. "Off Friendship Road?"

"That's the one," Ike answered. I wasn't sure of the road exactly. I didn't travel via road names.

"But how is that possible? The Virago is not allowed in Upper Pittsgrove."

"I don't know, but they were there. One of them has a bum leg now." Her eyes widened until I thought they might pop out of her head.

"And how exactly did that happen?"

"She had a run-in with a tractor trailer." I got looks of incredulity from them both. "What? They were going to kill them. I couldn't let that happen." Her head fell back and her gaze focused on the ceiling as she squeezed her forehead between her thumb and middle finger.

"What's going on?" Ike's mother asked as she walked in the back door carrying a milk crate filled with random items and a hair dryer on top.

"Ever interrupted a crime in Upper Pittsgrove."

"Oh." Gisel turned her full attention to me. I wanted to somehow sneak upstairs with Ike and avoid this entire conversation.

"The criminals were invisible women who mentioned us."

"Really?" I didn't think her attention could increase, but yes, it could. "What did you do?"

"They separated, so I threw one of them into a truck and then told the other one to go help her."

Gisel's mouth hung open a little. "You talked to them?"

"As little as possible. They didn't see me."

Gisel handed my mother the crate and took the hair dryer from the top.

"We're not done talking about his," my mother said and followed Gisel up the stairs.

"She's right," Ike said. "We're not done. You cannot get into fights with the Virago." He moved closer to me and stared down. My eye contact never faltered. "You were outnumbered. No one knew where you were." I wrapped my arms around his neck. "You shushed me." I stood on my tiptoes and kissed his neck. "I'm serious, Ever. You have to be more careful."

"I promise."

"I don't believe you."

I kissed him again in a way that finished his argument.

I
T WASN'T AS IF HE hadn't already been away. Ike reported to training camp in the middle of August, but today, the reality hit me that when I walked into Woodstown High School tomorrow, he would not be there. Reality was cruel just about all of the time.

He kept going over all the reasons we should be thankful. He wasn't that far away. Rowan University was a half hour drive and even shorter flight. Our families, at least mine and his mother and Gwen, literally lived together. It would be easy to stay in contact and see each other. We could talk in our heads was his final and most compelling reason why this should be an easy transition.

Talk, I did. Every morning, I'd speak to him before I even opened my eyes. I couldn't remember a time when I was able to get enough of him, when I didn't yearn to be close to him. Ruby would watch us as if we were set to implode if a spark came too close.

"He just seems to consume you. That isn't good," she'd say and smile as if she weren't alluding to the unhealthy nature of my relationship. If she were a "normal" friend, I would have thought she was jealous or fearful she'd be replaced, but with the four of us on top of each other in our attic, that would be impossible.

I knew Ruby loved me as much as Ike did. The sense of urgency that consumed me regarding him hit her, too. She was a part of me, and because of that, she worried that I'd be hurt, but my only nightmare was something happening to Ike. I didn't argue with Ruby because Ike did consume me and I had zero concerns about it compared to her.

I turned away from Ruby, inspecting Gwen's corner of the room, which was almost fully set up. A fourth twin bed was moved in as the love seat floated down the stairs from our room to Lovie's since it was the only one big enough to hold an additional piece of furniture. The four of us followed it down and found Lovie rearranging her dresser and vanity.

"It's only for a little while. In less than a year, you'll all be off to college," Lovie said as she moved a throw from the end of her bed and positioned it on the back of the couch.

"That's crazy!" Gwen squealed. "I can't wait to get out of this town." I was no longer sure how I felt. Since Ike was gone but not far away, staying around seemed like a great option. Plus, I was beginning to love Auburn. The tiny town perched on the hill. "I've been going to this same school since kindergarten."

"No you haven't," Ruby argued.

"Well, not the same building, but with some of the same people. Scott Adams sat by me in kindergarten. We have all been together forever." We followed her up the stairs, each with a box of her belongings from the second-floor landing. "We couldn't wait for the sending districts to come to high school with us. A little fresh blood to mix things up."

"Oh, that we did."

Gwen turned to the three of us. "You sure did. You can put the boxes down at the end of my bed." We stayed watching her as she unpacked. "Is this too much? I mean, you already have three people in this room."

"Three witches," Maya corrected. "And we will always have room for you."

"I was torn," Gwen rambled on. "I didn't want to leave my dad or my house, but I wanted to be here with you guys. My mom convinced me to come."

"I think, especially based on everything that's been going on with the Virago, that you should be here," I said. I hated to even say their name when we were enjoying ourselves, but Auburn was the only place I felt completely safe. Everywhere else, including her old house, I had my guard up.

I left them unpacking. There was more talking and laughing than actual productivity, which made it harder to leave than it should have been. Still, I wanted to see Ike, who would probably be hungry by the time I got to Rowan.

No surprise, he was sitting on a bench outside his dorm eating a sandwich. I leaned over and kissed him before sitting next to him. His backpack was on the ground. His lanyard hung from the top of it.

"That was quick," he said and took another bite. I sat beside him. "I think your flying is getting even faster. We should race sometime."

"How would we do that?"

"I'd ride my bike. See how fast you are against the rocket." He bounced his eyebrows at me.

"I'd be so worried about you dropping it and killing yourself that I wouldn't be able to properly beat you."

Ike stared at me until heat rose to my cheeks. "I'd take the beating." He wrapped the rest of his sandwich and put it in his bag.

"Keep eating."

"I can eat anytime. Now, I want to be with you." He put the lanyard over his head and stood.

"I'm jealous school has already started for you. You have a routine to keep you busy."

"Well, after tomorrow, you will, too." He led me toward his dorm.

I shook my head. "It isn't going to be the same without you."

"Maybe it will be better."

I stopped walking. "You being gone is not going to make anything better."

Ike turned and examined me. He looked me up and down as if he were deciding how much he would say. I hated the hesitation from him. "Are you sure this is all because of me?"

I had no idea what he was talking about. "*What* is all because of you?"

"You told me you're not sleeping, having nightmares, your dad has been coming up a lot . . . maybe you're on edge because the last person you loved who left you never came back."

I hadn't equated the two, and I wasn't about to start. Even though it was exactly what my tortured dreams predicted in the dead of night, I knew Ike wasn't going to die. To admit Ike was right would mean I created all of this in my mind. I couldn't be that cruel to myself. "I don't think so."

Ike pulled me against his chest. I let my arms hang at my side as he enveloped me with his warmth and security and love. "Did your father ever talk to you about why you never dream?"

"He talked to me about all of it. My powers were our 'only family secret' as he called them. He always made a game out of not letting anyone know how special my mother and I were, but he wanted me to tell him every detail I could comprehend about how things worked in witchcraft."

"Kind of like me?"

I was feeding into his theory, and I hated it. "I love you," I said to throw him.

He laughed, knowing exactly what I was doing. "Oh, Ever, you are a conniving witch."

"I'm your cross to bear."

Ike and I walked into his dorm and hit the stairs. He said hi to a few other students as we passed them. One practically dove on top of him as he was unlocking his room door. Ike had already settled into Rowan. He belonged there, but then again, I couldn't imagine a place he wouldn't perfectly fit in. Even in a house full of witches.

"How's my mom?" he asked.

"Haven't you talked to her?"

"Yes, but she seems almost giddy." He threw his backpack on the chair by his desk. "Like she's been sucking helium or drinking too much coffee."

Ike's mom had been floating around our house in Auburn for weeks. She'd even been happy to take the bedroom that we all had to trounce through to get to the attic. We almost offered the idea that we could go in through the attic window and not wake her, but Ruby squashed that before the thought left our mouths. No need for them to know about our "non-emergency exit."

"I think she's happy. I can't imagine how lonely she was the last twenty years."

"She wasn't alone, you know?" Ike feigned insult.

"By a witch's standard, she was. Her wedding. Two babies. All of that she did without her coven and without her powers." I crossed my arms at my chest. "I can't imagine."

Ike tackled me onto his bed and yanked me up like a blanket toward his pillow. Protesting was out of the question. I was rendered speechless as soon as his lips touched my neck. "Have you thought about Rowan for next year?"

"I keep trying to get my boyfriend to give me a tour of the campus, but the only place he'll show me is the inside of his bedroom."

He leaned back. "It sounds like he's trying to have sex with you."

"I know." I lifted my head toward him and kissed him before dropping back down to the pillow.

He stayed still above me. "Maybe if you gave in, he could concentrate on something, *anything*, else."

"Maybe I don't want him to focus on anything else."

III

AP ENGLISH. THIS WAS GOING to be a long year. I was starting to see the brilliance of stopping language arts classes once you had mastered reading. My schedule should be filled with science with a little bit of math mixed in to keep the day moving.

I dragged myself from English, down the hall, and up the side stairwell to modern media. The syllabus was sitting on my desk when I walked into the room. It was seven pages long and stapled on the wrong side. This class was painful, and I hadn't even sat yet. The thought of turning around and walking back out shot through my mind.

Instead of leaving, I chose a seat against the far wall three-quarters of the way back from the front. I was sure there was some logic behind the decision, but I didn't evaluate it. I just sat away from everyone else. Maya was right. This first day was infinitely better than last year's. Gone was the challenge of locating the cafeteria and remembering all my teachers' names. Everyone knew everyone else here. Their names were as common as streets we drove on. As few in number, too.

Billy walked into the room, and without seeming to even notice me, he took the seat to my right. He'd been two rows in front of me for AP English. Before that, I hadn't seen him since last June. He hadn't gone to prom. The note he left me was never mentioned, but the look on his face the Monday after prom made it clear he'd sent it. He'd been in my room, or at least near my journal, which I rarely took outside, let alone out of Auburn. I'd racked my brain for the opportunities he'd had to rip the sheet of paper from it.

I'd taken the journal to the shore when we'd first moved to Auburn, and it went with me to Marlton Park one day when we'd taken Carl there. Carl had tired himself out and lay next to me on a blanket. I could have fallen asleep, but I hadn't. I was sure of it, and there was no time when I didn't have a view of the blanket or someone else wasn't sitting on it.

Mr. Frank stumbled through a lengthy introduction. He was new this year. Hired to teach, The Impact of Social Media and Cable News on Society and Government, but the course title had been reduced to Modern Media. He rolled his eyes when he said it as if the shortened title was not agreed to by him.

Billy stretched his legs out from under the desktop hooked to his chair. He didn't say hello or any other smart comment. His quiet withdrawal from the spotlight put me more on edge than his usual command of the room. He took out a notebook and pen and laid them both on top of his desk. He manipulated the pen back and forth between his fingers, which drew my eyes to a purple scar on back of his hand. It was almost a perfect circle. As he twisted his hand, two more matching scars closer to his palm came into view.

I wrung my own palms together. History and Billy's demeanor told me they weren't from falling off his bike. Mr. Frank stood at the front of the room, discussing news outlets, print magazines, and social media, but I couldn't keep my mind off Billy's hands. He never looked my way and barely took a note. He was lost some-where that didn't include modern media.

How's school?

Good. Ike would have only known Billy two years more than me because Ike came from a sending district, too. Billy grew up in town, but I asked anyway. *What are Billy Roberts's parents like?*

Is he bothering you?

No. In fact, he's sitting next to me in modern media and hasn't looked my way once.

At least he's listening. I paid him a visit before I left for training camp.

Why didn't you tell me? Annoyed, I sat back in my chair.

Because it was between me and Billy.

No it wasn't.

Ever, leave it alone.

"Casting a spell?" Billy asked, and his question threw me. I left Ike alone in my mind and turned toward Billy. My reaction was controlled. It was the lesson I'd learned from Billy. That and how to disarm the enemy.

"What's your mother like?" I'd never heard a word about her. She hadn't been to the school for any events.

Billy stopped moving and stared at me until his glare began to actually hurt me. I shouldn't have asked. "Dead," he said just as class was dismissed.

"I'm sorry. My father died when I was ten," I offered. Billy may have been more of a tortured soul than evil.

"I know." I packed my things and avoided eye contact with Billy until he said, "Ayars is an unusual name. What was your father's first name?"

Some protective instinct rose up inside me. I didn't want to tell him, but that would cause suspicion where there was no reason for any. My father's name could easily be found on the internet. "Owen," I said and left Billy standing by our seats in the classroom.

At the end of the day, I went right to the source for information. I stopped by the office, which was unusually calm for the first day of school. If I asked my mother and she didn't know, she'd call her old friend Trish. My mom wasn't there, and if I waited for her to ask, I would probably get the edited version of whatever Trish said.

"Hey, Ever." Trisha looked up when she heard the door close behind me.

I held papers in my hand that would give anyone who saw me the impression they were the subject of my visit, but when Trish walked up to the counter I laid them down without referencing them. I lowered my voice and asked, "Can I ask you about someone?"

Trish mirrored my demeanor. "Sure." She leaned on her forearm.

"What is Billy Roberts's family life like?"

"Why?" she asked, and it was more of a clue than her blurting out everything she knew. Billy's story was to be protected by the administration. It must have been worse than I thought.

"I noticed some scars on his hands." I lowered my voice a bit more. "Last year, he had a cut above his eye."

Trish reached out and touched my hands. "Billy lives with his uncle. I'll check into his hands. There have been reports before." Trish squeezed my hands tighter. "Thank you for bringing it to my attention."

"My mother and her friends don't know him. Is his family from around here?"

Trish smiled just a little, as if the secret that everyone around this place knew each other was between the two of us. "They know him." She let go of my hands and whispered, "Search James and Rebecca Callahan."

Principal Jeffries walked out of his office and smiled at me.

I gathered my papers off the counter. "Thank you."

"You're welcome. See you tomorrow."

I walked across West Avenue and down toward Auburn Road. Before the intersection, I followed the train tracks into the trees, disappeared, and launched into the sky. The clouds darkened as I flew toward Auburn, and the first drops of rain fell as I landed on the other side of the tree line behind our house.

The kitchen was packed. With eight witches residing in one house, every room was always full. Lovie was busy rolling ham and cheese in dough squares on the counter by the sink as Ruby, Maya, and Gwen ate apple slices and cookie batter.

"You're back," Lovie said, her shoulders falling a little. They couldn't keep us from flying, but no one relaxed when one of us was out.

"I am." I dropped my backpack on the floor and greeted Carl, who was patiently waiting for my attention. The dog still had a slight limp after his attack at Marlton Park the year before. "Come here, boy," I said, and he almost knocked me down with his love. I let him jump up, even though that went against all his training. It was hard to resist him since he made every person just want to lay down and cuddle with him.

"Want some apple slices?" Maya asked.

"Better hurry," Ruby said and threw another slice in her mouth.

"No. Thanks." I turned my attention to Lovie. "Do you remember Rebecca or James Callahan?"

Lovie placed a dough creation on the cookie sheet with the other rolls she'd already completed. Her movements slowed, and she seemed to pick her words carefully. "Yes." She washed her hands and grabbed the towel while I waited for her to elaborate. "Jimmy was a few years ahead of us in school, but I'm not sure about Rebecca."

"Do you know what happened to them?" I asked. Gwen and

Maya kept chatting and eating, but Ruby was acutely aware of my conversation.

"No. I never heard."

I turned on the computer and waited for the home screen to come up. The hum of the kitchen returned as I typed the names into the search engine, but only literary characters, mixed names, and references to a brother and sister duo in England came up. I added Salem County, New Jersey, to the box, and the results changed dramatically.

Twenty-two-year-old Rebecca Callahan (formerly Rebecca Lane from Alloway, New Jersey) was shot to death in her home in Pilesgrove, New Jersey . . . Twenty-four-year-old James Callahan, Rebecca Callahan's husband, was arrested and charged with her death. He pled guilty to second-degree murder and was sentenced to twenty-six years in prison.

The couple had an infant son, who was placed in the temporary care of James Callahan's brother and his wife, Stanley and Jean Callahan.

I sat back in the chair and read the words on the screen again.

Lovie was mixing a concoction that smelled like vinegar, mayonnaise, and pickles. She walked over behind me, still stirring the pungent dressing as she read.

I waited for her input or her reaction to the horrifying story that was Billy's history.

"I knew Rebecca Lane," she said and kept reading. "She was lovely. Graduated with us." Lovie cried in such a way I felt it more than I heard her. "That's horrible."

"Her son is in my English class. He sits right next to me."

"He is?" She looked at me hopeful.

"Yes, but he isn't lovely."

IV

HALF THE CLASS WAS LOOKING at their phones under their desks. The other half was sitting and pretending to listen as Mr. Frank lectured us on society's use of social media.

"Someday, there will be a study done on the impact of all this connectedness." I stared straight ahead and focused on his words. Maybe if I listened, I wouldn't have to study. "How the evil of mankind is planted, cultivated, and spread through the world." Mr. Frank was dark.

I leaned to the side in my chair and took in my classmates. Mick was in the second row, a pack of Skittles sticking out of his pocket. He and Maya were still going strong. Although for them, that meant they spent Sunday afternoons fishing and then cooking dinner together. They'd somehow morphed into a forty-year-old married couple over the summer.

Billy was turned in his seat until his back was to me. His shoulders had broadened since the year before. He'd grown a few more inches, too. He no longer had the lean form of a soccer player. He was becoming a man—albeit a cold and distant one.

Billy barely looked up from the blank sheet of paper in front of him. No drawings, no doodles, no notes. He was sitting in the room but gone in his mind. The possibilities of where his thoughts wandered left me just as cold as he seemed. Billy needed a hug and a stern lecture all at the same time. He needed guidance and parameters, and judging by the way he stared off into the distance, he also needed a friend.

As if he could feel my eyes fixed on him, he swiveled in his seat, ripped out a piece of paper from his notebook, and began to write on it.

"Social media began as something, well, social," Mr. Frank kept speaking. "It was baby pictures, vacations, and nights out. Now it has become a political firestorm and nonconventional media outlet. Those are the two aspects of social media we're going to talk about this marking period."

Billy's hand swept across my desk, leaving the paper in its wake. His body tilted toward Mr. Frank again without ever having taken his attention away.

The last note I got from Billy was unwanted and nearly ruined the prom. I didn't want this one, either. Still, I laid my palm flat on top of it. The note was in my possession, so I might as well read it.

I pulled the packet of papers Mr. Frank had handed out at the beginning of class back toward my body with the note on top of it. I let it fall open and lay flat.

"I think we can be friends," it read.

Ike's warning to stay away from Billy was the only thing locked in my head as I read it. I didn't need Ike's direction. Billy repelled me, but the loneliness in his note struck me. He'd quit the soccer team at the end of last year. I'd overheard someone saying to him that he'd played since second grade and asking why he'd quit. Billy shrugged and walked away. The topic of soccer garnered no more attention than any of the subjects we sat through together in school. His quitting of the team, the bruises, and his complete disconnect from the student body this year made me think Billy was sinking into a new hole. One that he was no longer able to lift himself out of.

He glanced back over his shoulder at me. The papers were tilted toward my body still. I had no response in writing to give him. I should have had no response at all, but I smiled. It was one of those sorrowful gestures I always found myself giving to Maya whenever she spoke of her father. She'd entered year two without him and the sad smile still came out quite often.

"Your assignment for this week is to follow Fox News, MSNBC, CNN, and *Time* Magazine on your choice of outlets. You can use Facebook, Instagram, Snapchat, or just choose to receive notifications from their apps on your phone. It's all explained on page five of your packets."

A collective groan rolled through the room. Hadn't he said himself that social media was a personal thing. Yet, he was going to dictate what we followed for the purposes of school. High school could ruin anything.

The bell rang. I gathered my things into a neat pile on top of my desk.

"Ever and Billy, I'd like you to stay after class."

It wasn't Mr. Frank's request that caused the sinking feeling of fear to hold me in my seat. It was the terrified and small demeanor Billy had sunk into. I didn't think he could afford a call home from a teacher. I imagined the ramifications to be quite different in his house than in my own.

We both stayed in our seats as the other students filed out. Mr.

Frank came and stood between our chairs and the row in front of us. "While I appreciate the ancient art of note passing in class, it is not allowed in this one," he said.

Billy and I stayed similarly disengaged from his speech.

"This is a class about the modern media's impact on our society. It is about engagement and interactions both personally and with new access to our world leaders." I kept my sight fixed on him, hoping to feign interest. "Corporations have never had this type of access to buyers. Politicians are now able to connect with voters in a way that was unimaginable years ago."

What was he getting at? My neck was starting to hurt from the strain of paying attention. If Billy had held out his hand, I might have grabbed it and run out of the building with him.

"I need you both to pay attention." Ah. There it was. "There are juniors in this class and one sophomore." He rolled his eyes, making it clear he didn't feel Chris Nixon should have been allowed to take his class at such a young age. "Give me the note."

Billy was staring at me when he asked. His gaze formed into a plea not to let Mr. Frank see it, but it wasn't evidence of anything that could get us in trouble. He wanted to be friends. Billy's hands fisted at his sides. His white knuckles pressed against the sides of his legs. I thought he was going to cry and then hurt himself. Vulnerability was more punishable than a drug arrest or a drunk driving accident for Billy.

The folded filler paper was still on top of my folder in my arms. I closed my eyes for a second and removed the ink from it. Without a word, I handed the paper to Mr. Frank.

"You're both dismissed," he said.

I slipped my things into my backpack and stood to escape. Billy followed my lead. We were just about to the door, when Mr. Frank held up the paper and asked, "This is it?"

Billy looked at me. I shrugged as if my participation in this entire exchange was confusing to me. Parts of it were. Billy's eyes softened when he saw the paper. I left him in the room with Mr. Frank. He could answer any of our teacher's other questions. I'd already been involved more than I wanted to be.

"Ever," Billy called out as he ran after me.

"I'm going to be late." The hallway around us was empty. "I'm already late."

"I know." He grabbed my backpack, stopping me. Billy's lack of respect for my body or the space around it ignited an old instinct with him. I stared at his hand until he returned it to the side of his body. "I need to talk to you alone. We need to meet in private."

"No, we don't."

"Yes." He leaned down until we were staring into each other's eyes. "You can do things I know about. That paper had writing on it."

"What writing?" I lifted my eyebrows. I was more relaxed with Billy than I'd been the year before. My fear of him was dissipating and being replaced by a mix of emotions that together were more kind.

"Meet me at Stoners Lane on Thursday."

"I don't know what Stoners Lane is." I began to walk toward AP Calc. I'd never been late for a class before, and I didn't want to start.

"It's near your house. Before Seven Stars. Do you know where that is?" Everyone knew of the historic house on the corner at the four-way stop intersection. "After the field, Stoners Lane leads into the woods. Just follow it back until you get to the clearing. I'll be waiting for you there."

"For what? The last time I ran into you in the woods didn't end well. I think I'll pass on round two."

Billy's gaze dropped to the ground between us. "I'm sorry. I don't know what else to say about that." His desperation was swaying me. "We need to talk." He needed to talk to someone. Not me.

"No. We don't."

"We do if you want me to keep your secrets."

I took one step back and centered myself. "I don't have any secrets, but I'll meet you at Stoners Lane."

He exhaled, and his shoulders relaxed. My attendance on Thursday meant a great deal to Billy. Even more than me being his friend, I thought.

When I got home, I cuddled next to Carl and flipped through my journal until I got to the page that had been ripped out by Billy. I'd slipped it back where it had been torn from. I hadn't returned the words I'd erased. The pages before it were covered in drawings of birds flying and a poem about one disappearing. When Billy had taken it, he'd seen them, too. I flipped through all the pages to see what else he might have found, but there were only random drawings. Some with Ike's name incorporated. Some of Ike himself. I'd never even shown him, but Billy had seen them, I was sure.

I concentrated on the paper until I could almost see his handwriting there again.

I meant it when I said you were perfect.
I *let* your boyfriend hit me to see how strong he is.
You'll be the first to know when I hit back.

I'd take Maya, Gwen, and Ruby with me to meet Billy.

I wasn't willing to wait for Billy to show his hand. The next day after school, I followed him home.

Ike would kill me for being in Billy's house, so I didn't mention it, which wasn't lying, so much as withholding information. I disappeared after school and flew high over top of Billy's car. He pulled into the driveway on the other side of the lake. The lawn was mowed. The shutters had been recently painted a bright blue, and the whole outside of the house looked well kept. I followed Billy from his car through the backdoor.

The tended to nature of the yard was lost inside the walls of Billy's house. A faint putrid smell lingered about the room. At first, I wondered if it was Billy, but his movements only stirred it up. Dirty dishes overflowed from the sink. The top plate had a bright yellow crust stuck to it reminiscent of eggs. There were two gnats trapped in the mess. The floor was sticky, and I could hear the suction of Billy's shoes every time he took a step. I floated six inches above it to avoid the issue.

Through the doorway was a hall I presumed led to the bed-rooms. A hole about the size of a fist decorated the drywall, and there was no telling how long it had been there. The wallpaper shredded around it. The pieces were curled and browned at the edges. Nothing, not even the damage, looked fresh in Billy's home.

He opened the refrigerator door, but there was nothing inside but a small container of milk and a half full bottle of ketchup. Billy sighed before closing it. I started to think we could be friends. He obviously needed one. A friend, and so much more, judging from his living conditions.

My stance regarding whether there was any good in Billy began to shift. He checked his phone, smirked, and tossed it on the kitchen table. He found a can of cat food under the sink, took a dirty bowl from the pile under the faucet, and emptied the can into it. There was no sign of a pet of any kind in the kitchen. I leaned back to peer into the laundry room. No litter box in there, either.

Billy took the bowl and grabbed a box filled with random con-tents from the shelf in the corner. A spool of twine, scissors, and a hammer all stuck out from the top. He went out the back door. I slipped through before the screen hit the jamb. I leaned against the back of the house waiting to hear the name of Billy's cat.

"Here, kitty, kitty," he said and placed the bowl of food in the center of the walk that carved Billy's backyard in half. Billy came and sat on the back patio. He lit a cigarette and blew smoke into the air. I could have appeared and rung the doorbell. His loneliness was infecting me. A meow rang out before a yellow tabby cat came into view.

Billy smiled and melted me more to his situation. The cat was cautious, looking around before dipping its head toward the bowl and smelling the food that Billy had left out. I wondered how many days this cat came to eat at Billy's. He had a white collar around his neck, but I couldn't read the name on it. I tilted my head and focused, trying to decipher the letters as I waited for Billy to say the name.

Bang!

The cat fell to the side screeching and pawing at his eye.

I spun and glared at Billy, who was laughing as he lowered the BB gun. Before I could decide what to do, he traded the BB gun for a hammer and lunged toward the cat. He held it high above his head and dropped it onto the cat's skull. The screeching stopped.

I could not breathe. I clawed at my chest and turned my head from Billy as tiny gasps of air fed me enough to launch into the sky. In the air, I could inhale. The cat didn't move. Its body lay still in a small puddle of blood beneath it.

Billy came back to the porch and collected the box he'd brought outside with him. My stomach churned. I was going to throw up. He whistled as he strolled out to the animal, and I launched farther into the air high above his house. I couldn't look down. My heart couldn't take what he might do next. I flew straight to Rowan. I needed Ike.

I sat on the bench outside his dorm for an hour before he walked up the sidewalk path. His pace quickened when he noticed me, but his smile melted as he saw my face.

"What's wrong?" he asked before I threw myself into his arms. He held me tight against him. "Ever, what happened?"

I couldn't speak. The words describing what I'd seen wouldn't form in my mind. I shook my head back and forth against his chest. "You're scaring me." He pulled away and held my face in his hands. Ike leaned down and with an incredibly gentle voice, especially for him, he said, "Tell me."

"Billy Roberts is not a nice person."

The muscles in his jaw tightened. "Did he come near you?" He reached down and grabbed me by the arms. When I didn't answer he shook me. "Ever, what did he do?"

"Nothing to me. He didn't even know I was there." Ike exhaled and loosened his grip, but his attention didn't falter. "I just watched him murder a cat."

"What?"

"I know. It was awful. He lured it to his yard and then . . ."

"What were you doing in his yard?"

"I don't know." I started to cry. I hated the feeling of somehow being in trouble, but the repulsion I felt at Billy was burying all of that. "I felt bad for him. Did you know his dad killed his mom?"

"No."

"He lives with his uncle, who I think hurts him."

Ike shook me by the arms again. I stopped talking about Billy and focused on my boyfriend. "Do not go anywhere near him again. He's a sick f—"

"Ike." I should have said he needs help or that it wasn't his fault, but I couldn't shake the image of the cat sniffing the food from my mind. And the hammer.

Ike wrapped his arms tight around my shoulders. He pulled me close to him and kissed the side of my head until I felt myself exhale. I needed Ike to be careful. I had to know he was safe.

"Do you remember the note that was in Gwen's purse before the prom?"

Ike didn't release his grip on me. He kept me close as he

answered, "Yes."

"It wasn't blank."

"I saw it."

I stepped back from him having to face him with my lie. "It wasn't blank when I originally read it. I removed the ink."

"Why would you do that?"

"Because after everything we'd been through, I just wanted us to have a normal night. Just you and me at the prom. Nothing evil or murderous hanging over our heads."

The power of the lost words took hold of him. He grasped the nature of the message by my willingness to keep it a secret. "What did it say?"

"It said, 'I meant it when I said you were perfect.'" I steadied myself before the next line. "And, 'I *let* your boyfriend hit me to see how strong he is.'"

"That—" Ike shook his head. "How did he get the note in Gwen's purse?"

"I don't know."

Ike stopped thinking and stared at me. "Was that it?"

"No. It also said, 'You'll be the first to know when I hit back.'"

He exhaled loudly. "He's sick, but he knows better than to mess with me. It's you I don't like anywhere near him. I wish he'd just hurry up and rob a gas station so he ends up in jail like we all know he's going to. Just get it over with so I can relax with you in that school without me."

"I have my coven . . . and my mom's."

"Ever, I'm serious. Stay away from him. I can't be there every day."

"Which is the real problem." I pulled him close to me and wrapped my hands around the back of him. I wanted to forget about Billy. At least for a few minutes. "When is fall break? I want you to come home."

He lifted my chin until I faced him. "Is it really so bad? I'm not that far away."

"No. It isn't so bad. I just need you."

Ike held me tight and rested his chin on the top of my head. We fit together perfectly. "Just stay busy, and the time will fly by."

I closed my eyes in the security of my boyfriend's arms. "With eight women living in my house, that shouldn't be a problem."

"How do you fit in there? The six of you with my mom and Gwen?"

"It's like I never lived there without them." They melded into the family without a hint that twenty years had been between them. "How's your dad?"

"Lonely, I think." I held Ike's hand. I knew how his dad felt. "I think he misses Gwen and me more than my mom, or maybe he just misses not being alone. They got married so young."

"When my father died, my mother was sad for years. I hadn't known until recently that it was more than just his death, but she still missed him."

"Has she ever been with anyone else?"

"I don't think so. I've never even heard of another person except your father."

"The way he looks at your mom creeps me out."

"I know. It's like they're still in pain just from standing near each other." I stood on my tiptoes and kissed Ike's lips. "Your mother, on the other hand, seems fine."

He shook his head as if his mom exhausted him. "She's always fine."

"I have to go."

"No." His arms tightened around me again. "Stay for dinner." He kissed me right near my ear and whispered, "Stay the night."

My knees buckled, and Ike caught me with an arm around my waist. "I can't. I have to go home for dinner. House rules, and school just started. I don't want to mess things up already and I need to hug my dog."

"When are you sleeping over?"

I laughed. "I don't know."

"You don't think your mom still hates me, do you?"

"No. It's just normal mother-daughter stuff now. I think."

He kissed me again. It would have to hold me over until the next time I got to see him. "Be careful going home. Let me know as soon as you get there."

"I will."

"I love you, Ever."

"I know." I walked toward the parking lot and disappeared on the third floor of the garage before taking off into the air. Nothing could heal me like Ike.

"MOM, CAN I SLEEP IN Ike's dorm with him tonight?"

Solid.

Nothing.

Not even a blink of the eye. My mother had missed her calling as an interrogator of some kind.

"I know it's asking a lot." I really wasn't sure what to say. I wasn't technically an adult. I could tell her how much I loved him, but she'd already heard that a hundred times.

"I know I can't control who you see or where you are every minute of the day," she said. I stayed silent on my spot on the edge of her bed. "And I know you two love each other."

"But?"

"But I want him to be able to experience college for himself, and I don't want you to miss out on your senior year. There are a lot of adventures you'll have this year that will never occur again, and they're all with Gwen and Ruby and Maya. If you spend every weekend at Rowan, I'm afraid someday you'll regret it."

"I won't." The only thing I regretted was having to go into the high school and not see Ike in front of me in physics, on the stairs, or playing football every Friday night under the stadium lights. I was spoiled. He was close enough to get my hands on every day, but I wanted a whole night with him. To lay next to him and not worry about an alarm going off and having to fly home.

"How about we make a deal?" This sounded promising. She was thinking and not just saying no. Everything was negotiable. At least according to Ms. Garrison, my economics teacher. "You can stay the night once each month. From Saturday morning until Sunday afternoon as long as your homework is done. I won't ask any questions. I just ask that you answer my calls if I need you and that you're safe."

This was not a bad starting offer. She'd already exceeded my expectations for this conversation. I thought it was going to be a much more direct, "No," and then swift movement to the next topic.

My mother sat next to me on her bed. She smiled when she looked into my eyes. "And at least two weekends a month, you spend with your friends. Not just Maya and Gwen and Ruby, either. I mean Mick, Sam, and all the rest of the crew that texts you guys all the time. Go out. Stay in. Do homework, whatever, but I want at least two weekends a month to be completely Ike-free."

I inhaled as I considered her request. I should have known the second part would be painful when the initial offer was generous. I would not see him for a month to sleep with him. I exhaled and asked, "The other weekend I can see him?"

"Yes, but not overnight. Not every day of the weekend."

"Here or at Rowan?"

"Yes." She seemed to be equally as uncomfortable with the compromise, which according to Ms. Garrison, meant it was a good one. Neither party should feel they'd completely won or lost. "And you need to go on birth control."

My eyebrows raised at this. I'm sure my eyes were the size of half dollars. "I thought that was all up to the universe."

"When your little witch is born, yes, but other babies may come. Ike for instance."

"I guess I'll know for sure when Gwen, Ruby, and Maya are pregnant at the same time."

"That will probably be your first clue."

"I haven't had sex with Ike."

I threw that at her as she was lost in thought. It wasn't fair, but when the courage comes to say those words, you toss them out.

"Oh. Well, that's great." She took my hand in hers. We were having a moment, which made us both laugh. Moments weren't typical between us. I couldn't remember if they were a thing before my father died, but after his death, everything was a moment and few were recognized. We survived by just stringing moments together until they became days, weeks, and finally years. "There's no rush. I'm putting you on some type of birth control anyway."

"Okay. That's good. Then maybe we won't have to talk about this again."

"Ever, you can tell me anything. Even if I'm going to hate hearing it."

"I know. I'm just not sure I can if I hate saying it."

"Do it anyway." She stood and exhaled. Conversation done. We could go back to our lives, and I could take out a calendar and plan out the nights for the rest of the year that Ike and I could be alone. He was going to have to find out if his roommate was planning on any Saturdays away. Just the thought of multiple hours of privacy with him infiltrated every other thought I tried to keep in my head.

I fell asleep and the nightmares continued. Ike was lying on the side of the road. He was hurt, but whenever I got close to him, he moved. Sometimes a few feet, others times several yards. He hopped away, bloodied and bruised, and I kept running to save him. I could see his broken body, but I couldn't touch him. He would just keep moving until finally, he jumped and then never reappeared.

I sat up in bed awake, opened my eyes, and realized I was still in Auburn. We were all safe. Including Ike. I fell back against my pillow and settled myself until I heard Ruby roll over in her bed. She was always the first one up. Gwen and Maya would soon follow.

What are you guys doing after school? I asked with my head still on my pillow. Carl was still snuggled under the covers against my legs.

I'm supposed to go to Sam's.

I'm going to the mall with my mother. I need new boots. Gwen thought and rolled over toward us.

I'm doing nothing. I'm sure my mother will want me to cook something. Maya was awake, too.

Billy wants me to meet him in a clearing behind the woods between Auburn and Woodstown. Somewhere called Stoners Lane.

Billy, the cat killer who says he knows our secrets? Maya asked.

Go. I want to hear what he has to say, Ruby thought. *We'll be there.*

They would drop everything. As usual. I would do the same for them. I'd already filled them in on Billy's afterschool activities. As much as I could say aloud without feeling sick. The look on his face, his expressions, both of utter disregard for the cat's life and then enjoyment at its death would stay with me forever.

"If he smiles or seems to move from being completely disconnected to suddenly involved, strike. Before he does."

"Why would he want to hurt you?" Gwen asked.

"I don't know. He's always had some issue with me." I thought back over my and Billy's history. "I think at first, he wanted to be friends, but I don't think he's capable."

School dragged, and by lunch, my stomach was starting to knot. I should have told Billy the meeting was off. I'd go home to my mother and tell her everything about him. She'd do something to make being near him this year not so disturbing. I wasn't sure what.

"Thanks for agreeing to meet me. I think it will be a fresh start," Billy said as he let me leave the cafeteria before him. It was what a normal person might say when they'd gotten off on the wrong foot upon first meeting, but he wasn't a normal person—he was a cat killer.

We'd only been in school a week and new bruises showed up on Billy's face and arms. That day, he had been pulled out of English and sent to the office. Later, I heard he was being interviewed by a woman who wore a navy dress and carried a huge canvas tote filled with files. Nothing seemed to come of any of the attention Billy received except maybe a new injury. He needed help. Regardless of what I'd seen, that was true.

The four of us flew from the school to Stoners Lane. Gwen, Maya, and Ruby fell back when we reached Seven Stars. I felt them move to circle Billy, who was already standing alone in the middle of the space. I showed myself at the lane leading back from the road. A large tree blocked it. There was no vehicle anywhere in sight, but the other side of the clearing led to Kings Highway. Billy could have parked somewhere on that side.

I made my way toward him with Ruby chirping in my head about not turning my back on him. She was going to move in closer as I approached.

"You weren't afraid to come?" he asked. I didn't answer. I wouldn't let him lead this conversation down whatever path he'd planned. I was there to figure out what he wanted and how I could spend the rest of my life without him being in it. Billy nodded at my lack of response. "What are you afraid of, Ever?" He stepped closer to me, and I moved back.

"Why did you want to meet me?" His lips pursed. He wanted to toy with me, and I wanted to go home and eat dinner. "Our mothers knew each other."

"My mother knew of your father, too."

He lifted his hand to his chin, considering the information I'd just shared. It was more than the recognition of our parents' acquaintance. I'd just told him that I'd checked into his past, which meant I knew all about the tragedy that left him in his uncle's care.

He reached down into his backpack. His movements were swift. I responded by shifting my weight to my back foot. The aggressive stance wasn't lost on Billy. The corners of his mouth tilted up, obviously pleased by my reaction. He pulled out a faded purple book with a leather cord wrapped around the center of it.

"This was my mother's." The book had to have been twenty years old. "It details how she was able to fly, disappear, and move things with her mind." My eyes widened, but I didn't say anything. My instinct was to launch into the air and get far away from him. My heart raced at my family's secret being spoken by the monster in front of me. The air swirled around us as Maya and Gwen moved in closer to Ruby, who was only a few inches behind me. "My father thought she was crazy. My mother showed him her powers once after they were married, and he beat her for it."

I cringed and closed my eyes.

"Look at me, Ever." I still didn't understand why I was there. What was it that Billy wanted from me? "Violence comes easy to the men of my family. It is their power."

"It isn't right."

"There was someone my mother was more afraid of than my father."

The Virago, I thought. Maybe his mother had written about them, too. I'd want that information to be shared as much as my craft with whatever loved one read my secret book.

Billy watched me as if he were listening to my thoughts. "There was a man who my mother wrote about. He threatened her because of her powers. Someone other than my father." If it was a man, he wasn't part of the Virago. "She thought he might convince my father to kill her."

"That's impossible."

"Is it? A man that could punch his pregnant wife until her tooth went through her lip. Would it be so unthinkable that he could be used to kill her?"

"Billy, you need to talk to someone. An adult that can help you. This life. Your history. It doesn't have to be repeated in you."

"Shut up, Ever!" He held the book against his head.

I stared at the book. So little of our craft was written down. The fear that our secret would be shared with someone who could destroy us was a real part of our history. The Salem witches had no powers, and they were burned at the stake. Our ancestors watched in horror as the small-minded townsfolk murdered innocent women.

"She never mentioned her gifts again, but he caught her appearing in their backyard after a rare flight. That was the night he shot her. He thought she was insane, but when he told his defense attorney all of this, my father was the only one who seemed crazy. The rest of the town thought my mother was a sweet and loving wife and new mother."

"I'm sure she was," was all I added to the conversation. "I don't understand why you're telling me all of this."

"Because I think you're like my mother."

"I'm not." There was no need to add another word to the explanation. Billy could share as much of his family as he'd like. He could take out an ad in the yearbook and write down everything he'd read in his mother's journal, but he wasn't including me in any of it. My mother, and all the mothers before her, would kill me themselves before I divulged anything about the craft to this disturbed being.

"I want you . . ." He stared at the sky above us. "And your coven to give me the same powers you possess. I want you to fulfill the promise of my mother's hopes." He'd lost his mind. It was hard to reconcile the sad figure in front of me begging for power with the Billy I'd met last year.

"I'm willing to help you, but that isn't the kind of power you need. Counseling, police intervention, planning for your future away from your uncle should be your only concern. I don't have magical powers, Billy. I don't know what your mom wrote, or what she thought she could do, but that truth died with her. I have nothing to do with it."

"You're selfish." Billy dropped the book into his bag and lunged at me. Ruby flew from my right and threw him twenty feet away onto the ground without a word. Billy stood, brushed the dirt off his thighs, and slowly smiled. "What was that?" he asked as he sauntered closer to me.

"What was what?" I was done with this meeting, or whatever it was.

"I thought we were alone."

"You're about to be. I'm leaving."

"And how are you getting home, Ever? Walking? Or will you fly?"

"Billy, I think what happened to your mother is tragic and sad, and you've certainly been put in more than one situation that was not of your own doing, but you're creating one now that you don't want to start. I want you to leave me alone."

"And if I don't?"

"Why wouldn't you? A girl asked you to leave her alone? Why is the word 'no' not good enough for you?"

"Because of all the girls I've ever met in this godforsaken town, you're the only one I believe is like my mother." If he really knew, then he'd suspect Ruby, Maya, and Gwen were witches, too. As if reading my mind, he added, "I know all about your galère." He kicked a rock toward the trees. "You're the only one who's kind and fearless. That's the way she was."

"Honor your mother, Billy. Seek help. You're young."

"Nothing will ever stop us, if we're together. I can force you to be with me."

I laughed a little.

"You'll lose someone, the way my mother was taken from me."

I stood tall in Billy's face. Anger grinded from my teeth, down my throat, and rooted me to the earth. "Now you sound like your father. Where he is will be a gift if you don't stay away from me."

His shoulders shook with a laugh that made no sound and showed no emotion on his face. "You and your family have made enough enemies around here that I won't have to lift a finger."

"You're crazy."

My words caught him like a right hook to the face. It was the same claim his father had made against his mother. "Watch me do crazy." He disappeared, taking his backpack with him as the wind swept across my face.

Don't say a word, I thought. I wasn't sure how far he'd gone or if he could fly. I walked to the woods, ran behind a tree, and disappeared. If Billy were watching, I wouldn't let him see my power. I wondered if there were any limitations on his.

We flew back to Auburn in silence. We landed and stepped into the safety of our yard. Facing each other and the enormity of Billy's knowledge and his sick disposition.

"Gwen," Maya said. Her eyes were fixed on Gwen and enshrouded in fear. "What is that?"

"His mother's diary. I want to read it."

I stopped breathing. The reality of what she'd stolen set in. Billy would come for it.

VI

WE FOLLOWED GWEN WITH THE journal in her hands up the stairs. She sat on the floor in the center of our attic and opened it.

"Read it aloud," Ruby demanded.

Gwen leafed through several pages and then returned to the beginning. She ran her hand over the thick paper and concentrated while she ignored Ruby.

"Gwen?" I asked.

"When I first opened it, it was a normal journal. It described her wedding, her pregnancy, but . . ."

"But what?" Gwen handed the book over to Ruby who stared at the same page Gwen had.

"The page changes. It's black with silver writing and says, 'if you're able to read this, then you know. You're part of our secret sisterhood, or maybe you've been born with the power, but you never knew it. My baby will be here any day, and I'm hoping it's a she to carry on the craft because I'm alone."

She flipped through the pages reading off tidbits from each one. They explained flying, disappearing, moving things, and historical details about witchcraft.

"I could have used this," Gwen said. "I'm still trying to figure out everything."

"You're doing great," Maya said.

Ruby passed the book to me. I turned the pages until the word Virago stood out. "My mother's coven was decimated by the Virago. She died before I could walk, let alone fly. She left me one letter that was written similarly to this book. Only I could read it. To everyone else, it was a love letter to her newborn daughter, but to me, it was a witch's doctrine. I could fly, I could disappear, I could move things with my mind, and I knew I was alone because I could cast spells. I'm the only one left, and this baby will be a coven of one, too. How incredibly sad. Covens are meant to share all the elements of our universe. We are air witches, but I've never felt the power described to me that would come with knowing my Earth witch."

"Billy could read this book as well as disappear. He's always seemed to know more about us than he should. He has some power."

"Let me see it again." Gwen turned several more pages. "It describes her baby boy and her disappointment in not having a girl, until he disappeared one day. She was terrified. Her husband hated witchcraft and forbid her to ever use it. The second time the baby disappeared, she hid him until he came back. She was terrified her husband would kill him."

My chest tightened. Could it have been worse than what Billy's uncle was doing to him? "Billy has had an awful life," I said.

"Billy isn't human." Ruby would never hear a word of sympathy toward him, and I had few to say.

Gwen was silently reading beside me. She glanced up and re-
alized we were all waiting for her to share. "It says," she started
quietly. "His anger knows no bounds. A quiet calm comes over him.
He sinks into the evil before he strikes. There's no turning back.
It is the most terrifying form of rapture, and he inflicts it on me."
She turned the page. "It's been worse since the man spoke to him."

"What man?" Ruby asked.

Gwen flipped a few more pages and then stopped. "I don't know.
It doesn't say."

"Billy mentioned a man. He said whoever it was scared his
mother more than his father."

Gwen, Ruby, and Maya all just stared at me. They'd heard about
the bruises, the burns, and the cat. They were lucky not to have to
see the images of that day when they shut their eyes, but they trusted my account of the events enough to know Billy was disturbed.

Gwen slammed the book shut. She held it in her clenched hands
as a tear ran down her face. "She spoke to me," she said.

"Who did?"

"Rebecca. The woman who wrote the book."

"What did she say?" Ruby asked.

Gwen had told us her retched grandmother—the one who
cursed the fathers of our children to die—her Mimi, talked to Gwen
at her funeral, but we assumed it was something to do with her
connection to her grandmother. She had no connection to Rebecca.
The only similarity was that both who Gwen could hear were dead.

"She said to send him to her in heaven. He was evil on earth
because she was taken from him. To send him back, and she would
love him."

Ruby took the book again and held it close to her chest with her
eyes closed. "Nothing," she said. "Gwen, that's amazing."

"Is it?" Her eyes filled with tears again. She held out her hands.

Ruby placed the book back into them as Gwen closed her eyes. "Beware."

We waited for Gwen to tell us more. When it appeared she was through, Ruby began to speak, but Gwen interrupted her with, "Heed the second telling. The hunter as well as the hunted. The story that lasted well past my death."

"The second telling?" Ruby asked.

Gwen opened her eyes. "There's more than one book."

Our mothers returned home in Lovie's minivan. We met them in the kitchen with the book in my hand.

"What's this?" my mother asked when I gave it to her.

"Open it."

She did as we asked and leafed through the pages. They turned to black in her grasp. Sloane, Gisel, and Lovie looked over her shoulder as she read. "Is this . . ." My mother flipped back to the first page that listed the journal as belonging to Rebecca Lane Callahan. "It's Rebecca Lane's."

Sloane took the book from my mother.

"Do you guys know what happened to her?" Lovie asked our mothers.

"She was killed," Gisel said. "By her horrible husband, Jimmy Callahan."

"What?" my mother asked.

"I never liked him. He killed her. She had an infant, but I lost track of what happened to him. It rocked the entire county. I was eight months pregnant with Gwen at the time." Gisel stared at Gwen. Her eyes filled with tears as she let herself sink into the memories.

"His name's Billy, and he's in the girls' class," Lovie said.

"Rebecca's son?" Gisel asked us.

"He's Billy Roberts now," I said.

"I think they changed Billy's last name to protect him from this horrible history," Lovie said.

"But everyone knows you can't hide from history in this town," Gisel wiped a stray tear from her cheek.

"He's a really sick person." I thought of that poor cat again. "And he can disappear." Sloane lowered the book and stepped in front of us. Her eyes narrowed as I forced out, "He wants us to give him his full powers."

"How does he know about us?"

I shook my head. "I don't know. Not everything he said made sense."

"Like what?"

"He said there was a man his mother feared more than his father."

"A man?"

"She wrote that he would convince her husband to kill her because of her powers." I nodded at the book Sloane was holding.

Our mothers looked from one to another. If they had any thoughts on who the man was, they weren't sharing.

"Jimmy Callahan's in jail," Lovie said.

My mother placed the journal onto the kitchen table. "I never knew Rebecca was a witch."

"I didn't, either," Sloane said. "But I always liked her." Sloane's gaze dragged from the book on the table to the four of us leaning against the kitchen counter as if we were in a police lineup. "Where did you get it?"

Silence was the only thing that came easily. It invaded the room and clued our mothers into our guilt before we could come up with a proper response.

"Oh no," Lovie said. "Please tell me you didn't."

"It wasn't like that," Gwen was unconvincing. "We didn't break into his house or anything." I stayed silent about my visit and let Gwen keep going. "It fell out of his bag." There was no getting away with this completely innocent story, and Gwen knew it. "We just didn't hand it back to him the way we should have."

"You're giving it back tomorrow."

"Of course."

I waited for Gwen to tell them about Rebecca talking to her, but she never did. I didn't know why, but I followed her lead.

We decided Gwen would stay invisible for the beginning of first period and sneak the book back into Billy's bag. He had some powers. He could disappear, but based on the fact he didn't know they were with me at Stoners Lane and he didn't sense my presence at his house, he couldn't tell when we were near the way we could with other witches.

The plan was unnecessary. When we walked downstairs for breakfast the next morning, the book was gone. All of us, including our mothers, just stared at each other. He wasn't part of the Virago because he'd been able to set foot in Auburn, but that didn't mean Billy wasn't an enemy.

VII

THAT DAY, BILLY WAS LATE coming to school. His left eyebrow was swollen a little, but I might have missed it if I weren't looking for Billy's latest injury. Anyone else and I would have assumed he'd hit it on a cabinet door or the top bunk when they'd gotten up too fast, but I knew better.

Billy didn't say a word to me in AP English. He barely looked my way. Every time he reached into his backpack, I kept an eye out for a glimpse of the book or a second book. It was as if the day before had not happened.

Billy, I thought. *Billy, if you can hear me look my way. Stretch and put your hand behind your head.*

Billy sat with an open notebook on his desk and a pen in his hand, but there were no notes he wrote down.

If you answer me, I'll help you get your powers.

I was lying. I didn't even think it was possible to assign powers to someone else, even if that person was the son of a witch. Not that I would have given Billy any powers anyway. He was sick, and spells were used to change the universe forever and should never be taken lightly. The course of our existence was already set. Changing it had ramifications.

The consequences of granting Billy power, combined with his evil mind, were too frightening to consider. Billy stayed still in front of me. Neither he nor his mother had ever mentioned speaking inside their minds. Though, if she were a coven of one, she wouldn't have had anyone to speak to, so maybe she didn't know.

The bell rang, and Billy rushed out of the room. He went down the side staircase he never used this time of day. He wasn't in Mr. Frank's classroom by the time I got there. I took my seat as Mr. Frank marked each of us in attendance on his laptop. He stared at Billy's empty chair and then turned to me. His glare belied his warm welcome. Some accusation I couldn't figure out rested in his stare as I took my seat next to Billy's empty one. Besides the note the first day of school, Billy and I hadn't exactly come off as best friends.

"Has anyone seen Billy Roberts today?" Mr. Frank stood over my desk as he asked.

I kept my hands still on the top of my notebook and my gaze fixed on the board in the front of the room. He rested the tips of his fingers on my desk. The fan's breeze landed on the back of my neck with the eerie sense of peril. I tightened the core of my body to hold still, as the silence continued.

"Apparently not," Stacey Gruber said from across the room.

Mr. Frank tapped my desk twice and walked to the front of the room. I waited the entire class to escape. The fear of him holding me back and asking questions about Billy's attendance plagued me, which was ridiculous. I was a high school student with no idea where my classmate was. That statement should easily be accepted for the truth that it was.

Billy didn't reappear the rest of the day. I thought about flying past his house on the way home, but I couldn't bring myself to go back there. Instead, I went straight home after school, ate dinner, and packed to leave for Rowan the next morning.

"You don't have to be so excited," my mother said as she sat on my bed.

"Sorry." I packed shorts and a tee to wear to bed. "And thanks, Mom."

She paused for a second. I assumed she was acknowledging how far we'd come since last year. She put my toiletries bag on top of everything else as Carl jumped onto my bed. "What about this guy? Isn't he welcome in the dorms?"

"No dogs allowed at Holly Pointe Commons. Unfortunately."

Carl snuggled in next to my leg. "I guess it's good practice for next year." She rubbed his head behind the ears. "You're going to have to get used to sleeping with me." She left Carl and me to sleep in her own bed.

As long as I kept moving, Billy couldn't settle in my mind. Him. His cat. His request of powers. All of it stayed just on the peripheral of my thoughts until I lay in bed with the lights out. I listened to the sounds of sleep coming from the other corners of the room. Even Ruby was out cold.

When sleep finally took me, I was back at Stoners Lane with Billy. He was standing next to me. The sides of our bodies were touching. Instead of being full daylight, it was early in the morning and a thick fog hung in the clearing, making it almost impossible to see the surrounding trees.

"Don't worry, Ever," Billy said. He wasn't whispering, but I felt like I could barely hear him. He was standing next to me, but his voice sounded so far away.

"I'm not," I said and faced him.

"I'm going to kill him for you." Billy didn't smile. He waited for my response.

I set the ground around him on fire, leading the flames toward his body. As they crept over the ground, I remembered the words of his mother, Rebecca Callahan, in her journal. How she spoke of her powers and how she asked us to send him back to her, but it was against everything we stood for.

I woke clutching my chest and crying. If there came a choice between Billy and Ike, my honor wouldn't survive.

❧

"I think you should go to the homecoming dance," Ike said as he ran his fingertips up and down my bare arm.

I tilted my head toward him, but I still couldn't see his face to judge if he was serious. I pulled myself up his body until our eyes met. I kissed him because I could. "You have a football game. I want to go to that."

Ike pushed my hair back off my face and held it in a ponytail behind my head. He kissed my neck. "I know, but this is your senior year. You should be at homecoming."

"It's my senior year in a school I've barely been at a year. It doesn't feel like homecoming, and I don't want to be anywhere without you, especially a dance."

"These things may not seem to mean much right now, but they're important."

I studied his face for the reason behind his newfound concern for my high school memories. "This coming from the guy I had to convince to go to a dance in the first place." He almost smiled and melted me, again. "What's going on?"

"I don't want you to feel like you missed out. I don't want you to regret anything."

"Why don't you let me worry about what I might regret?" Ike

sighed. His chest rose three inches with me on top of it. "What is going on? Do you not want me at your game?" The hurt was rising inside me. It was a deep heat warming my cheeks.

"No. That isn't it." He pulled me closer to him. I buried my head in his neck. "I had lunch with my dad today."

"And he doesn't want me to go to your game?"

"No." Ike laughed a little. "He kept talking about giving you the freedom to enjoy your senior year with your friends and how I shouldn't put undue requests on you to spend your time with me instead of them."

"He did?"

"Yes. He wants me to encourage you to look at schools far away."

"What?"

"I know. The thought of it pissed me off, too, but he's right. You can't just be on the sidelines of Rowan University your whole senior year, and you need to pick a college that will make you happy no matter how far away from me it is."

"Why does your dad care?"

"He went on and on . . . and on about it." Ike rubbed my back. "I think he has a lot of regrets about the way he and your mother broke up. I'm guessing it has something to do with her going away to college and leaving him home."

"I got the distinct impression it had something to do with your mother, too." Mrs. Kennedy was absolutely a factor in the end of my mother and Ike's dad's relationship. I was too scared to ask exactly how, though.

Ike returned to caressing my arm. "Who knows? I don't even care, but if any of his advice is wise, then I'll take it. I don't want to lose you, and I don't want you to miss out on anything because of me. I love you. You have homecoming, your senior trip, and everything in between."

"Don't forget the prom."

"And the prom."

I sat up. He was so serious. "I'm fine. I don't feel at all suffocated by you, if that's what you're worried about. Ruby, Gwen, Maya, and I are all planning on touring each of our mothers' alma maters as well as plenty of other schools. We'll figure it out. What's right for us"—I pointed between the two us—"will be what's right for me."

"I don't feel like I got through to you."

I leaned forward again and silenced him with my lips.

"I don't know why you feel that way."

VIII

THE FOUR OF US WALKED in a line on the path of Marlton Park. We took the outside, longer loop near the fields, letting Carl lead us on his leash. I wasn't sure about him wanting to come back to the park, but he hopped out of Lovie's minivan as if nothing bad had ever happened to him. We remembered, though. The sounds of his cries as his limbs were practically ripped from his body in the air above us.

The leash was locked into place so he couldn't get more than three feet in front of us. Nothing was ever going to hurt this dog again. He'd become the center of our home, and every witch in it was in love with him. A man and a woman approached. They were walking at an aggressive pace and swinging their bent arms to burn more calories.

Carl stopped and stared at them. We moved off to the side to give them room to pass and kept Carl near us.

"Hello, Ever." It was Mr. Frank.

Carl leaned back on his haunches and ferociously barked at my teacher.

Mr. Frank stopped, stared at Carl, and then examined the four of us as if the dog weren't barking and pulling at his leash to attack him.

"Carl, no. Stop." I yanked him back toward me as I smiled at Mr. Frank. "Down!"

The woman with him never said a word. Just kept looking at all four of us.

"Have a nice night," Mr. Frank finally said and walked away.

Carl's barking subsided into a deep growl. His lips pulled back, exposing his teeth. I'd never seen him react to a person that way. He was always sweet and kind.

"Was that your media teacher?" Maya asked.

"Yes." I kneeled down and rubbed Carl below the neck. "Carl obviously loves him."

"He sure does," Ruby said.

"Carl has great instincts. I cannot stand modern media. That's one of the classes I have with Billy."

Ruby held her hand up and tilted her head to the side. I rubbed Carl's head to keep him quiet so she could concentrate.

"Our moms need us."

I stood. "Where?"

"They're with the Kingsway Coven. In South Harrison." She held up one finger and nodded her head. "They're fine, but they need us. I told them we'd drop off Carl at home and come, but they said to just bring him."

"I wish we could fly." I looked around the crowded park. Someone would notice the four of us and our dog disappearing. Plus, cars weren't allowed to be parked there overnight, and I wasn't sure how long we were going to be.

We jogged back to the car and drove toward South Harrison. None of us had actually been there before except Gwen. She seemed to know something about every town in South Jersey. She led us to the small intersection and down the road until we reached Maryann's house. It was exactly as Sloane had described it to Ruby. Right down to the circle of witches surrounding it. We pulled into the driveway and every single one of them came to the front of the house and stood between us and the front porch.

"We're from Auburn," Ruby said and the women directly in front of us relaxed their stance.

"Come in," Tara Jane yelled from behind them. She was standing on the porch and waving to us. "Thank you for coming," she said as we made our way through the crowd.

We followed her to the dining room table where our mothers sat. Past them on the far wall, someone had painted crude flames in red paint, which had dripped, making it look as if the flames were bleeding. I stepped back into the family room to find a similar image dripping down the mirror. The paint appeared to still be wet. I reached up and touched it with my fingers, and it dented in like hardening icing.

Gwen, Maya, and Ruby followed me past the front door, which I pulled closed.

A circle, or the number zero, took up the entire top half of the wood. Lovie took Carl from my arms and carried him out the back door.

"Show them," Maryann said from the dining room. "Show them what these wretches have done to my home. Take them upstairs." Her angry narrative was winding tight around the occupants of the room.

My mother led the way. We followed her to the second floor of Maryann's house where Roman numerals were painted on all but one of the bedroom doors in the hallway. The numerals one and two were on the door to what was obviously the master bedroom. Three and four adorned the door that lead to what could have been a boys room. The last door was still perfectly white. My mother pushed it open, revealing a toddler bed with a Roman numeral six scrawled above it. The twin bed next to it with the purple flowers quilt was pristinely made without a drop of paint near it. A piece of paper was lying on the pillow with a knife stuck through it. The note read: "You'll lose V."

"Maryann's daughter, Amelia, is a member of their next coven," my mother said. Her voice was dry and worn from the images she was presenting.

The dripping red paint ran right through my blood. A little girl, chosen from this home because of her powers, had a knife stabbed in her pillow. My jaw clenched as I tried to settle the contents of my stomach. I swallowed hard while I stared at every inch of the child's pillow.

"Is she okay?" Maya asked.

"Yes. She's with her coven in the backyard. Under close watch."

"What can we do?"

"The Kingsway Coven is asking us to make their homes sacred ground."

"Why not their town? Like Auburn?"

"They're spread out. Other witches reside near them. It isn't one area like Auburn or Upper Pittsgrove. Witchcraft and our spells are about balance. We can't just take over all the land and make it safe for us. There has to be a fair distribution of power and space."

"What are you waiting for?" Ruby asked. This was all clear to her.

"We were waiting for all of you. We'd like to have their coven and both of ours cast the spell." My mother hesitated. She was deciding how much to say, but I remembered my day in Upper Pittsgrove.

"You're afraid the spell no longer works."

She glanced up at the number above the toddler bed. "We don't know why Upper Pittsgrove is no longer sacred or how the Virago got into our house last year. We hope the power of the three covens will be great enough to make the difference."

"Disgusting isn't it?" Tara Jane said as she walked into the room. "I had to physically hold Maryann back. No one goes near her children." She walked over to the bed and ran her fingers across the top of the comforter. "Not that I'd blame her if she tore their heads off and threw their skulls in the river for fun."

"None of us would," Ruby said.

"I have the spell ready if you're willing to help."

"Of course," my mother said, and we filed back out into the hallway of Maryann's house. My mother put her arm around my shoulders.

"Love is our weakness," I said. "The more people we have in our lives we're unwilling to lose, the more weapons they have to use against us."

"You're wrong, Ever. Love is the hammer we wield against them."

"We'd be stronger alone."

She turned to me and grabbed me by the shoulders. "It's the love that makes a life." I stayed still. She was right. The terror I felt for Ike's safety was only a small part of what I felt for him. The rest couldn't be quantified or explained. It was a drop of dew on my soul and a half-beat of my heart. He belonged to me because I gave myself to him. I would kill for him. I would die for him, and I wasn't going to live another day as if it was guaranteed I would have him.

My mother and I were the last to enter the family room. The coffee table had been pushed under the front windows, making room for the three covens. Mine still had limited experience with the art of spell casting, but we'd witnessed the Kingsway Coven doing some magical things before.

"How do you think this should work?" Jennifer asked. She was already holding Tara Jane's hand.

"I'm telling you. None of this matters. Our kids are going to leave our houses at some point. I'm going out tonight and finding out who did this, and then I am going to jam that knife in each of their eye sockets." I watched in silence. The few times I'd been with Maryann, she'd seemed reasonable. Motherhood was the magic that turned a woman into a warrior.

"I'll go," Ruby said. She'd been ready to fight the day Carl was hurt, and I could tell just by the way she looked at Maryann that she liked her.

"This will at least allow you to sleep at night. We all need a safe haven. Some place that can't be breached, and then we'll talk about retaliation," Sloane said. "I agree. They've gone too far."

"Again," Lovie added.

The four of us sat in a circle on the floor holding hands.

Our mothers knelt behind us, forming their own circle.

The Kingsway Coven stood behind them, their arms stretched wide to circle everyone in front of them. The house fell quiet as every other witch inside observed every move we made. Ours were the only whole covens present. Except for the elderly woman in the corner. We'd met her the year before, and she herself was a coven, but for some reason she wasn't participating in our spell. She was just perched in the corner of the room, watching. Something about the way she looked at us made me think she knew why Upper Pittsgrove was no longer sacred ground.

Before I could think too long about that, Tara Jane spoke.

"I'm going to place the spell in your minds. Breathe in your power. Own this and how we will change the world tonight. United we are safe. A coven is our family of four, but honor and our histories will forever bind all of us together."

I closed my eyes and inhaled deeply. I was powerful. Witchcraft ignited inside the house even before we walked in and was about to be set on fire with the past. I exhaled, and the spell came into view.

Tara Jane, Maryann,
Jennifer, and Riley

A coven to one town
Scattered where they may be

The land which holds their four walls
The home of her family

Freed from evil or attack
Deemed sacred by our decree

Then, as quickly as the power surged around us, it stopped. The air in the house settled, and I dropped Ruby and Gwen's hands before leaning back on my own on the floor behind me. The Kingsway Coven helped our mothers to their feet. Tara Jane glanced at the elderly witch in the corner of the room, who nodded without a word. The spell had worked. Peace flicked through the atmosphere of the house in South Harrison.

Maryann poured shots in glasses lined up on her kitchen island. Every adult witch took one.

"To unity," she said and raised her glass. Everyone around her raised theirs, too. "Kill or be killed." The shots were drank and the glasses were banged on the countertop.

Amelia ran into the house and hugged her mother's legs. "Hey, sweet girl, don't go back upstairs, okay? Aunt Riley and Aunt Jennifer are fixing up your room."

"Why would someone paint our walls?"

"We don't know. Your aunts will make it perfect again, though."

"It smelled like summer in there," Amelia said.

My mother reached out and grabbed the wall, but her focus never left the young girl.

"What do you mean it smelled like summer?" Maryann asked and picked up her daughter. She lifted her to the counter and sat her in front of all of us.

"When we first got home. It smelled like summer. Honeysuckle."

Maryann hugged Amelia. She held her so close to her chest I thought she might suffocate the child, but she was smiling and playing with the curls of her hair when her mother finally let her go.

"Anyone?" Maryann asked the crowd of women around her. The room fell silent. My mother opened the sliding glass door and stepped outside onto the patio by herself.

Gisel sighed and said, "I've been visited by someone with that scent. He's invisible, but he's never hurt me or my family."

"He?" Tara Jane asked as if Gisel had spoken of an animal or some other species that could never "visit" anyone.

"Yes. I don't know what he *is*, but there's always a hint of honeysuckle around him. He smells sweeter than he acts."

"But if it were a man who came to your house, then it wasn't the Virago," a witch standing next to Maryann said.

"This was the Virago. Last year, they painted the Roman numeral seven near every accident they caused. Just never close enough for the police to put it together. They think they're clever."

"Have you ever heard of them leaving a trace? A scent of all things?"

"Only if they've wanted to. I've never heard of them making a mistake."

"Well, they have tonight, and they're going to regret it."

"What, Mom?" Amelia asked.

"Don't worry about a thing. Mommy will take care of it."

"I liked the smell. Not the painting."

"Can you still smell it? Even now? Can you smell the

honeysuckle?" I inhaled. I couldn't detect a thing. Just the remnants of the liquor drying in the shot glasses.

Amelia inhaled deeply as the room full of witches watched her. "No. He's gone."

"*He's* gone?"

"*It's* gone," Amelia corrected herself.

The rest of Maryann's family came into the kitchen. They were too hungry to pay any more attention to the fact that someone had come in and vandalized their house. It was a school night and she had four children to worry about, so we slipped out the front door. We had to leave, but we knew they'd all be safe as long as they were in their homes. I wanted the same type of bubble to surround Ike.

Billy. The Virago. God knew who else. Even an accident. I couldn't face any of it. I'd already lost my father. I wouldn't lose Ike. There should be some spell that I could put on a person so they'd never die, but I knew all the fables that dealt with wishes such as that. A human's mortality was not to be altered. It was set by a power higher than ours.

I lay in bed that night and called out to Ike in my mind.

I miss you more than I thought was possible.

I'm right up the road. Not going anywhere. Meet me at the tree house tomorrow?

I stared at the moonlight hitting the tapestry hanging from the ceiling above my bed. *All of a sudden, it's not enough.*

It has to be. For now, but not forever.

I didn't want to be his winey girlfriend who drove him crazy with worry and constantly needed reassurance. Actually, that was exactly what I wanted to be, but I wouldn't allow myself to become that. Ike made me strong, and I wasn't going to let Billy or the Virago change me. If they wanted a fight, we'd fight.

Are you still there? he asked.

Always. I'm always going to be here.

I love you.

I love you, too, I thought and let my eyes close.

Sleep stole me from my fears. It left me alone until the morning sun drifted through our windows. I rolled over and covered my eyes with my arm. Carl crawled up from my feet and laid his head next to mine. He didn't want to get up, either.

"You know this bed is not big enough for the both of us," I whispered, and he cuddled in closer. I spooned him with my arm over him. He'd been my sleeping partner for most of my life, I wasn't sure if I could sleep without him.

Thoughts of what the Virago had done to him the year before churned in my mind. Billy's attack of the cat followed. What was wrong with these people that they could take lives on a sunny afternoon?

No day was guaranteed.

He was standing on the balcony watching for me when I got to the tree house. It had only been a week, but it felt like a year since the last time he touched me. Billy's comments, Rebecca Callahan's journal, the Virago, the possibility of Ike being hurt were more than I could bear.

I landed next to him. He barely flinched as I appeared. He was getting used to me popping in. He reached up and threaded his hand in the back of my hair. My chest shook with my jagged breaths, and the heat spread through me. From where his lips touched mine to the very core of my being, I could feel Ike Kennedy hijacking me, and I gladly submitted.

I pushed him back through the door of the tree house. He ducked as he retreated inside where I threw myself against him. I pressed him to the wall, but Ike turned us around until I was the one trapped. He ran his hands up the sides of my body, letting his fingers linger over my breasts as he kissed me.

I couldn't ever say goodbye to this. To him. The commitment I'd made to myself to wait until some indeterminate date in the future to make love to Ike was incomprehensible at the moment. The sound logic and obvious moral sense flew completely from my mind. I no longer grasped what I was waiting for to give myself to him.

With my arms linked around Ike's neck, I pulled myself up so I could wrap my legs around his waist, and my lips grazed his neck. The ends of his hair fell over the tips of my fingers, and I pulled at them as he kissed me again, making me forget everything but the feel of his body against mine.

He wanted me. I could tell by the rasp in his voice when he said my name and the way he let his head fall back to expose his neck to me. I ran my fingers down the sensitive area from his chin to his collarbone, taking in every inch of his body as I went.

He lowered the front or my strapless dress until my chest was exposed. The cool air of the shaded woods touched me like a knife until he took me in his hands. "We should stop now if you're going to tell me to," he said. Ike was used to me only letting him go a certain distance in this area. Even my mother thought we'd been together. She took me for a birth control shot while swearing she believed me when I said we weren't having sex. "Ever." I could hear him say my name all day, every day, for the rest of my life. "Tell me."

With great effort, I dropped myself to my feet and lifted my dress up and over my head, leaving me standing in front of him in only my underwear. "I have nothing to say."

Ike stood back and considered me. I wasn't nervous or embarrassed. Heat rose to the surface of my skin as his sight swallowed my almost naked body. When his eyes met mine, I could feel his questions and concern before he voiced them. There would be no words. I took his hand and placed it on my breast. I inhaled his touch on my body and the power I fed off whenever he was near me.

He kissed me one more time before lying me down on the floor and climbing on top of me.

I'd waited so long, I wasn't sure what it was going to be like. I'd convinced myself it would be no different from the three thousand times I'd given my body to him in every other way, but the one that signified so much. I was wrong. There was a magic other than witchcraft surrounding each touch of Ike's fingers. He infiltrated me physically, emotionally, and took from me what I only wanted *him* to have. Giving myself to him was almost as intoxicating as the shudder of his breath and tightening of his muscles above me. I could do this with Ike all day.

We did just that. Ike and I spent four hours making love in his tree house until I could barely walk and I was certain everyone who looked at me would know instantly that I'd given myself for the first time to the man I loved. They'd be able to tell just from the air that surrounded me that I'd felt something different within the last few hours. Sensations that would bind me to him for all of eternity.

I was making too big a deal of it in my head. I wasn't Ike's first. To him, it was probably routine. The same thing everyone else did. I'd ask Ruby about it when I got home. She'd become my sexual advisor the minute she was the first of us to have sex. With experience came knowledge. I could trust her with my life, which made her a better resource than the internet. Even if it was typical, I wanted to do it again.

I can't get you off my mind. The heat vibrated across my chest and down my thighs at his words.

I know. I keep closing my eyes and remembering what your hands felt like on me.

Just my hands? I closed my eyes and inhaled.

No. I leaned against the wall in my bedroom and steadied myself as I dragged my mind through the memories of the past few hours.

I'll pick you up after dinner.

I wasn't sure how much more my body could survive.

I'm not sure I can take much more.

I'll be gentle. The sound of his words in my mind was close to a purr.

I shuddered a little and squeezed my thighs together. *I'll be ready at seven.*

LUST

Helene

MARYANN LEFT THE CAKE ON the center of the kitchen table. Her youngest, Violet, toddled around the room with Ever a step behind her, making sure she didn't find her way into the knife drawer without us watching.

"How's Amelia?"

Maryann waved her hand in the air in a no-matter gesture. "That girl moves from one thing to the next. She's fine." She exhaled and stood straight. "I may never be right again. I swear. It's like I can't calm down. I won't get over it."

"I don't blame you," I said. The thought of someone touching Amelia's bed, her pillow, had scarred us all. Even Ever and the rest of the girls were affected in a way I hadn't seen since Carl was hurt. "You didn't have to make us a cake."

"I know. I wanted to." She tapped her fingers on the edge of the table. I waited for her to say whatever she was holding back. Maryann rarely held something in. "I was ready to kill them."

It was a common feeling evoked by the Virago. I wasn't surprised by her admission. "We all were." She shouldn't have felt guilty about it. "My mother used to go on and on about the Virago, but they were quiet when I lived here. Now . . ."

"It's ridiculous."

"Do you remember Rebecca Lane? From Alloway?"

Maryann shook her head as she thought. "No."

"She was a witch and none of us knew. Her son's name is Billy Roberts, and he's in our girls' class."

"Have you reached out to her? Maybe she'd help."

"She's dead. Her husband killed her over the craft." Maryann took a slight step back. Her husband would have helped her rob a bank if she'd asked him to. He'd never deny who she was, so the thought of a husband killing his wife over the craft was as abhorrent to her as it was to me.

"And her son is demented," Ever said. The same tortured look of disregard I'd seen the last few weeks settled on her face. Maryann turned to her. "And he has powers. At least, he can disappear."

"Really?" Maryann picked up Violet as if by instinct to have her close. "I've never heard of such a thing. Is he part of the Virago?"

"We don't think so. He's dangerous enough on his own." Ever's eyebrows crunched together in pain. "He says, 'We're perfect for each other.'"

"Who is?" I asked.

"Billy and I." Her eyes hardened. "He threatened to hurt my boyfriend." She worried endlessly about Ike. She was as lost in Ike as I had been in his father. Her existence hinged on him. I'd stopped dismissing her boyfriend when I accepted they were going to be together. Instead of fighting with her, I let the memories of my first love back in. The feeling of only being able to take a deep breath because Isaiah was nearby. I exhaled. I'd been forced to breathe without him decades ago.

"Keep me posted," Maryann said as she put Violet back on the ground. She grabbed her hand and led her out the back door.

Ever was busy collecting the measuring cups Violet had played with when the phone on the wall rang. I hadn't heard it ring since Sloane's father was still alive. Ever rushed to answer it. The uneven bell was a siren from a bygone era. A phone call used to mean something. A cancellation, someone had skipped school, an invitation, a loved one had died. Time had replaced the ringing with silent texts and missing words. Typos and slang. Most meant nothing.

"Hello," she answered it as if she were on stage at a museum and demonstrating the odd machine for her classmates on a field trip. "No. She isn't here." Ever looked around the room and leaned over to check the cars that were in the driveway. "Just me and my mom." That statement was insane considering our current living arrangements. Eight witches in a house was more than enough. We needed to talk to a realtor about making an offer on another house in Auburn, even if the current resident wasn't ready to leave.

Ever held out the phone to me.

"Hello," I said.

"Helene, it's me." It was Isaiah. "I'm sorry to ask this of you." *Then don't.* "But I'm at my mom's, and she fell. She was in the shower. I need some help, and Gisel isn't picking up her cell phone."

"I'm on my way." I hung up, ran into the backyard, and launched into the sky.

Within seconds, I landed on the wooded lot I'd spent the last two years of high school sneaking onto. The front door was ajar. "Isaiah," I called out as I entered.

"In here. Back in the master bedroom."

The pictures on the mantle were the same, as were the wallpaper and the carpet. It was like stepping back in time, but the period was a dangerous one for me and Isaiah. I found him kneeling next to his mother on the bathroom floor. He'd covered her with a towel and was speaking gently to her.

"She won't let me lift her." The torture in his eyes bore down on me. It'd been so long since I had a mother to feel for, but his pain reached through the years.

"Hello, Mrs. Kennedy," I said and knelt down so she could see me.

"Helene." The tension released in the room with her gentle hello.

"Why don't you wait right outside the door in case we need you," I said to Isaiah before turning back to his mother. "Did you hurt anything?"

She tilted her head toward me. "I don't know." I wasn't sure whether it was safe to move her or even what other questions I should be asking. My medical knowledge was limited. I wished Xavier were there. Twenty years ago, he'd repaired my shoulder with barely a thought, so I had a feeling he would know exactly how to help her. He might have been a doctor or a paramedic for all I knew. The next time I saw him, I was going to point blank ask him what he did for a living. He couldn't just show up in my bedroom and not share the most basic details of his life.

Mrs. Kennedy tried to raise her head and winced at the movement.

"We should call an ambulance. What if you've broken something?"

"Well, no one is seeing me naked. I haven't kept things under wrap this long for some stranger to come in here and see the family goods."

"Understood." She was as feisty as I remembered. "Let's see if you can sit up first." I inched her up and helped swing her legs to the front of her before leaning her back against the tub. All of this was done at a snail-like pace ensuring she didn't injure anything further. "How is that?"

She exhaled. "Better."

"What would you like to put on?"

"My nightshirt is on the hook on the back of the door."

"How's it going in there?" Isaiah asked. His mother rolled her eyes.

"We're good. Give us a minute." All the times his mother and I had laughed behind Isaiah's father's back came flooding back to me. The man was serious to a fault, and I think she and I were both happy that Isaiah had gotten his sense of humor from his mother. Together, they used to entertain me until I almost forgot my mother had died. Mrs. Kennedy leaned forward so I could get the nightshirt around her back and her arms through the holes. I fastened the bottom buttons as she worked her way down from the top. "Good?" I asked her.

She only nodded. Her exhaustion was infectious. I wanted to rest against the tub with her.

"I'm going to lift you to your feet, but if I hurt you, you have to tell me right away." She didn't say a word, and I knew that her needing my help wasn't something she was proud of. "Okay." I wrapped my arms under her shoulders and stood above her straddling her body. Instead of using my muscles, I lifted her with my mind and the transition from the floor to standing was smooth and effortless. She relaxed in my arms. I wanted to fly with her to the bed, but Mrs. Kennedy would never be out of it enough to not comprehend that.

I walked backward, careful not to jostle her or move too fast. Isaiah supported her back as soon as we cleared the doorway, and when we got closer to her bed, he propped up pillows for her and pulled back the covers before I lowered her down into it.

"Thanks," she said, took a sip of water from the glass beside her bed, and turned on the television behind Isaiah.

"Mom, you're going to the doctor's."

She didn't even look his way when she said, "Can you get Helene some tea. It was so kind of her to stop by." She turned to me. "I always hoped you'd forgive him."

"You keep talking like that, and I'm going to need something stronger than tea," I joked.

Mrs. Kennedy smiled. "Whatever it takes. It's never too late, you know?"

I knew more than she thought, and it was most definitely too late for me and her son. I walked toward the front door, but instead of following me, Isaiah went into the kitchen and put the kettle on the stove.

"I'm okay. Really."

"You heard the woman. You're having tea."

I sighed and followed him into the kitchen. This was the one room I'm glad they hadn't changed because it had windows everywhere. Not one upper cabinet to block the view of the trees surrounding the house or the crick at the base of the deck. I leaned over the countertop and took in the familiar landscape. I inhaled the pleasant memory, which for the moment was lacking the bitter taste. I was healing. I could skip over that one night and bask in the moments before things went wrong.

"Do you remember when your father was out grilling?" I asked, and Isaiah laughed. He knew exactly what I was going to say, but I kept going anyway. "And he told your mother to shut up under his breath."

"She was nagging him about the flower beds." Both of us laughed together.

I was practically doubled over when I said, "So she squirted him with the hose."

"He should have known better."

"I was supposed to have dinner here, but she'd ruined the steaks with the water so she fed us all bowls of cereal because, 'Men shouldn't ever tell their wives to shut up.'"

"She's still just as crazy. I think he died to escape her."

The word "died" brought back the memory of my mother. I wouldn't let it quell the laughter, though. "She should have been a witch."

"Are you sure she isn't? Maybe just a different kind." The kettle whistled.

"I think she's the best kind." I looked out the window at Mrs. Kennedy's flower boxes lining the deck. They were empty. Only dirt was left in them to hold them down in a storm. They used to be perfectly placed with flowers that were watered every day in the summer. She was meticulous about her yard. It was sad to see the house lacking the color.

Farther back on the property, the crick flowed over the rocks, and branches lined the shallow area. I leaned over the counter so my sight could follow it. Pressure surrounded my heart as it beat against the wall of my chest. What was I doing? I tilted my head until I found what I was looking for. Perched so far up in the tree tops you'd never think to look that high was the tree house Isaiah and I had spent so much time in.

"I better go," I said and made my way to the door. "Call us if you need any more help." I barely looked back before lunging out the door. The tears were coming, and I wouldn't share them with Isaiah ever again.

At the end of the walk, I took three steps and launched into the air. I flew straight up and above the trees before landing on the balcony of the tree house. It didn't injure me anymore. I could stand there and look out at the woods without feeling the need to pull the dagger from my lung. A small herd of deer walked across the shallow creek to the Gloucester County side of the land.

I did the unthinkable and opened the door, letting out a deep breath as I stepped inside. I waited for the rush of pain, but there was nothing but a cool wind swirling around the structure.

I stood in the middle of the room and steadied myself by balancing on both feet beneath me. The floor didn't give out. I'd left him. He married her. I fell in love with Owen. Ike and Ever and Gwen were born. This tree house was nothing but a distant memory. The same as the first time I fell off my bike by the church in Auburn or the time I forgot to take off my bra before putting on my suit and jumping in the pool at the Melissa's graduation party. The pain didn't linger the same as the ache of my mother dying. Isaiah hurting me was a part of my youth. It was a memory I shared with a man that was still alive. My mother was gone forever.

The door opened behind me, and Isaiah leaned down to walk in. "I saw the door open," he said. "From the kitchen window, I saw the tree house door."

I stayed still. Afraid to move. Terrified the delicate balance of memory versus pain would be upset by his presence in this, our lover's hideaway. He closed the two steps between us without ever taking his eyes off me. Whole thoughts were pressed from my mind, leaving only Isaiah in front of me. I couldn't speak. The birds squawked a warning outside, but I wouldn't listen.

Our bodies were mere inches apart. My gaze rested on his shoulder. The same one I'd laid my head on so many times before. I forced my hand to stay by my side and not reach up and run my fingers down his body. His neck was still tan from the warmer months, his chin . . . his lips.

Isaiah reached up and held my face in his hand. The birds' noise was replaced by complete silence as Isaiah kissed me. The woods around us held its collective breath, waiting for my body's response to Isaiah's touch. His lips rested on mine as his heat infiltrated me. I tried to breathe, to think, but there was a trembling beneath my surface I had to fight to control. I stared in his eyes one last time before closing mine and pressing my lips against his again.

He forced me back against the wall, and our bodies melded together as he leaned against me. I wrapped my arms around his neck and pulled him closer. I wanted him to touch me everywhere. My fingers found the back of his head and knotted in his hair. The air surrounding us grazed my skin and reignited a twenty-year-old obsession with Isaiah's body.

Breathless, he kissed my neck and dragged his lips up to my ear. My head fell back as I let go of the exhaustion and hate I'd held between us. I turned my head to the side until Isaiah relented and stepped back.

He waited for me to say something, but his knowledge of my thoughts wasn't exclusive to high school. My body told him what he knew to be true all these years, and his memory of the person I was would tell him the rest.

He was a man. Not some young kid who'd let me go because he couldn't figure out how to keep me. He would let me fly away this time. We both knew it without him saying it, but the words were toying with the tip of my tongue. My hands were clenching at my side, fighting to touch him again. I wanted him. I'd wanted him my entire life. The memories I'd endured made me feel some entitlement to whatever was about to transpire.

I took one last look at Isaiah and disappeared. I flew back to Auburn and to the sisters I'd never risk losing again. I let the air and my speed rob me of the thoughts and emotions connected to Isaiah's kiss. I twirled and dove through the wind until I had to focus solely on not crashing. The strategy worked until I landed behind the tree line at the back of our property. I ran my hands up my arms and chased the heat from his touch. I closed my eyes and let myself sink one last time into my youth and what it felt like to be loved by Isaiah Kennedy. I had to let it go. My first love, the kiss, and the nagging fear that I'd flown to the tree house in hopes he'd follow me.

Gisel was out back, planting mums in the beds next to the fire pit. "I'm sorry I wasn't here. How is the old bat?" she asked and barely looked up.

I waited next to her until she stood and faced me. "I just kissed Isaiah."

Her eyebrows rose. "Okay."

"It isn't okay."

"This isn't because of me, I hope."

I thought about it while I stood, trapped within her stare. How could it not be about her? It was more than just the screwed-up members of our family and the vicious past we'd endured. Unbelievably, there were others to consider with us. Three children had been born into our love affairs. The wind blew, and the treetops swayed with it. "It's about you and me and him and a lot of other things. It's about everything, but I don't want there to be any more secrets between us."

"Do you still love him?" she asked. *That* I wanted to keep a secret.

"Yes, but not the way I used to, or maybe exactly how I used to, which is not the way I feel today. I don't know."

"Well, I know better than anyone that he still loves you. I don't think he ever stopped." She smiled a little. "Try to figure this out so you don't hurt each other again. A love like that shouldn't cause this much pain."

I left Gisel in the yard and dragged myself inside. Everything felt heavier, including my footsteps. The burden of Isaiah came back with a vengeance.

"What's wrong with you?" Sloane asked.

"I just went to Isaiah's mom's. She fell."

"Oh no. Is she all right?"

It wasn't her I was worried about. "Yes. I helped her up and into bed, and then I kissed Isaiah."

I looked to Sloane, who was only watching me. She crept into a chair at the kitchen table without taking her eyes off me, and I took the chair across from her.

After a few minutes of silence, Sloane finally said, "We all loved Isaiah." Her voice was low. Secrets would be exchanged. "He was our friend and *funny*. Some of my favorite memories from high school include him." Sloane's gaze focused on me, holding me. Trapping me there with her. "I know Lovie, you, and unbelievably Gisel, have all forgiven him for the damage that occurred . . . but I haven't. I still want to kill him." Our joint laughter broke through the dense confusion in the room. "I like to think the entire situation was his fault."

"That's big of you."

"I know, but to think of it any other way would mean admitting we're not perfect, and life is short. I have no time to address our imperfections. I choose to ignore them."

"The appeal of your position is not lost on me." My laugh trickled off as I faced how imperfect Isaiah and I must have been.

"I never want to see you hurt that way again, and I don't think there's anyone alive who could injure you to that extent besides Isaiah."

"I don't want to be with him. I don't want to go back."

"Then don't."

X

"**WHAT ARE YOU DOING DOWN** here?" I'd heard the footsteps on the leaves behind me and prayed it was Lovie. I knew it was Isaiah, though. He'd seek me out and find me if I were on the other side of the earth. Since I'd let him know the secret that I still wanted him, he'd let himself in everywhere else.

"Hiding."

He sat on the tree trunk next to me. "Not very well."

"No." I kept my eyes on the crick. I'd gone over what I'd say to him dozens of time in my head, but seeing him as I tried to speak erased all my eloquent plans.

"Helene—"

"Isaiah." I wrung my hands in my lap. He reached out and placed his palm over my fingers to stop me from fussing, as my grandmother would have said. He'd done the same thing when he'd sat by me at my mother's funeral. Heat traveled from his hand, up my arms, and settled in the center of my chest. "I'm sorry."

"What do you have to be sorry for?" His voice was light. It brought the weight of the subject to the surface with it and made it easier to speak.

"I should have let you apologize twenty years ago. I kept us all in a state of regret and hate because I was too broken to resolve anything."

"You have nothing to be sorry for, Helene."

"I'm not saying I should have forgiven you back then. Just that I should have listened. Now we've been married, had children, lived through many deaths, and we're still here dealing with the same thing."

"I'm thankful we're here and have a chance to deal with things." I lifted my hands, and his palm fell to my thigh, making me jump as if his accidental touch had set me on fire.

I faced my first love. "Isaiah, I want to move forward, not backward. If we never discuss that time again, it will be too soon for me."

"I'm fine with moving forward." He stood, too.

I took another step back toward the crick. I'd fall into it before I let him touch me again. "I want to be friends."

He looked at the green growth between us on the ground and let the truth in my words sink in.

"The way we were freshman year. I want to laugh with you again and go fishing . . . maybe." I knew that would be too much, but if we were just discussing what I wanted, then that was part of it. "Together, I want to watch our children build their lives. You and I, and Sloane and Lovie and Gisel."

"I want that, too." The dense blue of his eyes was pulling me back to him.

"That's all I want." I held my hands up between us. It was either a defensive position or a retreat, but I didn't think I could hold my resolve if he kept moving toward me. I was committing to him in the only way I could, and he would have to be okay with that.

Isaiah ignored my hands and took a step toward me.

I disappeared but came back in the next second. "I'm not going to run and hide. We're too old for that."

He shook his head. "Don't ever run from me again. I promise, Helene, I'm not going to hurt you. My God, I will die before I do. You have to believe me."

I did believe, but I'd trusted him before. What was I thinking? None of that mattered because we'd never be close enough again for Isaiah to tear me apart the way he had back then. "There are many more people to consider now. Not just us." I looked him in the eyes. I faced our entire past and said, "I don't want to love you like that again . . . and I'm not going to."

He leaned down and whispered in my ear, "You already do." Isaiah stood straight.

I kept my eyes low. My sight was fixed on his chest as I steadied myself against his claim. When I looked up, he was smiling as if this, too, were one of the hilarious jokes of our freshman year in high school.

"I'm going to go now. Not running. Just leaving."

"I'll follow you," he said and moved out of my way.

We traversed the crude path from the bank of the crick, up the hill, and into my driveway in silence. His truck was parked near the house, blocking the path for any other vehicles.

"It's like you live here," I said and patted the quarter panel.

"I could. Everyone else does."

He made me laugh. Just like old times. "Goodbye, Isaiah."

With tremendous mercy, he did not follow me inside. I wasn't left broken and exhausted the way I usually found myself after a conversation with him. Ever was lying on the couch with Carl curled at her feet and our mothers' old notebooks and journals all around her.

"Where did you find all of this?"

"In the basement. When the three of you used to read these every night, you were looking for a way to overturn the curse, weren't you?"

I flipped through the pages of a faded yellow legal tablet until the paper turned black and the ink turned silver. Sloane's notes on spell casting covered the page. I nodded. "And now what are you searching for?"

"Anything about a hunter." She sighed, leaned over to the coffee table, and switched the journal she'd been studying for another one.

"Find anything?"

Ever's smile lightened the dismal tone of the conversation. "There was a man named Hunter who Poppy was secretly in love with. They cast a spell for him to find love in hopes it would be with her."

"Ruby's grandmother was something."

"It runs in the family," she said. "Judging by the fact Ruby's grandfather was not named Hunter, it doesn't appear to have worked out how Poppy had hoped it would."

"Well, if there is a record of someone called the hunter, it would be here." That didn't seem to relax her at all, and I set the notebook down and asked, "Anything else going on?"

She sat up straight against the arm of the couch. "You heard about the police officer who had the accident? The one who died?"

"I did."

"Well, I flew out there this morning."

He'd been killed. Instantly, I hoped. "Why would you go there?"

"I had a dream about him."

I froze. Witches never dreamed, but that condition didn't seem to apply to my daughter. "Before he died?"

"I don't know." She exhaled. "I think the night after, but I didn't really know it. When I saw his picture on the news, I remembered the dream."

"It was tragic. A single car loss on a bright sunny day. Maybe it affected you to the point of thinking you had some connection to it. I wouldn't worry about it."

"I wasn't really, but something told me to go to the accident scene and look around." Ever held still as if her mind needed a moment to process what else the forest had told her. "The Roman numerals three six seven were painted in red on a trunk a quarter mile from the accident."

The details turned in my mind as I tried to process her account. She pulled something up on her phone and handed it to me. It was a picture of the fallen officer. It listed his rank, name, and badge number. Three six seven.

They were never going to stop. "The Virago have no morals. A police officer." I shook my head.

Dainty flashes, like that of a sparkler, flew from a journal Ever had abandoned on the coffee table. She looked at me before picking up the book. Her eyes widened as she turned it over in her hands. It opened to a page three quarters of the way from the beginning, and the sparks halted.

"I didn't see this before."

"What is it?" I slid to her end of the couch and read over her shoulder.

Know your enemy.

With knowledge comes destruction.

Not all family can be trusted.

Not all honor is to the craft.

"This handwriting doesn't match anyone's," Ever said and reached for the other notebooks.

I recognized it as a part of my youth. "It's Clara's."

"What does it mean? Not all family can be trusted."

I stared at the words. "It's rich coming from Clara." Ever flipped through the pages of the book again, and Clara's words disappeared.

"Where did they go?"

"I don't know. We need to write down what she said. I don't think it was from when she was alive." Ever only stared at me. "She's trying to warn us of something."

I wrote down the warning on a sheet of paper I'd ripped from the back of a notebook.

"Not all honor is to the craft," Ever recited. "What other honor is there?"

"The world is full of men and women who fight to the death to honor their beliefs. Just because their views are opposite of our own does not mean their actions are dishonorable to them."

"The Virago?"

"I don't think so."

Ever stared at the words until I thought she was going to cry. She swallowed hard and closed her eyes.

"Ever . . ." I caressed her arm.

"I can't stop thinking about that couple in Upper Pittsgrove. What if Auburn is no longer sacred, either? What if the Virago have found a way to overturn the protection?"

"A witch's spell cannot be overturned," I said.

My daughter and I only looked at each other in silence.

I'D PUT ALL THE WITCHES' secrets back on the shelf in the basement the night before, but I couldn't get the conversation with Ever out of my head. I hung the fall wreath on the front door. Black and silver ribbon wrapped around it and secured a large witch's hat hanging from the bottom. It was a gift from Sloane for my and Owen's first Halloween together. He'd hated it. I was in love the minute I pulled it out of the box.

Lovie stood in the middle of the empty family room with three laundry baskets by her feet and folded laundry on nearly every square inch of the sectional.

"Need some help?"

"I think we need less clothes. No one would believe how many articles eight women could wear in one week."

"I'll get some water and help. Do you want a drink?" I opened the refrigerator and found all four girls' lunches staring back at me from the shelves. "They forgot their lunches."

"Oh no."

I poured myself some water from the pitcher and replaced it on the refrigerator door. "They were running late." I stepped into the makeshift laundry room with Lovie. "Said they couldn't find anything to wear."

"That makes sense." She laughed as she checked the clock on the television. "I'm going to run them in."

"You shouldn't do that. They have to take responsibility, and dealing with consequences is a great way to learn." I was shaking my head as I spoke.

"I know, but it goes against my personal beliefs for them to eat cafeteria food, and today is Salisbury steak." The meal's grotesque nature was evident in her curled lip and tilted head. Lovie couldn't even stomach the idea.

"Suit yourself. I'll keep folding."

Lovie moved to the kitchen, checked to make sure all the lunches were balanced and fresh, and loaded them into a tote bag. She'd missed her calling as a chef. I folded Ever's favorite hoodie and started a new pile for her clothes next to Gwen's.

When the silence of Lovie's absence hit me, I put on the old boom box on the kitchen counter and music filled the downstairs of the house. I sang along as I pulled the basket of towels toward the empty chair in the corner.

The hint of honeysuckle hit my nose and paralyzed me as I bent down.

"It's just me," he said casually, as if I shouldn't be alarmed that he was in my home with me.

"Have you ever considered knocking?"

He leaned closer to me. His leg brushed against my arm that still rested on the basket. "Wouldn't that be strange? Having someone that you can't see ring the bell?" Air swept by me as he sat back in the chair. "What if you weren't alone? How would you explain that to one of your . . . sisters? Or worse, to Ever?"

"Okay." I raised my hand. I folded a towel and dropped it right on where I imagined his lap was.

"You're annoyed," he said.

"I'm annoyed or you're annoying?" I kept folding the towels.

"Touchy. What has gotten into you today?" I didn't answer.

I dropped the next towel and sighed. "It's just becoming less appealing not being able to see the person I'm talking to. I know nothing about you, and you just show up here whenever you want." If Xavier was doing anything besides concentrating on what I was saying, I couldn't tell. "It feels like I'm a toy you play with at your whim."

"I apologize." The towel I'd dropped disappeared and became visible again when it was tossed on top of the pile perfectly folded. "Perhaps if I contribute." Another towel followed. "It isn't wrong, it's different."

"What is?"

"Our relationship."

"Is that what this is? A relationship?"

"I brag to everyone who will listen that you are my best friend." I threw a towel at him. It blinked in and out of view before landing at our feet. He leaned down to pick it up, and the hint of honeysuckle moving past me brought back my latest questions.

"Xavier?"

"Yes, Helene?"

"Have you ever been to a witch's house in South Harrison? Her name is Maryann. She's a part of the Kingsway Coven."

Silence. I let the towel fall to my side. I didn't really want to know. Not the truth if it meant he could hurt someone or threaten a child. Whatever Xavier was in my mind, it was good.

"I have been there." I disappeared, too. I moved back a few feet until I was standing in front of the television. "Are you afraid of me?" His voice was barely a whisper and filled with hurt.

"Why were you there?"

"I'd heard about a plan some acquaintances were concocting." He was moving closer to me. I couldn't see him. I *felt* him, and instead of moving away again, I stood my ground.

"Acquaintances, as in friends?" His answer to this question would determine whether I ever spoke to him again.

"No." He grabbed me by my upper arms in a firm grip. His fingers loosened right after he held me. "Helene, you have to believe me. I am not a part of those you hate. I wouldn't be here if I was."

"Have they ever seen you?" I longed to see him.

"No." I exhaled at his single word.

What was he? Who was he? None of the details of Xavier made sense, not even the sense of safety I felt when he was near. "Do you know a boy named Billy Roberts?"

Xavier let go of my arms. "Yes." He stayed directly in front of me. "He has issues."

"Did you know his parents?"

"Yes. Didn't you?"

Didn't everyone in this town? "What kind of issues?"

Xavier waited before he answered. The delay was another reason not to trust him. If there were no alliance with the Virago or Billy Roberts, the answers should be easy for him to give me.

"High school is difficult enough without being different from every single one of your classmates in basic physical ways. Billy struggles with confusion and isolation." I wished I could look into Xavier's eyes. At least then I'd be able to judge the thoughts behind his words. "And his uncle abuses him."

I lowered my head. Some shame for my hatred of a boy who'd been abused his entire life because his mother was like me fell on my shoulders. He needed help. Not more hatred.

"Not everyone can be saved, Helene."

I stepped back out of his hold, picked up a towel, and continued with my folding. "Why *are* you here?"

"I told you." He moved closer to me again. "You're my bff." I reappeared so he could see me roll my eyes. Xavier only laughed at me.

"Are you hungry?" I asked.

"No. Are you?"

"Not especially."

"Did you have a good morning?"

"Were you watching me?" My words were harsh again.

"No." Xavier was indignant. "I was just asking a question. What happened this morning?"

"Nothing." I was going to leave it at that, but something forced me to admit, "Yesterday, I spoke with Isaiah."

"Oh." Xavier returned to folding towels from the basket and piling them on the chair. "Wouldn't it just be easier to continue hating him and never speak to him again?"

Somehow, I was smiling even though our entire conversation was ridiculous. "I've tried that. It didn't work out so well, and it was far from easy."

"I think you should keep working on it. Perfect your silence."

"I kissed him the other day." Xavier embraced his own silence. There were no more signs of movement, as if time stood still when Xavier did. "In his tree house. I kissed him like a teenager." I inhaled deeply the memory. "Like myself as a teenager."

"Do you still love him?"

"Yes." I didn't have to hesitate with Xavier. He wouldn't use it against me the way Isaiah would. "But nowhere near enough to have a relationship with him under the current circumstances. He is in the middle of a divorce with a member of my coven. Our children are dating. Our daughters are best friends. Isaiah was my past. Now, he'll be a part of my future, but not in the same way."

"I'm guessing he's disappointed by that."

"He hasn't said exactly."

"I'm sure he didn't have to."

"I guess that's what old friends are like. Do you have many old friends, Xavier? How about work friends. Got a lot of those?" All the questions ran through my mind. I wanted to tie him up and keep him here until he answered every single one of them.

"Plenty of friends," he said. "I think it's time for me to go." Of course it was. Why talk about Xavier when we could delve further into the intimate details of Helene's life? "Thanks for having me, Helene."

"Sure." I let the sarcasm drip from my words. "Anytime. Just let yourself in. Don't bother to knock."

Xavier left. I thought. I continued to fold the laundry. I should have asked him about his first love. He certainly knew plenty about mine.

The girls remembered their lunches every day the rest of the week. The fear of Salisbury steak was more of a learning experience than starvation. The air was deliciously sweet and crisp like the apples that were being harvested from the orchards. October was my favorite month. Sloane had always shunned it because a witch's favorite month shouldn't be the one with Halloween, but I was fine with being perfectly predictable and ordinary, and I happened to love Halloween.

The weak sun warmed me in the afternoon light. I leaned my rake against the tree and wiped my brow with the top of my wrist so the dirt from my work glove didn't cover me. The days were flying by. The hours of sunlight dwindled. Mondays became Fridays before dinner had been served. Time would propel us into the holidays, and the snow would soon arrive.

"Helene." Xavier's voice came from behind me. I looked over my shoulder, knowing I wouldn't see him. "I didn't want to scare you."

I turned around. "You didn't."

"Is Gisel, or anyone else, home?"

"No. They're with the girls at the movies." I'd needed a day alone.

The silent pause was awkward. If I could have seen him, it would have meant something, but I was always in the dark with Xavier. He finally said, "There's been an . . . accident."

I straightened and forced air into my lungs. Ever.

"Ever's fine."

"Xavier." The silence that always accompanied him was killing me.

"It's Isaiah." The name was stifled leaving his mouth. "He's in his yard behind his house."

"What happened?"

"He'll tell you."

I disappeared and launched toward Alloway. I couldn't tell if Xavier was with me, but that was often on the ground as well as in the air.

Isaiah was at the bottom of the hill by his house, lying by the water's edge where the pictures had been taken for the prom last May. I flew around him twice. No one was near him or in the yard. The house appeared empty from the outside. I dropped down and showed myself next to him.

"Isaiah," I whispered and touched his arm.

He rolled over. A hole near his right eye spewed blood down the side of his face. "Helene." His voice slipped out the corner of his mouth.

"Don't move."

"Helene." He reached for my arm. "Don't leave me."

"I'm not. I just need to get something to stop the bleeding." I ran into the house, grabbed the dishtowel that hung from the handle on the stove, and dialed 9-1-1. I gave them Isaiah's name, address, and what I had seen of his injury, but I couldn't stay on the phone or answer any more questions. Isaiah needed me outside.

I knelt beside him and placed the folded towel over the hole in his head.

Gisel. Sloane. Lovie!

"What happened?" I asked him. He tried to raise his arm. At first, I thought he was reaching up for the towel, but he was covering his head. He was protecting himself.

Gisel! Ever, Ruby, Gwen, Maya.

I remembered, they were all inside a movie theater, probably too enthralled with whatever celebrity was on the screen to listen.

I patted his cargo shorts and pulled his phone out of the left pocket. "Isaiah, what's the lock code on your phone? I have to call Gisel and Gwen." His lips parted, but the words didn't come. "Isaiah, can you hear me?" I held the towel tight to his head and leaned down so I could speak softly in his ear. "Isaiah, it's Helene." I tilted his head toward me.

"It's your birthday."

I was losing him. He might have had a brain injury. "No it isn't."

"The code. It's your birthday. Zero, one, one, zero." His chest rose as he inhaled deeply.

"Oh." I ignored the significance and typed the numbers into the phone. His home screen opened, and I sent texts to everyone. My coven, Ever's coven, and Ike. Isaiah's phone was all I had beside my powers.

There were only two other people with me in the waiting room—an elderly man in a tuxedo and a middle-aged woman holding a carved pumpkin in her lap. Emergencies didn't come when you were prepared to address them. The pumpkin's design was a cat with a long tail climbing to the top near the stem.

My own outfit was just as confusing. Cutoff jeans, which were covered in a dusting of dirt from the leaves, and an old Woodstown Athletics tee I was sure Ike had left at our house at some point over the summer. No makeup, and my hair pulled back into two ponytails at the base of my neck because no one was supposed to see me.

Ike was the first to arrive. He came tearing into the room ready to rip the automatic doors off the front of the ER when they didn't open fast enough. "Where is he?"

"He's with the doctors." I kept my voice calm and level, but Ike's response was more appropriate. My time in the waiting room had given me the horrible space to properly assess Isaiah's wound, but nothing made sense considering the lack of another scratch on him. At least not one that I could see.

"What happened?"

"I don't know." Ike sat beside me. "I found him lying on the ground. His head was bleeding." I left out terms like "gushing," "pouring," and "profusely." "I have no idea what happened before I got there."

"Did he call you?"

Ike's question was a glimpse into my future. Questions would be asked about how I found him. I looked around the room, wondering if Xavier was with me. I wasn't sure what he would want me to say about how I found Isaiah.

"No." I lowered my voice. "I was out flying and went by your parents' house." Was it even Ike's parents' house anymore? Gisel lived with us in Auburn. Divorce made all of the tiny details as confusing as the big ones.

"Did you see any signs of someone else having been there?" Ike was not some frantic or shaken kid. He was solid. I didn't know if it was maturity or a central part of his personality because I hadn't known him when he was a child. My coven had already lost so much. Time was one of the greatest prices we'd paid.

"No," I said, and Ike and I sat in silence until the others came. They poured into the room, bringing life to the small group of somber strangers.

"What happened?"

"Where is he?"

"Is he okay?" They peppered me with questions.

"He was talking a little. He knew who I was and seemed to know where he was," I said.

To Sloane, Lovie, and Gisel, I thought, *He has a head injury. There was a lot of blood.*

What happened?

I have no idea. I didn't see where he fell onto anything. There was nothing around him that could have caused it. We're going to have to wait until he can tell us, I think.

The doctor came out and took Gisel back with him. Gwen began to cry. Maya and Ruby held on to her, but there was nothing anyone could say. She needed to see her father.

Gisel didn't speak a word to us from the other side of the doorway. I assumed she was lost in a conversation with a doctor. I stood and walked toward the window. He had to be okay. We couldn't lose someone else from our family. Not even Isaiah, who had been such a source of pain for so many of us. We needed him, though. Gwen, Ike, and Gisel needed him.

I needed him.

Gisel appeared and told Gwen and Ike to go back and see their dad. "He's going to be fine. He just doesn't look it." The color was gone from her face. Tense lines dug in above her eyebrows.

I waited for Gwen and Ike to disappear before walking toward

Gisel. She met me in front of Sloane and Lovie and thought, *This was a message to us.*

None of us responded. The knowledge that this wasn't an accident, that we'd somehow caused his pain, rose inside me.

All he can remember is a woman on top of him. She surprised him. He was about to take out a canoe. She said, "Tell them to leave," and then everything went dark.

What did she hit him with? Sloane thought.

The doctor is assuming he fell onto something sharp, but he marveled at the fact it looked clean enough to have been an ice pick.

Three chills ran down the back of my neck and over my spine, chasing each other.

"I think you were right at the Goddess Gathering last year, Helene. This is going to be a war," Lovie said. None of us answered.

The next day when Isaiah was released, Gisel brought him back to our house. She made Isaiah comfortable in her bed and cared for him as if they were still married. In this situation, he felt like all our husbands.

Lovie cooked Isaiah's fall favorites. Butternut squash soup, garlic bread, and apple pie. He was gracious and kind and joked about how he was going to get hurt more often if Lovie was going to cook and Sloane was going to be nice."

"Don't push it," Sloane said, and only Isaiah laughed. His injury had brought us even closer together, and with the excitement, no one questioned how I was able to find him so quickly after the attack occurred.

My mind was lost between the Virago's threat and Xavier's part in the whole thing. I needed to see him, but I had no idea how to contact him.

Xavier, if you can hear this, I thought, shutting out everyone but him. Even as a woman who often had entire conversations in my mind, I felt ridiculous. *I need to talk to you.*

I thought the same thing a few times throughout the day. The girls arrived home from school, and Ike came down from Rowan. For dinner, Lovie made lasagna, another of Isaiah's favorites. Isaiah never mentioned the threat. He'd only told Gisel, and none of us were going to bring it up in front of the kids.

Isaiah went to bed in Gisel's room. She assigned herself to Lovie's bedroom for the night.

"I don't want to disturb Isaiah by rolling over," she said and left us in the kitchen. We all knew she just didn't want to sleep next to him. I understood her stance. Sloane did not.

"What is the big deal? They were married for almost twenty years?"

"The big deal is now they're not, or at least, they won't be soon," Lovie stepped in on Gisel's behalf.

"So?"

"So, endings are hard enough. When you finally come out on the other side of one, why begin again?"

Amen, I thought, but only to myself.

That night, I couldn't sleep. The sight of Isaiah lying by the lake haunted me every time I closed my eyes until I gave up and went down to the kitchen. I left the lights off. My eyes adjusted to the moonlight just enough to make out the teakettle. I filled it with water and fumbled around with the stove knobs until I was sure I had the right burner turned to high.

I leaned on the edge of the sink and looked out the window up to the moon. It was three-quarters full and perfectly placed in a clear sky, but because of the angle, only a sliver of its light made it to the kitchen.

"Why are you in the dark?"

I turned toward Xavier's voice and let my eyes adjust. The faint outline of a man several inches taller than me came into focus. "How come you're not invisible?"

"Can you see me?"

He was facing the door with his head turned toward me. I couldn't make out his eyes or the lines of his cheekbones, but I thought his hair was thick. He certainly wasn't bald.

Xavier laughed a little, but I wasn't sure at what.

"More of you than I ever have before."

"And that makes you happy?"

"Is it so much to ask? Knowing what a friend looks like?"

"In this case, yes."

The kettle whistled, and I rushed to take it off the burner before it woke anyone. "Would you like a cup of tea or hot chocolate?"

"Yes."

"Which one?" I found two mugs in the clean dishwasher that had been run after dinner.

"Whatever you're having."

I poured the water over herbal tea bags, being careful not to burn myself. When I replaced the kettle on the burner, I realized Xavier had moved. He was so close I could lean against him without moving my feet. His silence softened the enormity of his stature. There was something delicate about Xavier. It was the vulnerability he wouldn't share that kept him hidden in the shadows and never fully with me.

"Lemon? Sugar?" I managed to say with him so close.

"No, thank you."

"How did you know Isaiah had been attacked?"

He took a sip of his tea, taking his time as if he knew exactly what I was going to ask and it was of no bother to him. "I'd heard their plans. They, of course, couldn't agree on anything." His head shook a little, I thought. "I followed them to make sure you weren't the target."

"You were there when they did this?" How could he let it happen? He knew who Isaiah was to me.

"I was around. I flew over and made sure you weren't anywhere near the house. I wasn't even certain he was home until they flew away and I saw him lying there."

"Why didn't you help him? Stop them?" I was whisper-yelling and ready to unleash the full volume of my disgust. I didn't care who heard.

"If it had been you, I would have."

"But not him?" I couldn't have watched anyone be hurt that way.

"You don't understand how things work. Outside, in the real world where there are no more covens or codes of honor."

I never thought Xavier could have the gifts of a witch. He was a man, but he was so much more than that. With the knowledge of his powers came the possibilities he could be something other than honorable. He could be an enemy. "Explain it to me then."

"These witches are lost and bitter. They've been angry for most of their lives. Just not long enough to forget how things used to be for them. They're alone and isolated and shunned."

"I know that." He needed to get to the part where a decent human being stands by and lets someone be assaulted with an ice pick.

He inhaled deeply, obviously reading my disgust. "I've been alone my whole life, Helene. I know of the Virago. Who they are. *What* they are, and I am hellishly familiar with the absent limits to the evil they will cause."

"We can stop them. We're not going to let them terrorize us or this town."

"How will you stop them? Are you willing to kill them, the way they will you?"

I didn't have a retort. He knew that wasn't an option.

Unfortunately, the Virago did, too.

Xavier sipped his tea. I could feel him breathing near me. "Show me you, Xavier." I couldn't understand keeping his secret from me. I already knew about his powers. What else needed to be kept a secret? The details of his life I was asking for we shared with everyone.

"I'm sorry. I can't," he said. I put down my cup and stood in front of him. "I live two lives, and the way I survive is to keep them separate. Only my mother knows the man that I am and the secret that I live." I reached up and laid my palms flat on his stomach. The fabric of his shirt was a thick flannel. "The rest of the world knows me as Jason."

"I want to know Jason and Xavier." It was either the silence or his closeness that made the kitchen feel small with the two of us standing next to each other.

"You've always known exactly where you belong. Right here in Auburn. An entire town protected for your family. I've been an island raised on a farm in Upper Pittsgrove with barely a word about my powers. The ones that were said were all warnings to keep it a secret." He placed his hands on top of mine. "I've observed the Virago for years, and although they know I exist, we've managed to cohabitate this area without a problem. I mind my own business, and they stay out of it."

I'd always had Sloane and Lovie. No matter who else we'd lost, I'd never been alone. Xavier's upbringing was certainly not like my own, but did that excuse him from helping where help was needed? I would have died before standing back and letting someone be attacked the way Isaiah was today, but I also had my coven to fight by my side.

"Now do you realize why I don't share my identity? With anyone."

I stepped back from him and wrapped my fingers around my mug and let the heat seep into my body through my hands.

"I always understood why you don't share it with anyone." I focused until I made out the shape of his body next to me again. "I just want you to share with me."

He tilted his head to the side, and the moonlight from the window revealed his thick black hair. He whispered in my ear, "I'm going to go. Before I do something stupid." Heat coursed through me and followed his breath down my neck. He'd replaced my anger at him with frustration.

The warmth settled between my shoulder blades. I inhaled a shallow breath and exhaled, trying to regain control of my emotions. There was too much unknown about Xavier.

His lips rested on my cheek close to my ear. I closed my eyes and heard him say, "Good night," before he moved, and all of my senses confirmed he was gone.

THE SECOND NIGHT ISAIAH WAS there, Gisel slept with me instead of Lovie. This was something we had done when we were younger. If one of us were hurting, we would gravitate toward the counter balance. If it was a clear understanding, you went to Sloane. For love and support, a back rub, or the scent of muffins, Lovie's bed was the only option. Gisel and I would giggle the night away. That was what I always sought from her. I wasn't sure what she needed from me or why she was rolling over and staring at me. I could feel it even though my eyes were fixed on the cracked ceiling above us.

"I'm scared," she said. Her voice was low, but she wasn't whispering.

"I know." The hole in Isaiah's head punctured me again. "He could have been killed."

"They picked him because we both love him." I didn't argue her point. "And Gwen."

"He's the most central to all of us."

"He isn't, though. Ike is." I turned and faced Gisel without a word. Fear was choking me. "Gwen adores him. I can't live without him. He is Ever's world."

"And the rest of us consider him a son," I said.

"Isaiah was just the beginning. They'll come for Ike next."

"We don't know that."

"I do. I can feel it."

I inhaled through the tightening of my chest. "What do you want to do?"

"Kill them."

I waited for her to laugh a little or elaborate. The hole in her husband's head had reached deeper into Gisel than it had Isaiah.

"They tortured Ever's dog. She was ready to kill them then. If they so much as come near Ike, I won't be able to stop her. I don't think our honor will mean anything to her." Hot tears welled in my eyes.

"It won't. She was willing to give up being a witch for him. She'll kill for him, too, and I'll stand right by her side while she does."

Gisel hadn't come into my room to sleep. Her presence was going to steal every moment of rest I'd ever hope to have again.

Two days after that conversation, Isaiah returned to Alloway. I wasn't comfortable with him leaving. At least no more so than I was with him staying. The town of Auburn was our haven, and we'd bring whoever we needed into it to protect them.

We went through the motions of the second Saturday in October. The girls had their final SAT prep class and were up and out of the house early. They returned home exhausted, starving, and thrilled to be free of the "timed torture," as they referred to it. The stress was taking a toll on Ever. She was wilting before my eyes. She didn't want to talk about anything, but in saying nothing, she increased my level of concern.

"Tonight is the Goddess Gala," Lovie told them.

"What's that?" Gwen asked.

"You'll love it. It's beautifully bizarre and educational and somehow makes sense of what we are," Maya told her.

"Then I will love it."

My full coven had only been once before when our mothers took us as teenagers. We'd go every year from now on as long as Tara Jane and the other Kingsway witches would have us. We flew to Mullica Hill. It seemed fitting that instead of fitting all eight of us into the minivan somehow, we should fly, eight strong, to a party celebrating witchcraft. We landed in the backyard and all the women standing near turned in our direction before we even showed ourselves.

"Lovie," Riley said and ran across the lawn to hug her. The rest of the Kingsway Coven gathered to greet us. They made lifelong friendships look easy. Gisel and Tara Jane moved closer to the fire. Two Earth witches reunited after all these years apart.

"Mom," Ever called to me. She was standing next to Gwen, who was bent at the knees, gripping her head between her hands.

"What is it?" I asked as I leaned over and put my hand on her back. "Gwen, what's wrong?"

"The voices," she said. She raised her head up for a moment, inhaled sharply, and returned to hiding it in her arms. "There are too many."

I looked around for Sloane or Gisel. With my arm around Gwen, I led her back from the fire. Sloane was by the back door. I called to her, but she was deep in a conversation with Maryann. "It's going to be okay."

"Let her go," the elderly witch we'd sought help from a year ago demanded as she stood over both of us. Her eyes were fixed on Gwen.

I stepped back. The woman held both hands up in front of her with her palms facing Gwen. *Gisel*, I screamed in my head. Everyone at the party stopped and stared at the old witch bent over Gwen. Gisel ran toward us with Sloane and Lovie behind her.

"Don't be afraid, sweet child. They talk to you because your heart is pure. They need you." I had no idea what she was talking about, but Gwen calmed in front of my eyes. "There are many here tonight. They've come for you. They're tired of talking to me."

Gwen looked up, her eyes heavy with pain. "Too many," she said breathlessly.

"Silence," the witch ordered, but no one around us was speaking.

Gwen stood straight. Her breaths were heavy for a long minute before they returned to normal. She appeared exhausted. "Thank you," she said.

The woman took her hand. "Like all gifts, you must learn to control it." Gwen nodded. "You can make them stop talking, at least to you, by telling them to silence." The "them" she referred to wasn't us, which could only mean one thing. "And you can share their voices."

Gwen's attention shifted around the yard before landing back on the woman. "How?"

The elderly witch waved me closer and took Gwen's hand. "Hold her hand," she said to me. I did as I was told. "I'm going to give their voices to you, and then, as if you're pushing them down a pipe, you'll share them with her," she said to Gwen. "They won't be as powerful when you receive them because they're coming through me."

Gwen seemed to brace herself as she nodded her acceptance to the old witch. She closed her eyes and jolted while the witch kept her focus on her. She never took her eyes off her, and neither did I. "Now send it. Share it. Open your mind and let your aunt hear."

My mind filled with voices. Each of them was calling out to the elderly witch. Asking her to listen. Some had information to share and others had loved ones they wanted messages delivered to. Most of all, they just wanted to talk. It was chaotic and overwhelming and I wanted to hold my own head in my hands the same way Gwen had done when we first landed in the backyard.

"I'm going to let go now," the elder woman said.

The voices shifted and called out to Gwen. The volume increased. I made out, "It's Mimi," but there was little else I could decipher.

"Silence!" Gwen shouted, and her mind cleared. She opened her eyes and stared at me. I didn't let go of her hand.

"She's a bridge," the elderly witch proclaimed.

Gasps, cheers, the chaos in Gwen's mind was replaced by the crowd around her. She squeezed my hand.

"It's okay," I said, but I didn't know what any of it meant.

Gisel wrapped her arm around her daughter's shoulders and pulled her tight against her. "I should have known. I thought it was just Mama, and that she was being stubborn not talking to me, but only Gwen could hear her."

"How often do you hear them?" the elderly woman asked Gwen.

"I've never heard anything like tonight. Sometimes I hear things, and I don't know why, or who, or what it even is."

"They're all the departed trying to reach you."

"Why me?"

"Why any of us." The witch waved her hands around, taking in the entire backyard where some witches were floating in the air. "Any of this?"

"Let me spend some time with her." The elderly witch directed to Gisel. "I'll teach her what I can."

"We'll go with you," Ruby said.

The elderly witch scrutinized each of the girls as they moved forward and stood next to Gwen. She smiled back at us as she recognized them. "Very good," she said, and the five of them went into the house.

"A bridge, that's amazing," Maryann said.

"Do you have a bridge among your girls?" I asked.

"Not that we know of." Their daughters, the next generation of coven were still young. The night we'd been to South Harrison, Amelia's baby blanket still lay at the top of her bed. A last memento that moved from a crib to a big girl bed.

"How old are your daughters now?" I asked.

"They're ten. God help us. We're praying to make it through the next ten years."

The memories of trying to keep Ever away from Ike the year before plucked at my mind. "I'll say a prayer for you, too. It isn't pretty."

"Have they decided what they'll do next year?"

"No," Sloane said. "They're all over the place with possible colleges."

"How will you deal with them being out on their own?"

"I'm not sure they won't be safer away from here than they are with us," Sloane said, bringing up the subject we needed to talk to them about.

"We heard about your ex," Maryann directed at me and then tilted her head to Gisel.

"Is there anything that isn't *heard* around here?" Gisel asked.

"It'd be scarier if there were."

We followed Maryann to the patio furniture out back and each took a seat.

"The Virago hurt him," Tara Jane said.

"Whoever it was told him to deliver the message for us to leave."

"That's what we heard."

Sloane rolled her eyes. She'd had years in Las Vegas to forget how quickly information was disseminated in our small towns.

"We've been on high alert ourselves. After you left, this area became a stomping ground for exiled witches. I wish there were a way to find exactly how many and who they are. They have no regard for this area or the people in it."

"Like Maryann's house," Tara Jane said. "Even ten years ago, they would have been too scared to go near her. Their numbers increasing have given them courage, and now, they want freedom to do whatever they want." She tapped her fingers on the side of her glass. "They're completely out of control. Some of them have lived a long time like this. They don't remember what it was like to be civilized."

"How can we stop them?" Lovie asked. "If we're not willing to sink to their level."

"They're forcing me very close to being exactly like them." Gisel's words hung on the darkness in her voice. Considering consequences and planning were not her forte.

The enemy of the Virago would have to be like them to defeat them. I practically whispered as I thought aloud, "It would be best if they would somehow destroy each other."

"It would be perfect." Tara Jane sat back in her seat and pondered the idea.

The dagger in Amelia's pillow. The hole in Isaiah's head . . . I didn't know how we were going to evict the Virago from South Jersey, but attempting to inflict the greater torture was a dangerous way to proceed. Their evil had no bounds, and they felt they had much less to lose.

"We're having a Halloween party this year and would love you all to come," Lovie said, drawing us to a lighter topic.

"With dates?" Tara Jane asked.

"Yes. Not that we'll have any, but please bring whoever you'd like," Sloane offered.

"I actually have someone in mind for you," Jennifer said to Sloane.

"Me?"

"My cousin, Sean Watts. His wife just left him, and he always had a crush on you in high school."

"Why'd she leave him?" Sloane was skeptical.

"I didn't ask. We just put a spell on her that she'd sweat profusely from her feet whenever she kissed someone other than Sean."

"I'm not sure I should get involved with a relative of yours."

"Nonsense," Jennifer said. She peaked into Sloane's cup. "I'll get you more wine."

"I'm still not going out with him. When I leave him, and I will, you'll make me smell or something."

"That isn't true. We never liked this one. I told him a hundred times to move on, but men *never* listen."

XIII

I WAS DRESSED AS THE Wicked Witch of the West and Sloane was Glenda. She was ironically lovely and sweet in her blue sparkle ball gown. None of us could stop laughing at the wand. Where did that prop come from in the story of witches? We invited everyone we could remember from high school, the few people we'd met since we moved home, Gisel and Isaiah's friends, a few of the girls' classmates, the Kingsway Coven, and the entire town of Auburn. A good Halloween party needed a lot of people, and ours met that one criteria.

Sean Watts was dressed as a fireman, making it hard for Sloane to ignore him. They were sitting on the couch together talking about the nights my coven had flown to the county above ours to party with the Kingsway witches in high school.

Maya dressed Carl in a shark costume, which he hated. Ever

told her after twenty minutes she was springing him. I had to admit that it was impossible not to laugh as the dog slash shark made his way through the crowd. Lovie had set up a corner of the room as a photo booth. She'd left a box with oversized sunglasses, feathered boas, crowns, and conversation bubbles attached to sticks for everyone to use. She also painted an old frame to be held up in their pictures. It was a popular attraction. Guests took an abundance of pictures, picking their favorites and posting them online while the party was still in full swing.

The Stormtrooper in the corner of the kitchen, sipping scotch through a straw into his helmet, caught my eye. More like the outline of his shoulders drew me in and reminded me of my favorite invisible friend.

"Lovely night," I said as I approached him.

"Yes." His voice was unmistakable. "Would you like to check out the fire?"

Without a word in agreement, I walked out of the kitchen, knowing he would follow. The fire was surrounded by people so I chatted on about grabbing some more wood as he followed me to the tree line without anyone caring where we were going.

"You shouldn't come to parties you're not invited to."

"I thought you told me once that I'm always welcome."

I shook my head while I smiled at him. "No. I never said that. Perhaps you're hearing voices in your head." He chuckled. "What's so funny about that?"

"Nothing."

"I'm glad you're here, though. I need your help."

His helmet tilted to the side. "Anything."

"With the Virago."

His shoulders slumped. "Why can't you just leave them alone?"

"They stuck something in Isaiah's head." I remembered where I was and lowered my voice as I stepped closer to him. "That's why.

It isn't safe here. For anyone."

Xavier exhaled loudly. I frustrated him. It wasn't my intention, but I needed his help.

"What do you need?"

"Information. I need to know how they're organized. Who is in charge? If they have a means of communicating."

"Planning on joining?"

"You're cute."

He moved closer to me and took the split wood from my arms. He leaned down until I could see his lips through the hole in his mask. "Am I?" he asked, and suddenly it was difficult to breathe. "How about I meet you in your room after the party?"

Isaiah and half of Salem County would be sleeping over. There was a chance Gisel could end up in my bed. Or Sloane. Or Lovie . . . I didn't let myself think of the other scenarios.

"Come away with me right now." he said and sounded almost desperate.

"To where?"

There was a long pause. He didn't know, either. Where exactly could a Stormtrooper take the wicked witch? "I know a spot. Bring a pen and some paper. Meet me back here in ten minutes. If that's all right."

"Okay."

I told Lovie I was going out to get some air and that there was nothing to worry about. She looked worried, of course, but Sloane wouldn't have believed me, and Gisel would have somehow tagged along.

I pulled the first notebook I could find out of Ever's backpack, which sat on the bench in the mudroom. I unzipped the front pocket and reached around until I found a pen. I hooked it on top of the notebook and disappeared into the shadows before flying out the back door. I landed exactly where Xavier and I had been moments before.

He was there. I couldn't see him, but I knew he was near me. I felt the exhilaration of his presence. "I'm here," I said, and he reached out, fumbled around my waist and side, and took my hand. "Anything crazy in the skies tonight?"

"The Virago loves to party on Halloween as much as anyone else does. We should be fine since it's the Saturday night before the holiday. I'm sure they have their own affairs."

Xavier held my hand until we reached Marlton Park. "Let's land here," he said. We stayed invisible next to the concession stand. The lock on the door clicked. The door opened only a few inches, and we slipped inside before Xavier closed the door behind us. I listened to the lock click into place again.

"We're trapped," I whispered.

He appeared. It was dark except for a few cracks that let in light from the lamppost by the sidewalk. I held my breath as he reached up and removed his helmet. He disappeared just before his face was revealed.

"I thought you were going to show yourself."

"It's like you don't know me at all."

"Exactly." I didn't let myself wallow in the disappointment. I let Xavier see me. I thought setting an example might move him. I hopped up on the table in front of the large wood-covered service window. I assumed Xavier was standing somewhere near me since I hadn't felt him get up on the table.

"I'm right here," he said and took my hand. He was directly in front of me. My legs spread as he moved between them.

"Yes," was the only word that came out of my mouth.

"What do you need to know?" he asked. The sound of his voice caressed my neck until I dipped my head on one side to stop the sensation that was traveling down my shoulder. I couldn't think with him this close. "About the Virago." He helped me remember.

"Can you step back?"

"Am I making you uncomfortable?"

I inhaled his closeness. "Yes, but not in a bad way. I just need to think." He let go of my hand. His body was missing from between my legs, and I could formulate a question. "Are they organized?"

"They have a governing body and meetings, but I'm not sure I'd describe them as organized." His voice came from across the tiny room. "There are always five women in charge. They are supposed to represent original covens born in this area, but there is tremendous infighting, collusion, trickery. I'm never sure who will be in charge next."

"Are attacks random or planned out?"

"Both."

"If something is planned, does the entire Virago ever participate? Do they have to approve it?"

"You're giving them too much credit. Imagine a group of women who hate each other, every other woman, and themselves, trying to work together. They couldn't plan a bake sale, let alone an organized attack." I took notes as he spoke. The paper shifted from a pale white that I could barely see to a deep black that was almost invisible in the darkness. The pen's ink turned to silver and lit up the page as I wrote. "But that doesn't mean they can't put their differences aside for a common goal once in a while."

"Have they ever been defeated?"

"They've never even been challenged until you moved home. They outnumber the witches who belong to covens. At least in Salem County. Their numbers are growing. Women are apparently going through a period of discourse rather than unity." I kept writing. "They have an Instagram account they use to share information. The pictures are usually of terrain around the area with a caption only they can understand. It denotes a target, and if anyone is available and interested in participating, they do."

"What is the name on the account?"

"Are you going to cyber bully them?"

"Maybe."

"The crafty ones."

"Do you have Instagram?"

Xavier laughed from the other side of the room. "You never give up, do you?"

"Would you like me to?"

"No." I focused my thoughts on him until I swore I could make out exactly where he was standing. I willed him to come closer. "We should get back."

Being friends with Xavier was bruising my self-esteem. He was the first man I'd wanted since Owen died, and I'd never seen what he looked like and he was perfectly content with our relationship being that of a child's invisible friend forever.

"We should." I hopped off the table. "Thank you. I know you want to remain neutral. I won't share who gave me this information."

"I trust you."

Just not enough to let me see him.

"I'll fly you back."

"You're not going to stay for the party?"

"No. I was just curious about your costume. I actually have another gathering I'm supposed to attend."

I don't know why that upset me. He wasn't my boyfriend. He never even claimed to be more than a friend. I was wishing for a commitment from a man I knew nothing about, including who he spent his time with when he wasn't with me, which was often. "Oh."

"It's at a colleague's house. I can't imagine it will be anywhere near as interesting as your soiree in Auburn, but I'd already promised him I'd go."

Him.

"And since I wasn't actually invited to yours."

"Of course." I still wouldn't tell him he was welcome anytime. He was going to have to give a little, too.

"You're very stubborn," he whispered near my ear.

"You should talk." He pulled me into a hug, and I let him. My head on his chest, and my hands roamed up his back to his shoulders. "And show yourself." *And maybe take off your clothes.* He was robbing me of all common sense.

"I have to go," he pulled away.

I'm sure if anyone could see me, I was blushing. "Me, too."

"Take the lead. I'll follow you back, and when I see you appear in your yard, I'll go."

"And when will I see you again?"

"When would you like?"

Later tonight came to mind, but there was still the problem of the enormous sleepover that would be taking place at my house. "Perhaps we can go for a flight on Monday night? It will be dark out early. We can go to Philly and see the city lights."

"I can't go on Monday," he said. I was glad he couldn't see the rejected expression I was sure was on my face. "How about Saturday?"

"Saturday is the homecoming dance."

"That sounds perfect."

"Yes. It does. I can go after the girls leave."

"I'll come get you at eight."

The lock clicked on the other side of the door. I disappeared and walked through the narrow opening Xavier created for me before closing it and relocking it.

A man stood under the pavilion. I could only make out his outline, but it was clear he wasn't turned toward us.

"You need to do more," he said. Xavier pulled me close against his body. "Make her demonstrate what she's capable of."

"She hates me, and she keeps saying I'm crazy," another voice said, but the second person wasn't visible. Xavier inched us back until we stood flat against the side of the concession stand and out of the light from the post.

"That's what they all say." The man walked away and toward the exit of the park.

I took a step forward, but Xavier grabbed my hand and pulled me back. The air shifted. Someone I couldn't see walked past us.

After a few minutes, Xavier whispered, "It was Billy Roberts."

"Who was he with?"

Xavier held on to me a moment longer, as if the danger hadn't dissipated. "Not someone we want to know," was all he said before I launched into the air with him behind me.

Maryann and Sloane were sitting around the fire when I landed, and I took a seat next to them.

"Perfect. I wanted to talk to you guys."

"We're free. Have a seat," Maryann said. She rested her leg with the torn jeans and rotted skin of a zombie over the arm of the Adirondack chair and leaned back facing me.

"I've been thinking about the Virago." Sloane groaned. "If they have no honor, if they're willing to kill us, we will never be able to defeat them."

"That's why I think Ruby is right. If they're not behaving like witches, we shouldn't treat them like ones," Sloane said.

"You have to be careful," Tara Jane interjected. "Without honor, this whole state will go up in flames. The Virago does seem to have a line they haven't crossed. You've all left the safety of Auburn since you've been home, and they haven't killed you."

"Yet," I said.

"I think they know it will bring witches from everywhere to finish the war they would start. That's why their coercion is small and short. It sneaks in with incidences well-spaced so no one alerts the rest of the world's covens to the eradication they've planned."

"Do you think it's that strategic?" I asked.

"I don't know. From what I've heard, they are moving in from all over, though. There has to be some kind of planning in that."

Maryann rolled her eyes as if outsiders of any kind exhausted her.

"I have an idea."

Sloane shifted until she was facing me. "I'm listening," she said.

"In order to defeat the Virago, they need to fight each other, not us. They can thin out their own numbers until it's a more manageable group of women to work with. There must be some of them that want peace. They can't all be crazy."

"Don't get your hopes up," Maryann said. "I think most of them are. Look at Gisel." She waved her hand toward the corner of the yard where Gisel and Gwen were standing.

"Exactly. We left her in Auburn, and she isn't crazy . . . at least she isn't evil."

"But she also never joined them. Think of what type of woman could live her whole life hearing the same stories of the Virago that were passed down to us and then still join them. Why that witch would be impossible to defeat when it came to battle."

"Which is why I'm recommending deception."

Everyone looked at me confused. Except Maryann, who leaned back in her seat with a satisfied grin and one eye that appeared to be hanging from its socket. "We're in," she said, and the rest of her coven stared at her.

XIV

HE FOUR OF THEM WERE stunning. Even without their powers they would have drawn attention standing next to each other, but the fact that they belonged together on a cosmic level made them an extraordinary group of young women. Sam, Mick, and Dave arrived to pick them up. Dave Anzaldo brought his friend Gregg, and all of us fell silent as he walked into the room.

"He's just riding in a car with us," Ruby said and dismissed any thoughts of Ike being replaced. "Relax people." It was one more occasion when our family ties made normal everyday situations more complicated.

The kids left in two cars. Lovie was busy putting pictures on social media and tagging us all. Gisel, Isaiah, and Sloane were sitting around the kitchen table as Sloane and Gisel poured more wine in their glasses. Isaiah just seemed to be there, not really engaged in any of the events of the evening.

"How is Ike with not going to homecoming?" Lovie asked.

"He has an away game tonight," Isaiah said. "If it hadn't been Gwen's senior homecoming, I would have been there, too."

Lovie was being kind by continuing to chatter and include Isaiah as a part of our family. "Any word on what Gwen wants to do for her birthday?"

Isaiah glared at Gisel.

"What?" she asked with her hand on her chest. "I did not say a word."

"The whole thing is ridiculous," Isaiah said.

"Gwen wants us all to go away for her birthday. Some place warm." My chest tightened. "She said she'll wait until after Thanksgiving if it works better with everyone's schedules."

"Doesn't she get enough of all of us under one roof?" Sloane asked, hitting on the first point that came to my mind. What we needed was space, not more time together.

"She's turning eighteen and preparing to move away, possibly forever," Gisel argued. "I think it's sweet."

"I think it's crazy," Isaiah weighed in.

"I'll go," Lovie said. We all laughed at her. "Especially if it's some place warm."

"Maybe we should save it until this summer and all go away somewhere together. A graduation gift," Gisel said, and it sounded much more appealing as a plan in the distant future. "Or maybe we can rent a shore house. Something big that we can spread out in."

"I'm in for that," I said. I emptied the last of the water from my glass into the plant on the kitchen windowsill. I put the glass in the dishwasher and closed the door. When I turned to walk out the back door, it became obvious everyone in the room was watching me.

"Where are you going?" Sloane asked.

I swallowed hard. "Flying." I kept my eyes on Sloane and

thought, *Please don't ask anything else.*

She paused for a half second before saying, "Well, be careful." She shared a knowing smile and then addressed the rest of the confused house with, "Anyone want to play rummy?"

I slipped out the back door before anyone else decided to ask questions. Why? Where? Who? None of it I wanted to address. Xavier wasn't ready for me to see him, and I wasn't ready for my family to know about him. Maybe we were even. I wouldn't press him anymore to share what he wasn't willing to. I'd be patient. Like Lovie always was.

"Ready." His voice came from behind me.

"Yes," I disappeared and launched into the air before flying north out of Auburn.

Xavier stayed close to my left. I listened to the wind and followed the changes in his location as the gusts blew across my face. We dipped low over the Ben Franklin Bridge, flew between the towers of Liberty Place and over the top of the Comcast Center in center city before soaring south and following the river. We landed on the banks of the Delaware River in Pennsville, New Jersey. The warm weather was still holding and the Riverview Inn had their large doors open to the outside as a band played near the bar.

I showed myself next to Xavier in the shadows of the building. "Are you thirsty?" I asked.

"I'll get us drinks," Xavier said with the ease of any other man on a first date. I paused and looked his way. "Oh. Maybe not."

"Is it difficult to get used to being the invisible man?"

"Apparently."

"I'll be back," I said.

I ordered us two seasonal beers on draft and carried them back outside. I wasn't sure where he was. I'd left him near the building, but I kept walking toward the water.

"Over here," he whispered from the shadows near the retaining wall. I looked back toward the building and disappeared before walking toward the water.

"Here," I held out Xavier's beer that was still invisible in my hand. He fumbled around, touched my wrist, and my arm before grasping the beer and taking it from me. "Let's sit. This is confusing."

I didn't have to worry about eloquently sitting on the wall and swinging my legs over the side in my maxi skirt, because no one could see us. It was quite freeing. The beer in my hand was ice cold. It froze my fingers and chilled me to the bone. I tightened my elbows to my side seeking heat. I wished I'd brought a sweatshirt.

Xavier shimmied over closer and put his arm around my shoulders. I melted into the space between us. A bride and groom floated out of the back door to the reception hall with a photographer following. He positioned them in front of the water with the bridge in the background. Without direction, they kissed.

"How long were you married?" Xavier asked. His voice was almost drowned out by the music coming from both sides of the building.

I took a sip of my beer and put the cup down next to me, but then it appeared. Like litter on the ground, it was sitting all by itself on the wall, and I worried someone would come over to clean it up. I picked the cup back up, and it disappeared again. "Almost eleven years." I wasn't used to talking about Owen. Everyone knew my husband had died, but no one had the courage to bring him up.

"Have you ever been married?"

"No." His voice gave nothing away. No regret. No hint of sarcasm.

"Did you ever come close?"

"I don't think so."

"Never?"

"Never. Did you know you were going to marry your husband when you met him?"

The first night I met Owen, a date seemed unlikely. I'd almost thought he'd hated me. "No." I laughed a little at our first meeting. "He was a scary guy. Very large and abrupt. He wasn't interested in me except to share some unwarranted anger when he first ran into me."

"That's impossible. I can't imagine anyone, especially a man, not loving you from the minute he first saw you."

"That's very kind." I warmed a little and leaned in closer to Xavier. "Owen was different from most men. His severe take on the world was what attracted me to him in the first place. I needed someone who was stronger, angrier, and meaner than anyone else."

"Because of the curse?"

"You knew about that, too."

He inhaled deeply, and I found myself wanting to rest my head on his chest. "I did. I found it hard to leave you alone after I found you in the woods that night."

"So you heard what Clara did?"

"Yes, and I couldn't believe it. I'd never heard of a witch cursing her own coven line."

The familiar bitterness rose in my throat. I'd worked so hard to forgive, but the memories of my former life still snuck up on me. "I know. I needed a husband that had a chance of beating it. It was ridiculous. There's no defeating a witch's curse, but there was something about Owen. He hated witchcraft. Anything not 'real' as he used to say grated on him in a way I'd never experienced before. Quija boards, wands, children's costumes, he hated all of it. Until Ever."

"Was he religious?"

"At first, that was what I thought. I was willing to leave him rather than tell him, but then I got pregnant, and he asked me to marry him." The fear of telling him was still vivid in my mind. "He was down on one knee, proposing, and I had to make a decision.

I moved the ring from the box to my finger using only my mind."

"I'm surprised he didn't run."

"I wasn't sure what he was going to do. He said he loved me, grabbed me by both shoulders, and made me swear never to do anything like that in front of any member of his family."

"I'm guessing you behaved."

"Of course, but getting Ever to stay in line was difficult. When she was a baby, she'd disappear or move things whenever she wanted. I had to keep a close eye on her."

"Did they ever catch her doing something?"

"No, but Owen's father watched her like a hawk. It was as if he'd been in love with a witch before because he could anticipate when I'd use magic. I had to be careful whenever he was around."

"What happened to him?"

"My mother- and father-in-law both died in a car accident. They went together, which is sad, but I don't think either of them would have wanted to live without the other."

"Did you feel that way when Owen died?"

"No," I said, watching as the water lapped against the beach below us. Poor Owen had always come after our daughter. He would have wanted it that way. "I have Ever, and nothing or no one will ever make me want to leave her here alone." I inhaled boldly the fall air and held it in my lungs before releasing it.

Owen had been completely unreasonable the first few years of Ever's life. He'd obsessed over keeping her powers a secret. It was one more reason to never tell him about the curse. He was already skeptical of the love associated with our craft.

"Have you ever told anyone about your powers?" I asked.

"I've only ever talked to my mother about them. My adoptive mother."

"Is she still living?"

"Yes, as is my adoptive father."

"Is she a witch?"

"No, and that was a major reason why my birth mother asked her to raise me. She'd known the families that lost their husbands and fathers and their beloved witches to the violence of the war with the Virago. My birth mother needed to know that someone understood exactly what they were protecting me from."

"Did your mother know you had powers before she gave you up?"

"I don't think so. No one knew. I kept everything a secret."

"Until?"

"One night my adoptive mother found me in my room. I was considering what the rest of my life was going to be like. Never being able to tell another human being about what I am, and how lonely a life that would be. She came in, sat on the chair by my desk, and told me everything she knew about my history and the events that had left me alone without a coven."

The thought of Xavier alone and afraid tore at me. I'd known about my powers and my history since before I could walk. I was celebrated for my witchcraft and born into the most loving relationship that would endure time and transcend this life.

"That was quite a gift," I said.

"She gave me my dignity and my sanity back. For so long, I was different to the point of being a freak, but when she explained my powers as a gift, I could believe in the goodness of the world again."

"How much do you know about your birth mother?"

"My mother's last name was Sickler." He sighed. "I never asked her first name. Isn't that crazy? I don't even know her name."

"Did you not want to know?"

His silence made me fear I'd offended him. "I guess not."

I searched for another subject. "I've never heard of a man who is a witch. I'd been raised to believe it was impossible. There must be others out there like you."

"If they're lucky, they were raised by a mother like mine. Otherwise, how could a person make sense of this?"

"I'm sure it's difficult." Owen was as conflicted about my powers as Xavier had been about his. "My poor husband."

"He realized how lucky he was." I took a long sip of my beer and let my eyes focus on the barge floating up the Delaware in the darkness. "He was, Helene, and I'd bet he knew it."

"He loved Ever more than anything he believed in before he met me. She changed the way he thought about the world."

"I've heard children will do that."

"Do you think you'll have a child someday?"

"Are you offering up your services?" I held my cup tight so I didn't spill it as I shook with laughter. "Shh. Don't let anyone hear us." I stifled myself. "Is that a no?"

"I often think Ever will be the death of me. She's almost eighteen. I think I'm done having children."

"Me, too, then. I'm following you."

The music's volume increased and more people moved to the tables outside the tented area where the band played. They were still far enough away from us that no one could hear or sense we were nearby, but I wasn't relaxed. I couldn't let my guard down and just enjoy the peacefulness that surrounded Xavier because we were a secret. Or he was. Maybe it was him out with me that was a secret. I didn't know.

"Helene," he said. "I know I ask a lot of you." He reached out, fumbled around until he found my hand, and then pulled it onto his lap enclosed in his. "But don't overthink us."

I released the thoughts. I let it all go. Things were rocky with Owen at the start, too, and had he lived, we would have been just fine. Witchcraft didn't exactly make relationships easier, and there was no precedence I was aware of for a man and woman who each had their own powers. Xavier and I were just friends, and that was exactly how it seemed he wanted us to stay. "Helene," he whispered sharply.

"What?"

"You're not talking. I know you're thinking about all of this."

"Would you want me if I never thought?"

There was silence as if he himself was considering the proposal. "No."

The band announced it was last call. I had to get back. There would already by questions about this flight, and I knew I wouldn't be able to avoid telling everyone about Xavier much longer. "I have to go back."

"I know." He stood next to me without letting go of my hand and then pulled me up by his side. We walked over to the trashcan and threw our cups away. They appeared as soon as they left our fingers. A bird digging through the can looked our way and focused back on the treasures inside the receptacle again.

We flew home next to each other and landed in my backyard. Through the kitchen window, we could see Sloane, Lovie, Gisel and Isaiah playing cards. They were laughing and carrying on. Isaiah had his baseball hat on backward, as if it helped him think. I knew without seeing the cards that Sloane was winning. She always won when I didn't play. The sight of them together warmed me.

"Did you go to homecoming with him?" Xavier asked.

I stared at Isaiah through the window. Not that man. The one sitting at the table inside was my best friend's husband. My date for homecoming was someone totally different.

"Yes," I said.

"Were you happy back then?"

I thought back over the memories from a different point of view. One of an outsider looking in. "I'd buried my mother six months before." Isaiah had literally held me up on some of the days following her funeral. "I was as comfortable as a girl in my position could be."

"I absolutely hate him for you."

I laughed a little. "Well, you only knew the worst of us."

"I saw enough in one day to know that I hate him."

"I'm not sure I choose the right men," I said and reached out in the direction his voice had come from. He grabbed my fingers in his hand and pulled me to him. I rested my head on his chest and tried to memorize every inch of him as I let both hands slide down his stomach to his waist. He was trim, and his button-up shirt was untucked. I reached down farther to check if his pants were denim.

Xavier stopped my hand. "I have to go."

"You always have to go."

"I know. Thanks for the flight."

"When will I see you again?"

"When would you like?"

"Well, if we're talking about what I'd like, the topic should be information. I'd like a cell number for you, a place of employment, a last name, and last known relationships." His chest vibrated with a silent laugh. "And an address . . . oh, and we cannot forget, I would love to see you."

"What fun would that be? Then we'd just be a normal couple."

Couple. Normal didn't seem so bad. Noise erupted from the kitchen as Sloane threw her cards at Isaiah. "She's a terrible loser."

Xavier stepped away from me. I watched my best friends in my house without me. I turned to say good night, but he was already gone. I could feel his absence more profoundly than his presence. It hit me in the pit of my stomach. The way I felt about him was unnerving. I was only going to get hurt, but I was going to put myself through it again because with Xavier, I couldn't stop.

XV

JUST MY COVEN, OUR DAUGHTERS, and Ike and Isaiah were a crowd, but somehow we all folded into the spectators of the Thanksgiving Day game at Woodstown. The same game had been played against Salem High School for the last one hundred years. I loved how Ruby rolled her eyes whenever the age of the school was mentioned, as if the years alone annoyed her more than the facilities or the curriculum. Ever told her she had ageism against the building. The way they joked was different this year. When we'd first brought the girls home, they were outsiders, this year they joked about South Jersey as if they were a part of it. The way only you could make fun of your mother, but if anyone else did, you wanted to punch them.

Is Billy Roberts here? I thought to all the women of my family.

Gwen and Ruby surveyed the crowd.

No, Ever thought as if she were always aware of his whereabouts.

"You must be Ever's mother." The voice struck me, but I let any familiar reference be replaced by the outstretched hand of the man who appeared to my right. "I'm her modern media teacher, Anthony Frank."

I shook his hand. "Nice to meet you." I couldn't remember if Ever liked his class or not.

"Likewise." He held my hand for a second too long. I glanced behind him to Gisel, who was calling my name, and when I looked back, Mr. Frank had the strangest expression on his face. As if he already knew me.

"Have we met before?" I asked.

Mr. Hathaway and Mr. Strozyk interrupted his answer with Thanksgiving greetings at the same time Gisel pulled me away.

"He's cute," she said as she appraised Mr. Frank. It was a comment I dismissed right before heading off to get a cup of hot chocolate from the concession stand. Instead of maneuvering my way back up the bleachers, I leaned on the fence and drank the thick, warm drink. The aroma, my knit hat, and every person around me brought back memories of high school.

The three people behind me were talking about a possible trip to Vegas before the year was over, so I assumed they were not high school students. I turned to see if I knew them, and they appeared to be in their twenties.

One woman of the group stared at me until a cold air swept across the back of my neck where my scarf had separated. She was familiar in a crafty sort of way. I turned back and kept my face toward the field as I listened to them go on.

"It won't be warm enough in Vegas to lie out," the one girl said.

"Then we need to go somewhere else," the man standing between the two women said with a tone that suggested he would have elbowed the guy next to him if there had been one.

"Vegas is fine."

Their laughter stopped.

"What's wrong with you?" The guy asked her. I couldn't help myself. I glanced back again to see a jealous scowl being thrown at him. The other girl stepped back, and the air belied her as well. They were both witches, and I knew nothing of them.

"Nothing. How about you not beg Megan to wear a bathing suit on vacation with us."

"How about you chill out. It's cold. I want to go someplace warm."

"Yeah. That's what this is all about. The weather."

"Syd, you are being ridiculous." Anger shot from her and almost knocked him over. He took a step back with his hands in the air. He knew what she was capable of. "Sydney Anne Collins. Calm down." His voice was steady.

Gisel walked up next to me. She smiled while I asked, *do you know the witch behind us?*

Yeah. That's Sydney Collins. She moved here a couple of years ago, and her boyfriend, Kevin Shimp, has lived here his whole life.

She's a bit jealous.

Pity, was all Gisel thought back as we watched the couple continue to argue.

It was Gisel's first Thanksgiving without her mother. She was going to her mother-in-law's house with Isaiah and the kids, and then they were coming back for dessert. Lovie, Sloane, the girls, and I held our usual Thanksgiving, which was easier than last year. There wasn't the heavy blanket of dread over our family, and we all seemed more relaxed. We were back in Auburn with futures to look forward to.

Ever helped me set the table. We'd combined all the china that we'd carried from Auburn to Vegas, Hawaii, and Vermont, and then back again. The unmatched plates and crystal glasses were the perfect accompaniment to the deep-red tablecloth Sloane had put out.

"Do you think Ike's parents are going to get divorced?" Ever asked. I noted she asked about *Ike's* parents. Not Gwen's—her sister's—or Gisel and her husband.

I cleared my throat and tried to come up with an answer. "Why do you ask?"

"His mother told him they were going to."

"I'm sorry." It felt like there were several people I should be apologizing to, but I didn't know why. "I think they will then. Ike's mother is known for her decisive action." I placed a fork on the left of each plate.

"Do you still love him?" She threw me. Everyone else, including Isaiah it seemed, already knew that answer.

"I don't think I'll ever *not* love Isaiah in some way, but the kind of love you're asking about can only exist in our past."

"Because of what happened?" She stopped folding napkins and waited for my answer.

"No." I shook my head determined for someone to believe me. "Because you get one chance at a love like that, and we screwed it up. It's as if it died. It can't be brought back from the dead."

She stepped into the sunlight beaming through the window. Dark circles drooped from my daughter's eyes. Her cheeks were sunken in a bit, and her lips were chapped. She was wilting right in front of me. "Ever, do you feel okay?"

"Yeah. Why?"

"You look tired. Exhausted even."

"There's just a lot going on."

"Like what specifically? Is Billy Roberts still bothering you?"

"No," she said, but she didn't convince me. "Senior year. College visits. Homecoming. SATs. You know, basic life trajectory changing things an eighteen-year-old experiences."

"How are you and Ike?"

Her breath caught a little, and I didn't miss it. "We're fine." She grazed her fingertips across the tablecloth. "I just worry about him."

"That's understandable, but I think Ike can take care of himself." I smiled lightly at her. She returned my carefree look, but it didn't touch her eyes. I needed to keep a closer watch on her.

"I have nightmares he'll be hurt." Ever pursed her lips together to fight back the tears forming.

"Oh, Ever." She was a woman now, but seeing her hurting or afraid would always turn her right back into my little girl. "You're still dreaming? Are they always about him?"

She shook her head and wiped a tear from her cheek. "Mostly." She looked at the wall to her right. "You told me once that your mother thought we didn't dream because we were closer to our subconscious than most people. Do you think I'm trying to avoid something obvious?" Her gaze bore into me. My daughter had been thinking a great deal about this question. "Do you think I'm trying to dismiss in my waking hours what I know is going to happen, but my mind won't let me hide from it in the night?"

"No." I rubbed the tops of her arms. "We don't know exactly why we don't dream. That was just her theory. Is this what you've been so worried about? That your nightmares are predictions? That Ike—"

"Your mother is atrocious!" Gisel yelled toward the driveway as she swung open the back door, letting Gwen slip in before her. "Have fun spending the rest of your holidays with her. Just the two of you!" She slammed the back door behind her.

"Where's Ike?" Ever asked.

"Oh. Sorry." Gisel pointed behind her at Isaiah's truck pulling out of our driveway. "He's at his grandmother's. We were on our way, too, but then Isaiah thought today was a good day to tell me what his mother actually thinks of me." She went to the counter, pulled the cork on an already opened bottle of wine, and poured herself a glass. "So, I get to spend the day with my sisters." Gisel seemed pleased with her new plans. She took a big gulp of wine and plopped into a chair at the table we were setting. "What can I do to help?"

Ever slipped upstairs. I watched her walk away and wished I could make everything better the way I did when she was five. "You can help me find serving spoons for everything."

"Perfect." Gisel was back on her feet and searching through the drawer of the china cabinet for different utensils. She turned around when she asked, "Did Isaiah's mom like you when you were together?" Her ability to completely disconnect from any emotion related to the question caught me off guard and made me laugh. Gisel had moved on from her marriage. It was a clean break. I never seemed to be completely free of anything.

"Well, you have to remember that when he and I got together, I was the girl whose mother had just died. It was hard not to like me."

"And I was the harlot that slept with him. I'm guessing I went the other way with her affections."

"Even after twenty years?"

"That woman can hold a grudge."

"Must be the generation." I thought of Gisel's mother, but I didn't dare bring her up. Today was about being thankful.

The doorbell rang. No one used our front door. Not even when we'd been little. The sound of it ignited some instinct of defense. Whoever was on the other side wasn't close enough to our family to come in through the kitchen so they must be strangers.

I opened it to find no one there. A long basket filled with deep red, yellow, and orange flowers sat at the edge of the stoop. The envelope attached to the flowers had my name on it.

I slipped the card into the back pocket of my jeans and carried the flowers inside.

"Oh, they're beautiful. Where did they come from?"

I shrugged. "Don't know. They were on the front porch. Perhaps they're a peace offering from your mother-in-law."

"Yeah . . . right. She's ecstatic I'm gone."

"Maybe the church sent them," Lovie said. She was showing Maya how to mold a piecrust. I should be showing Ever something. I wasn't sure what. She'd already mastered everything I had to teach her.

"Helene, can you check the turkey?" Lovie asked.

I basted it, closed the oven door, and waited for my next task. Lovie's kitchen was a machine. She had all eight of us in motion until the food was on the table and she was leading us in grace.

"Speaking of God, I have really enjoyed going back to church since we moved here," Gisel said. "Hasn't it been so nice, Gwen?"

"I guess."

"It reminds me of my childhood. The songs, the pews, all the people. It just feels like God's at home and so am I. Finally."

I passed the mashed potatoes to my left and took the stuffing from Ruby, who was seated to my right.

"That's the thing, Mom. This is your childhood. None of it reminds me of mine because I grew up in *Alloway*." I set the bowl down. We all stopped what we were doing. "I'm sorry. That wasn't polite."

"There's no need to be polite with this group," Ruby said.

"It's just, I know you love it here, but it isn't my history. There is no feeling of comfort outside of the people sitting at this table. We could build a huge house in Alloway that all eight of us could fit in, and I'd be just as happy."

"But you wouldn't be in Auburn," Gisel said.

"Exactly." Gwen passed a bowl encouraging other conversation as she did.

I had no other topics to address. "Auburn is special," I said. "I realize it has nothing to do with your past, but it is the only place in this world that a coven has deemed protective land for us. It belongs to us, even if you weren't raised here."

"It may protect us from the Virago, but evil has taken place here. The worst kind of curse was levied right across the street. Don't you have any memories of that?" Gwen persisted.

"Of course we do." It still terrorized me late at night. "But it was because we all came back to Auburn that we overcame it."

"I think you just miss Dad," Gisel told her daughter. "With Ike moving out and the two of us moving here, this has been a huge transition. I should have talked to you more about it."

"Well, thinking through something has never been part of your process."

Gisel glared at her daughter. "I'll let you have that one," Gisel said. "We still have a lot to be thankful for."

We ate the rest of the meal in virtual silence, only breaking it to heap praise on Lovie's hard work. The food was delicious, and when we started to clear the table, I wished I could have enjoyed the feeling of family a bit more. The curse of living with a teenage daughter left a bad taste in all our mouths. It reminded me of the holidays last year. I stared at Ever across the table. I could not go through another year like that.

"Are you guys on Instagram?" I asked. I was only on the bare minimum of social media.

Ruby stared at me as if I'd asked if they were comfortable crossing the street alone, which I assumed meant yes.

"I need your help looking up an account." No one rushed to assist me. I moved over to the computer at the kitchen desk. "I think it's linked to the Virago."

"Really?" Lovie asked as she turned off the water running over the dirty pots.

"Yes. I think they use it to communicate somehow, and if we can pull it up, we might get a better idea of who is aligned with them."

"It can't be that easy," Sloane said.

"Don't underestimate social media," Gwen said. "It's a world-wide phenomenon that has overthrown governments and been accused of rigging elections. Certainly, a group of bitter women could find plenty of places to congregate on there."

Maya scooted me out of the way and sat in the chair in front of me. Her fingers flew across the tops of the keys, and within seconds, Instagram was up in front of me.

"I'm not that impressed."

"It isn't designed to be used on a computer." Maya went to the online app store and downloaded it. We waited for whatever is was to download. "Once we set you up, we can switch it over to your phone. Then maybe you'll be impressed."

I doubted it.

She set us up an account using the name Janine Smith.

"I like it," Lovie said. "It's the name of a girl who knows everyone and somehow has no enemies."

Maya searched for the name on the internet. "There are also thousands of them, and the name is close enough to sound like a few others. So people will think they remember it, even if they really don't."

"People are not going to be friends with this woman online," Sloane said.

"Just wait. Once she gets three friends in common, everyone will let her in."

For our profile picture, we held Carl up in front of the camera.

"He is the cutest out of all of us," Ever said.

"Okay, now what is the account name you were given for the Virago?" Gwen asked.

"The crafty ones," I said.

"Oh, clever little witches," Sloane said from her perch over my shoulder. It took Maya six tries of different variations of the name to finally find what we thought was the Virago's Instagram account.

"That can't be right?" I pointed to the followers number, which was three hundred and twelve.

"I'm afraid it is, but they're not all witches. I hope," Maya said and pulled up the list of names. "We can rule out any of the men."

"Okay," I said, but hesitated in my mind. I wasn't completely sure we could. Especially based on Xavier's powers.

"I don't think we should," Ever said. "Billy can disappear. We don't know if he can fly."

"We'll keep the men for now, but some of these followers will follow anyone just to get followed back."

Sloane pinched the bridge of her nose and shook her head. "Complicated."

"See, look at this one." She pointed to a small thumbnail picture. "This is Mrs. Ryan She's Jay Ryan's mom. I'm sure she isn't a witch."

Sloane leaned over me again. "What makes you so sure?"

"Because she isn't evil," Ever said. "I would know, wouldn't I? I'd be able to at the very least to sense that she's a witch." Ever stood and glanced around the kitchen as she thought. "I could feel the witches in upper Pittsgrove. I knew where they were without even seeing them."

"That's not always going to be the case. The Virago is devious, and witches who are alone keep to themselves. We can't trust even our own instincts when it comes to who might be an enemy." Sloane pointed to Mrs. Ryan again. "She isn't evil to Jay's friends from school, who she doesn't realize are witches. That's all we really know about her."

"I can cross reference all of these followers with their Facebook accounts and any other social media they're on. We can create a list that would help us determine who is most likely to be a witch." Lovie, Sloane, Gisel, and I stared at Maya as if she'd just laid out the plans for the next space shuttle. "Give me a couple of hours."

"We can help. I'll get my laptop," Gwen said.

Gisel handed me a glass of wine. We were about to unveil the women of this town who wanted us to leave.

"Hey! This lady is the preacher's wife."

I took a gulp from my glass.

Long after lists were made, dessert was eaten, and the girls had gone to bed, I headed to my own room. When I changed my clothes, the card from the flowers fell onto the floor of my bedroom. I opened the envelope and pulled out the card. It said:

> *I hope your holiday is perfectly normal and safe and delicious.*
> *Happy Thanksgiving,*
> *X*

Just a few simple words that touched me. Made me think of him and possibilities I'd let go of long ago. I was young and alive, holding the tiny card in my hand. It also gave me an idea. I found the stationary and a black felt pen in the box under my bed. Words had power.

I wrote, "The world is a better place because you're in it," across the center in an obviously feminine script.

I didn't sign the card before I put it in the envelope and sealed it. A simple message of kindness that I'd leave on Kevin Shimp's windshield when he and Sydney Ann Collins were out some place. I thought she'd appreciate it for what it was. The first attack.

XVI

I HAD MY DOUBTS ABOUT our plan to infiltrate the Virago through their own posts on social media. With the girls' research and Maya's spreadsheet, we had a list of sixty-one possible members of the Virago living within a twenty-mile radius of us. Our mothers never would have believed it. The stories they told us as little girls made the Virago sound like three lone witches who barely talked to each other.

We split the list into territories by their residences, where they were from originally, and if their husbands were from the area if they were married. Some witches were outsiders, not because they were members of the Virago, but because they weren't born in South Jersey. One member had recently moved onto a farm in Upper Pittsgrove. According to Denny Taylor, the family was renting the old farm house from the owner. The witch should have barely been able to drive through that area. We needed to find out why Upper Pittsgrove was no longer safe.

Two witches were identified as possibly belonging to the Salem City Coven. It seemed unlikely they'd join the Virago if they had each other, and I hadn't heard any rumblings about turmoil in their coven. We moved them into a separate list.

"We'll watch them," Gisel said.

"They'll know. Won't they sense us near them?" I asked.

"I don't think so," Ever said. "When I ran into those witches in Upper Pittsgrove, they didn't know I was there until I spoke to them. The only reason they managed to locate me was because my shadow gave me away."

"They don't seem to feel the essence of a true witch," Gisel said, but it still seemed like a lot to risk.

"As long as we remain unseen, it shouldn't matter, I guess. If we're wrong, and they can sense when we're nearby, they still won't know exactly who we are."

"Let's start with these two," Gisel pointed to the names of two women.

"I already started." They looked at me. "I left a note for Sydney Collins saying 'the world is a better place because you're in it.'"

"The witch from the football game?" Gisel asked. "Why would you tell her that?"

"I left it on her boyfriend's car. Anonymously."

"You're evil."

"What? He seemed like a nice guy. I'm going to tell him again as soon as she calms down."

"Absolutely corrupt," Gisel said. "Give me someone to focus on."

"Take those two." I searched the list for the names she'd originally pointed to. "Jolie and Desirae." They were both active on Project Graduation and all the other committees parents were still asked to participate in even though there was only one year left of high school.

"They were in swim lessons with us when Gwen was a baby. They could barely get along *then*. I have been listening to how perfect their children are for eighteen years. All A's, gifted athletes, even when they were infants, they pooped purple glitter." Gisel made a fake gun out of her thumb and finger and shot it at her temple. "It will be my pleasure. The entire town will thank me. Tomorrow. After the girls leave for the chorus trip."

We pulled up the witches' profiles on Facebook and stalked each of their posts. Most were about their children, who were involved in many of the same sports and activities. Maya tracked likes and comments for both women. "They didn't like each other's pictures for these posts." They were shots from the school play. Both their children were in it.

"Competitive," Sloane said with a smile. "Can you look at the profiles for the dates Isaiah was attacked? See if it gives anything away."

The girls found nothing obvious, but they still entered every detail in the journal they kept before returning it to the hutch and heading off to start packing. Tomorrow, they were headed to spend the night out by Hershey Park with the school choir. Lovie was mixing the ingredients for banana nut muffins, and Gisel was making Isaiah a sandwich. He sat at our table reading the paper with the comfort of a man who lived with us rather than my ex-boyfriend who was in the process of divorcing my best friend. I inhaled, turned, and let the air out. I could be comfortable, too.

Gisel spread mayonnaise across the tops of the rye bread and sliced tomato to top the turkey and Swiss. Pickles, salt and pepper, and oregano were added to the strange concoction that I still remembered the recipe for twenty years later. Every day that I'd been gone, Gisel was there, making Isaiah a sandwich.

Without a word, I slipped out the back door. I ran to the tree line behind the house.

"Whoa, my friend. Not tonight." His voice stopped me just before I disappeared and launched into the air.

"Xavier."

"It's stormy out tonight. Not good for flying."

The sky was crystal clear. The more my eyes adjusted, the more stars I could see. "The weather's fine."

"I'm talking about the people. The Virago loves Woodstown by Candlelight. It's their night to celebrate." The town's open house tour of historical homes brought people from all over South Jersey. There was music, hot chocolate, and dozens of residents opened their homes to share their history with strangers.

"That's ridiculous. Our mothers always went to the tour. Since when has it been *their* night?"

"It will be seen as an aggression."

"Me? Flying alone? They can't keep me from flying. What has become of this place?"

"You left it. It's best to stay in Auburn."

It wasn't the first time he'd mentioned Auburn as if he knew its history. "What do you know about Auburn, Xavier?" I moved closer to his voice until I could feel the heat of his body. I reached out and felt his arm next to mine. I held on to it as I moved in front of him. I was always searching for Xavier. I let go of his arm and disappeared.

"Why did you do that?" I tiptoed behind him without a sound. "Helene?" He was impatient.

"I'm over here."

He spun around. "Why?"

Because I shouldn't always be at a disadvantage. "Come find me," I said and moved two steps to the side.

"Marco," he said into the night sky.

"Polo."

He moved in my direction. "Marco."

I waited until he was only inches from me and replied, "Touch me." I focused on the sound of his breathing.

Xavier's palm awkwardly found my head. He laughed as he dragged his fingers down the side of my face. He pushed my hair off my shoulder and rested his hand there before slipping it down my arm and taking my hand in his. Heat followed his touch along the left side of my body.

"Why the sudden urge to fly?" he asked. I closed my eyes and basked in his touch. Safely unseen, I let every cell of my body respond to the way Xavier made me feel. "Does it have something to do with your company?"

My eyes flitted open, and I glanced back at the house. He'd stolen the moment of preoccupation from me and replaced it with reality. My least favorite thing these days. "I'm just having trouble with all the changes." I showed myself. "With the last twenty years, I guess."

"Disappear again." It wasn't a request. I obliged. Xavier reached up and caressed my face with his thumb. His fingertips rested on my neck, and the heat returned and stole the air from my chest. "Focus on the next twenty, Helene." His lips touched mine, and all I could think about was him. His hand slipped to the back of my neck and cradled my head as he kissed me. The front of his body pressed against me, and the only thing I knew for sure was that I wanted him right there.

Xavier released me, and my mind exploded with thoughts and questions. I was hiding in my backyard like a schoolgirl, kissing boys, and playing games. I took a second before I spoke to recognize the emotion. It was joy. Xavier being near me made me happy.

He kissed me again and asked, "Are you . . . is this okay?"

"I was just thinking about that."

"What did you conclude?"

I kissed him again in lieu of a response.

I took a step back and launched into the air.

"Helene," he called out, but within seconds, he was by my side.

We flew next to each other until we reached the fields on the other side of Seven Stars. Then I soared past him.

Helene

His voice was in my head. I paused and floated above the livestock. *How did you do that?*

I don't know, but we should turn back.

I want to see the town with all the candles lit.

No!

Well, then I want to know how you can talk to me inside my head.

Helene.

Tell me or it's Main Street for me.

I couldn't see him, and there was no response, so I flew at full speed toward the center of Woodstown. Hordes of people crowded the sidewalks. There were lines on the front steps of each of the houses on the tour. The crisp air had everyone bundled to their eyes as they navigated the crowds and patiently waited their turns inside the homes. I hadn't been on the tour in decades, but I'd bet little had changed. Static was a mainstay in Salem County.

Ugh, came from Xavier as I dipped low and landed on a stately front porch on North Main Street. A group had just been taken inside and the next group chatted on the veranda.

"Do you have any more wine? My cup is empty," the bundled up woman next to me asked her friend. I recognized her as Andrea Ford.

"That probably means you've had enough."

"Really?" She held out her cup as her friend rummaged through the tote she was carrying. A group of boys navigated the packed sidewalk on their skateboards and finally gave up, carrying their boards as they walked in front of the house.

Andrea Ford stared at the spot I was sitting. She was on the Project Graduation Committee, too. She never scowled at the meetings, though. I realized the light from the lamppost shined with an outline void where my body was unseen. She glared in my direction and then stared at the outline on the front of the house before she disappeared. The whoosh of air hit me first, followed by something—an arm, a leg, a board—across my head. It threw me from my perch to the siding on the front of the house. I crouched down and covered my head in anticipation of the second blow.

Helene! Xavier yelled in my mind before the light above the door was knocked out and a thud sounded against the house. Everyone around us stopped their conversations to figure out what was going on. The wind picked up again as something hit the tree between the house and the street.

Xavier? I floated off the stairs and toward the tree, but I couldn't feel him or anyone else near me. Glass broke behind the house, and I headed in its direction. Every sense in my body was on edge.

The unmistakable screech of a woman in battle came from behind the barn in the backyard. I flew toward it and found her lying on her back and bleeding.

"Get me out of here!" she said, and the wind whooshed by me. They couldn't tell where I was, and I couldn't find Xavier. "She could see me," she said, and I didn't understand. She disappeared as I flew to her. Her friend must have covered her with her touch, but I still couldn't *see* them. "She knew every move I made. She could see."

The air cleared when I reached the backyard. I turned in the sky searching each corner of the yard and the ones around it. In the neighboring backyard, near the corner of a brick garage, a man was on his knees with his head on the ground, his arms covering it. He blinked in and out of visibility. *Xavier!* I screamed inside my head.

Go. His voice was weak. His image held, but I knew he'd never want that. *Now. Fly!* He said as I flew closer. His hair was dark and his shoulders were broad. He pulled the hood of his sweatshirt over his head and rolled onto his side and groaned. The honeysuckle infiltrated my mind as I closed in on him.

Xavier, hold still. I landed next to him and covered him with my body. Xavier disappeared with me. Our corner near the building was dim, but the backyard was well lit. I concentrated on the bulbs until they twisted in their sockets and darkness fell around us.

Xavier. He was breathing, but I couldn't tell if he was conscious. I could have us both appear, or just him, and finally see what Xavier looked like. It would be forgiven. I needed to see how badly he'd been hurt, but that wasn't what Xavier wanted.

"Wake up," I whispered in his ear. I rolled him over with my arms and legs wrapped around him. From the spot where we lay, I tried to lift off with him. We moved a few feet farther into the yard, and I wished I could just fly with him. It was out of the question. A low, hideous groan was the only sound he made.

My hand drifted down the side of his head until my fingertips were wet and I knew they were covered in blood. *Xavier, wake up. You're too big. I need your help. Again.* Xavier turned his head toward me in silence.

"You're awake," I whispered.

He stiffened in my arms and sat up next to me. Xavier disappeared on his own as a winter breeze rushed between us.

Where do you live? I can help you get home.

"Did you see me?" His voice was rough and filled with accusation. "Did anyone?"

"No. I don't think so." It meant so much to him. "When I found you, you were visible, but I hid you." I crawled over to him until I found his thigh and rested my hand there.

"Why?"

"Because you don't want me to know who you really are."

"You already know, Helene."

I reached up and pulled him to me in a hug. I wanted him to trust me, to feel the same way about me as I did about him. "Can you fly?" I whispered and then changed to speaking with my mind. *If not, we can walk. I can call someone to come pick us up.*

I'm fine.

I don't believe you. I knew he was bleeding. I wasn't even sure what had happened, but the sounds of the collisions would haunt me in my bed later.

A light guffaw rang in my ears. "I completely believe you." He stood, but I stayed on the ground, trying to make sense of Xavier and his secrets and the way I felt about him. "Helene, thank you," he said as if he knew how lost I was and was trying to bring me back.

"They said you could see them." I wasn't sure I wanted to know if he had even more powers than I already knew of.

"No. I can't. I just knew where they were." He reached out his hand and pulled me up beside him. "I really wish you could find a way to stay out of this. You can't defeat them."

"They've left us no choice but to fight."

He sighed. "Well, I wasn't raised to hit a girl, but that one had it coming." He laughed a little, and I felt him flinch.

I don't think you're okay to fly.

I'm fine. My wounds heal quickly.

I wish I could say the same.

You've come a long way since the night I found you in the woods. I wasn't sure I had, and the thought of returning to my house in Auburn left me cold. *I wish I could take you home with me.*

Me, too.

I'm sorry.

The back door opened and a man and woman walked into the yard. I moved closer to Xavier, and he took my hand in his.

"See, there's no light back here. I don't know what happened," the woman said as she and the man looked at every light on the back of the house.

"There was a cat screeching back here, too. Sounded like

something awful was happening."

The man held a beer in his hand and a disinterested look on his face.

"Well, are you going to fix it? It's Woodstown by Candlelight. We need light!"

"Light a candle," he said and carried his beer back inside.

She followed him, still nipping about the lights. I could hear her switch to his general lack of accomplishment and his overriding laziness. The light in the kitchen turned off right before a door slammed inside the house.

We should go, I thought.

I'll follow you home.

That isn't necessary.

Even if it isn't, I'm going to.

Xavier flew with me back to Auburn and left me when we passed the firehouse. Loneliness saturated me until I landed in my drive-way. My family still moved about the kitchen. Isaiah was leaning on the counter, laughing at something Sloane was saying. Time stood still when you were with your childhood friends. I could never feel alone in Auburn.

XVII

JUST AS LOVIE PULLED OUT of the driveway with all four of the girls in her minivan, hot tea sloshed over the side of my cup and burnt my hand. I extended my arm in front of me to reach the table without dropping my mug. Waving my hand in the air, I raced over to the sink to run cold water on it. It dripped down my wrist almost to my elbow and finally found the bottom of the sink.

"It's like you barely pay attention to anything anymore," Sloane said as if she were commenting on an impending rain that was moving across the fields. "Where have you been going . . . alone?"

Lying would never work with Sloane, and I wanted her to know the truth. It just wasn't my secret to tell.

"Last night, on the Woodstown by Candlelight tour, a witch named Andrea Ford spotted me in a group of people."

"I know her." Sloane was searching her mind for the face that went with the name. I'd give her this information first because it belonged to her, too. Any attack against our coven was ours to share.

"She noticed my shadow when I wasn't visible to have one."

"Wow. She's good."

"Yes, and a bit violent."

"What did she do?"

I remembered the blow. "Hit me with something. We flew all over the yard. She collided with an out building, and her friend helped her get away."

"Why didn't you call us? Did she know it was you?"

"No. I never said a word. I only knew it was her because she was on the tour with her friends before she spotted me."

"That's crazy."

"From what I hear, the Virago consider Woodstown by Candlelight *their* night to play."

Sloane leaned down, caught my eye, and forced me to face her before she asked, "Where did you hear that?"

"I am exhausted," Gisel said as she walked into the kitchen.

Sloane released me from her scrutiny, which I would have never survived without telling her everything.

"Has Gwen asked for a car?" I asked Gisel. Eight women in this house. We had one minivan and Gisel's BMW. We'd spent our whole lives trying to give the appearance of normal, and most teenage girls wanted cars more than anything. It was their freedom, but for a bunch of witches, a car wasn't necessary.

"No, but this morning she asked if we could go home for Christmas." I turned back to Gisel with no idea what to say. "She wants me and her to at least sleep there for Christmas Eve."

I'd tried to avoid the subject of Gisel's marriage ending as much as possible. "What did you say?"

"I told her I'd think about it. Her father and I are fine with this arrangement."

"I think that must make it easier to forget Gwen's thoughts." I was treading lightly. Maybe not lightly enough. "If you were at each other's throats, you'd be ultra-aware of Gwen and Ike's feelings, but maybe, because this seems so right to the both of you, you forget how wrong it must seem to them."

"It's true. Isaiah and I have come to terms with what we've missed out on the last twenty years, but for our kids, we were always their parents. We had no lives before they were born. I don't think Gwen has any interest in us having a life now that she's grown."

"I don't envy you navigating this." When Owen died, there was no one else to coordinate or include. We just were, and Ever and I clung to each other because of it.

"Ruby doesn't remember what Christmas was like with her father," Sloane said without another word of reference. The statement made Gisel pause with her cup almost to her lips.

"Do you think I should go back? Spend one last Christmas with Isaiah and my children?"

"It probably has a lot to do with the house, too. That's the only place Gwen has ever known Christmas. It was her home her entire life. The corner you put the tree in, the holly dish towels, the garland around the front door." I thought of all the little things my own mother had done that felt like Christmas. I tried to emulate so much of her for Ever. "She's probably afraid it won't be Christmas unless it's the same as it's always been."

Gisel's lips pursed into a fine line as she thought. She inhaled deeply, settled into her chair, exhaled, and said, "I think we should go home for Christmas."

"Are you sure?"

"We have the rest of our lives together. There's no need to force these changes down everyone's throats. I think Isaiah will like it, too." She looked around the room, and then her focus settled on me. "Maybe."

"Well, you are truly welcome here. Anytime. Even Christmas. Do what's best for your children. It won't be long before they'll have their own homes to wake up in Christmas morning. We'll miss these days."

"I'm already starting to." Gisel turned toward the scraping of the bush's branches across the kitchen window. "It's been a year." She didn't have to say since what. This week was the girls' holiday chorus concert, which meant it'd been a year since the first time we'd spoken in twenty years. A year since her powers were fully restored.

"It flew. Just like everyone says it does."

She turned back to me. "Life dragged without you guys, but the time has slipped through my fingertips since I saw you last year. I'm still grateful."

"I am, too."

"We all are," Sloane said as she moved to the computer desk, dragged the computer mouse around in a circle, and checked the Virago's Instagram account. While she waited for Facebook to load, she said, "You know, there are tons of other sites. Snapchat, Reddit, Twitter. We could be going in the wrong direction."

"We can't chase them down on the internet. What makes them turn on each other will have to happen in real life."

"I know. I left a candy bar on Simone's husband's car with a note that said, "You inspire me." She leaned back in the computer chair and lifted her feet to the corner of the desk. "I also sent a letter to the school commending Lisa's son on helping little old me cross the street yesterday in hopes he'd be considered for the civics award that Tanya is banking on her kid getting. I signed it with my mother's name." Sloane rolled a pencil between her fingers. "I snuck into the wrestling match and when Donna's husband put down his phone, I scrolled through and liked one of Amanda's posts."

"Just one?"

"You can't be too obvious. One like says I'm watching, a bunch says either "I'm desperate," or "My toddler got his hands on my phone."

"Who's Amanda again? I'm having trouble keeping them all straight."

"She's the one who just moved to Upper Pittsgrove. Oh, I also told John Wilde that I liked his new haircut in front of his wife. I still can't believe she's a witch, though. She has no . . ." Sloane searched for the word. "Style," she said with great disgust. "She must have been born into the Virago or something."

"Sloane, you're crazy," I told her. "This whole town is going to be like Melrose Place."

"I'm just spreading the love. If the Virago can't handle it." She held her hands up in the air as testimony to her innocence.

Ever ate dinner in Alloway the first three nights Ike was home from college. According to her, they decorated the tree, sat by the fire, and even ice-skated on the shallow portion of the lake. With every detail, memories of my young love flooded back. I avoided Isaiah at all costs. If I heard his voice downstairs or caught a glimpse of his truck pulling in, I was suddenly in the shower or taking a nap. Even if I'd taken one just a few hours before or wasn't tired.

Ever took the helm from Lovie on our own tree decorating. The girls, plus Ike, crossed the street to Mr. Crawford's tree farm and picked out what they referred to as "the one." Ike and Isaiah carried it across the street, up the hill, and into our living room.

"Are you sure you've got your end?" Isaiah asked, joking with his son. It was unbelievable I was a witness to it. I found myself captivated by any interaction between a father and their child. Especially one where I'd loved the father as much as I had Isaiah.

"Yeah. I'm sure," Ike answered back through the stray limbs that were in his face. Isaiah definitely got the better end of the deal. They placed the tree in the stand Lovie had readied in the corner on the opposite wall of the television.

Isaiah pointed to the floor, signaling Ike to get down on his belly and tilt the tree left and right while the rest of us chimed in on the straightness before he tightened the screws of the stand.

"It's perfect," Ever declared. Even as a little girl, she'd always loved our trees. In Vermont, there were trees everywhere for her to adore, but to have one of her very own inside our house enchanted her. I had to wait until she was in school to take the tree out and promise her it had been made into chips and mulch that would feed the earth again and make new trees.

When we drained the last drops of wine and hot chocolate, and the tree was lit with the lights dimmed, Isaiah and Ike finally called it a night. Ever watched with Carl from the window as they drove away. Tomorrow would be Christmas Eve. Her second in New Jersey, and her mind was lost somewhere other than the here and now.

"You okay?" I asked with the gentleness of a breeze. I wanted to entice her to turn around and talk to me.

She only nodded as the truck drove down the street.

"Well, you don't look okay. Ever, I swear. I know there's something going on. I can help. You can tell me anything."

"I know." She turned away from the window and smiled at me, but it was in response to her knowing I was there, not to the hope she might let me in. "I just worry about Ike."

"Why? Because of school? Football? He did great."

"I don't know. It's just a feeling." I moved to her with care. My steps were soft and light. If we made a big deal out of anything, these girls fled. I pulled my daughter into a hug. "I want to be there to protect him."

"Protect him from what?" I leaned back, begging her with my

eyes to share her worries with me.

She was silent for so long that I thought she was going to tell, but then she took a glass out of the cabinet and filled it with water as she said, "Nothing." She shook her head. "I'm just being emotional because of the tree."

I waited, just like I did when I knew she had something to tell me when she was little.

"It could have been Ike, when Mr. Kennedy was attacked. He means as much to us as his dad does," she finally said. "I know you're going to tell me I worry too much."

"I'm not going to say that at all, but let Ike's mom and me worry about this. We'll take care of him."

There was more on her mind. I could tell by the way she looked across the room dazed.

"What else?"

"Billy Roberts looks at me sometimes like he can read my mind. If I even think one kind thought about him, he retaliates with something awful."

"Like what?"

"The other day, Mr. Frank told him to stay after class, and Billy looked like he'd rather die. I must have had a sympathetic expression because he whispered, 'Get out.' He's cold . . . forgotten."

"Ike is right. You should stay away from him."

"Mr. Frank just assigned us as partners for a Facebook project."

"Keep your distance, Ever. He knows too much."

"Billy or Mr. Frank?" Ever left me by the tree and walked upstairs, wondering what exactly Mr. Frank knew about us.

I made my way to my room. My eyes darted to the window as soon as I opened the door, and my stomach dropped. It was closed, and there wasn't a hint of honeysuckle in the air. I missed Xavier. I wanted to see him, but I had no idea how to get ahold of him or where he lived. The questions went on and on.

What he looked like?

How he knew me?

What he was?

How he could fly?

Who else could he talk to in his head? I pulled back the coverlet on my bed and let the real question linger as I ran my hand over the cool sheets. Why wasn't he there? I wasn't sure if I'd ruined our friendship the night of the candlelight tour. I'd certainly risked more than he was willing to, and I did so after he had warned me not to fly there. He knew too much about what else was out there. About the Virago, and he knew too much about me. Even so, I wanted to see him.

I cracked the window and let the December freeze slip into my room. It swept across my stomach and thighs. I gazed up at the moon, and like a schoolgirl, I willed him to come to me.

If you're out there, Xavier, come. I miss you.

"What are you doing with the window open?" Sloane asked as she swung my bedroom door toward me. "Trying to freeze to death?"

I shut the window and locked it without an explanation. "Are you going to bed?"

Sloane's brows furrowed. She examined every inch of my bedroom before returning her gaze to me. "Do you want me to go to bed?"

"Sloane, I'm tired."

"No, you're not. You're up to something. Tell me now, or I will torture you with it when I find out."

"You'll think I'm crazy if I tell you."

She stepped further into my room and closed the door behind her. "Try me."

"Have you ever met a man that can do things?"

"Yes. Rob. That's why I married him."

She always made me laugh. "No. Things like us."

Her head pulled back like a chicken ready to peck, and her eyes widened. "Like us how?"

"Like he can fly." She tilted her head. "And he is invisible." I decided that was all I'd share. It wasn't my secret to tell.

"When did you meet this . . . person?"

"The night Isaiah told me he'd been with Gisel."

"Twenty years ago?" Sloane was irate. We'd never kept anything from each other, so my keeping something from her for twenty years was unthinkable. "Why the hell—"

"I had a lot on my mind that night. He helped me." My shoulder. The tree. My flight home in his arms came rushing back. "He was kind, but I never knew what he was."

"Not one male witch growing up. It's like peanut allergies. Where are they all coming from? Ike, this kid Billy . . . I've never heard of any man who had any power." Her anger switched to a smug smile. "Not unless a woman gave hers up to him. They're kind of at our mercy. Don't you think?"

"I did until I met him."

"Ike's house is on fire!" Ever yelled from the hallway. Sloane leaned out my bedroom door. "The tree is burning inside their living room, and they can't put it out."

"Did they call 9-1-1?"

"Yes. I'm going over," Ever said.

My instinct was to tell her she was staying right there and out of danger, but I couldn't keep her from leaving. "I'll go, too."

Sloane touched my arm where Ever couldn't see her. "We don't know how the fire started." Her voice was level, which filled me with terror more than Sloane yelling something.

I turned to Ever. There was no stopping her. "I'll get Gisel. In fact, we should all go."

"Let's go!" Ever left us and ran through the house rousting

everyone. Maya was already in her pajamas. She didn't want to go.

"No one gets left behind," Sloane said. The safest place for any of us was in Auburn, but I let Sloane take the lead.

We flew with the girls in front of us. Gisel and I were in the middle and Lovie and Sloane stayed a few feet back. The smoke billowed from the side of Gisel and Isaiah's home. The tips of flames jetted from the roof. The fire had reached the attic and had begun raging out of control next to the lake. Isaiah and Ike had already moved their car and motorcycle out of the garage and down the street. The word "Leave" was spray painted on the side of the house.

Water rushed from the lake and formed an arc before hitting the house. Neighbors' lights were turning on and people were beginning to open their doors.

Stop! I wasn't sure who was dousing the fire with water. I removed the painted words of hate. Each particle of paint I sent floating into the black smoke emerging from the center of Gisel's former home.

We can save it, Gisel thought back.

The blare of the fire engine approaching grew louder as the seconds dragged by. There needed to still be a fire when they got here, even if it meant helplessly watching the house burn to the ground.

You have to let it burn.

We stayed invisible, not able to explain how we'd all gotten there. Sloane and Lovie flew around the property, looking for any signs of how the fire started or who started it.

Couldn't it have been an accident? Christmas trees do sometimes catch on fire. Keep it watered, and all. Ruby thought. She hadn't read the message on the side of the house.

Accidents are much rarer than people believe. I'd been beating this into Ever's head since we moved home to Auburn.

Isaiah's best friend, Tommy, was a fireman. I hadn't seen him since I'd left town, but he was the same. He and the rest of the station helped Isaiah and Ike secure the unburned portion of the house. Even without the fire touching every square foot, the water and smoke damage could total it.

They're coming home with us, Ever thought.

It wasn't a question. Of course, her boyfriend and his father would spend Christmas Eve and Day with us after their house was tragically burned down. Ever's voice was on edge. Her anxiousness was more than any of the other girls' responses to the fire. I stayed close to her, just in case she did something rash. She moved toward Ike as he pulled out on his motorcycle.

I'll see you guys at home, Sloane thought.

Where are you going?

Every night for a week, I've put some message of love on Donna's husband's car. A heart carved out of the snow, a note. Tonight, I'm going to clean off his windshield.

I'm going with you, Gisel thought and they both took off.

The rest of us flew home and prepared for Isaiah's arrival. Lovie cracked eggs into a bowl and chopped vegetables for omelets. It was only four fifteen in the morning, but no one was going to sleep at this point. Isaiah arrived, Sloane and Gisel following moments behind him, and the kitchen filled with people who didn't know what to say. We bumped into one another as we spoke sentences about anything but what caused us all to be there. Ten people in this old house were too many. Isaiah and I together in any house was one too many.

"Thanks for letting us stay," Isaiah told Sloane when he got out of the shower. "We'll be out of here tomorrow. I just don't want to wake my mom this late. It might kill her."

"Nonsense. You'll crash here as long as you need to, but at least through the holiday." I stayed facing the kitchen cabinets so no one could see the pain on my face. "You're family."

"Thank you, Sloane."

We ate breakfast and lingered at the table until the sun rose. The girls had all fallen asleep late with Ike in a sleeping bag on the floor of their room. We had Gisel's bed or a couch to offer Isaiah. Neither of which seemed to hold any appeal as a legitimate plan.

"I have an air mattress we can set up in the laundry room. It's only a twin, but it will give you some privacy."

"That sounds good." He stared at me until I almost melted under his attention.

Without another word, I ascended the stairs and dug through the things under my bed to find the mattress and the pump. When I pulled it out and cleared the bed rail, Isaiah was laughing in the doorway behind me.

"Something funny?"

"It's just your organization system hasn't changed. You used to store half the world under your bed."

"It's great space that should be utilized." I dropped the items in his arms and pulled a plastic container out from the other side of the bed. I found the twin sheets, extra blanket, and pillow before closing the lid and hiding it again. "I'll follow you," I said and waited for Isaiah to move. It'd been a long night. I was grateful he turned around and left without an awkward conversation.

We worked together to unfold and inflate the mattress. When it was filled enough, I spread the fitted sheet out, and Isaiah grabbed one end. He pulled it so hard, it flew from my hands.

"Sorry." He reached over the bed and met me in the middle to hand my corner back to me. "Do you remember the night my parents went away and you snuck out and slept over?"

My breath caught. I shouldn't have, but I looked him in the eyes and let his words penetrate every wall I'd built to avoid him. Memories of the soft flannel of his sheets back then, the navy comforter that matched the wallpaper in his room, and his one pillow that we'd shared all surfaced in my mind. Fear of how far he'd take this tightened my chest.

"You rang the doorbell at twelve thirty as if it were noon." We'd never been alone like that before. I knew when my finger pressed the button next to his front door that it would be the first of many nights that I gave myself to him.

"Isaiah—"

"I know." He moved from the other side of the mattress, which was where he belonged, to right next to me in the hollow corner next to the washing machine. "I want you to tell me what you're thinking . . . and feeling. Because for all these years, you wouldn't let me hear a thing."

"I'm still not allowing it." I could barely breathe with him this close to my body and inside my mind.

"I know you remember. Every second we were together. I know the past haunts you the same way it does me."

"You know nothing." I wasn't angry anymore. I was lost somewhere between the memory of loving him and the loneliness without him.

"Tell me then. Explain to me what this is like for you. Let me in, Helene."

I stood and straightened my shirt. "It's been a long night."

Isaiah pulled me down on top of him. "It's been a long life. Don't run away again." He rolled over until I was lying underneath him on the blow-up mattress. Our location, his wife, and my daughter's relationship with his son were all the universe's cruel reminders that we didn't get to plan things out in a neat and tidy way.

"I'm not running away." He shifted until the bulk of his weight moved off me. "I'm trying to come home, but you're making it impossible." I reached up and touched his arm. My eyes clung to my fingers against his bicep. "I'm always tripping over you somehow because you block any forward progress with the past." I tried to push him away from me, but he was a concrete wall. "It can't be the same with you as it is with Gisel. I'm not just going to wake up one day and hug you or cuddle close to you on the couch while we watch television."

"Why not?" He truly could not understand.

"Because I don't love you the same way anymore. When you were with her . . ." I inhaled deeply to settle the sob that was building in my chest.

"Helene, you have got to believe me. I'm sorry."

"I know. Let me finish." I let my hand drop from his arm. "When you were with her, you made me question everything about the world, not just you. Whether I could ever trust someone again. If I was a good judge of character? If true love really existed? If good people, honorable and kind people, are always capable of making a mistake." Isaiah took my hand in his and squeezed it until I looked at him. "I'd never wanted anything the way I wanted to be with you. When it was over, I was scared to want another thing again . . . until Ever."

"That still doesn't explain how you can forgive her."

"Gisel is a part of me. I never wanted or needed her. She just was. From the minute she was born, we were together. Having her back is the equivalent of regaining my sight or the ability to hear. It is the same as before I left." I placed my hand on my lap. "Having you back is a reminder of how disappointing the world can be. I know it isn't fair, but it's as honest as I can be with you."

"It isn't fair."

"We were young. It was amazing." I'd give him this one night in hopes that he'd give me every one in the future to breathe. "I am still haunted by what we had." He leaned in closer, and I feared he'd kiss me, or worse, that I wanted him to. "But the ending of every memory tears my heart out the same way it did so many years ago. So, I need you to be my friend, not my ex-boyfriend."

"I'm a horrible friend," he whispered and flashed me the same smile he used to convince me to skip school or go skinny dipping with him.

I took a deep breath. "The worst," I whispered back. "Good night, Isaiah."

XVIII

FELT GUILTY. I DID. Sloane and Lovie were reading the news about Amanda Lawson's freak accident that left her drowned in the Delaware River near the bank behind the Riverview Inn. The author of the article speculated that she'd slipped on the ice, hit her head, and fallen into the water. We all concluded that Donna had something to do with it. Sloane attended the funeral without anyone seeing her and there were whispers among the crafty women in the back that confirmed they believed it, too.

"They weren't happy about it, either. Three witches I hadn't seen before were only there to check out the scene and gather information."

"Did you get any names?" Maya asked.

"Dina?" Sloane said. Maya took the journal out of the draw-er, waited for the names to appear, and then dragged her finger down the list of witches as she read. "Dina Reynolds." She took the book with her to the computer and pulled Dina Reynolds up on Facebook. She, of course, was Janine Smith's friend. Our fake profile had befriended almost every witch and half of the town. "Was this one of them?"

Sloane stared at the screen as Maya flipped through some more pictures. "That's her. Donna should watch out for her. According to the photos, Dina really liked Amanda."

"As much as they really like anyone," Ever said.

Sloane tilted her head toward my daughter. "Now that you mention it, she did seem angrier at Donna for killing her than she was that Amanda was dead."

"Of course she was. They're evil, which is why I don't want to have a party," I said with my arms crossed at my chest. The subject had already been brought up five times, and no one listened to me. I was adamant. Isaiah's house burning down still left a mark. As far as I was concerned, we should be spending every waking moment monitoring our plan to rid the area of the Virago.

"Bah humbug," Sloane said.

"Wrong holiday." It wasn't that I didn't want to celebrate the new year. Actually, it was. I didn't feel like I could relax. I rolled my head and rubbed my neck. Maybe the stress was getting to me.

"We're safe here. We should enjoy it. This town was given to us by our ancestors. If nothing else, that's reason alone to celebrate another year beginning."

Lovie started preparing the food that night. She worked for three days. I cleaned the house. Gisel went to the party store and brought home enough horns, hats, and eyeglasses in the shape of the year for fifty people. Even though it was only going to be a family affair, the guest list had crept up to include Denny Taylor, the Hitchners, Maya's boyfriend, Mick, and his parents. The girls also invited Ike—of course—Sam, and Paul Wentzel, whose parents had been invited, too.

Sloane invited Sean Watts and made me wonder if he was the whole reason in the first place for the party. A few others we hadn't seen in twenty years made the list. Not surprisingly, Lovie somehow had contact information for each of them. Trish, Kevin Flitcraft, and Gwen's obsession, Dave Anzaldo, rounded out the party. It was, actually, perfect.

There were plenty of people to talk to, which made avoiding Isaiah an easy task. The stories of our heyday flowed freely with the drinks Sloane kept preparing. The girls and their friends manned the couch and the television show that broadcast celebrities leading up to the ball dropping while the adults congregated in the kitchen. When the trash was full, Isaiah emptied it as if it were his responsibility. He was at the house so often that I could almost see the logic.

When the countdown was chanted from the living room, we all squished in beside our children and watched as the ball slowly made its descent into the new year. We counted along until Ruby began blowing her horn, and then everyone else with a horn in their hand followed. I waited for Ever to kiss Ike, and then hugged her myself. The coming year was a gift. I kissed Gisel and wished her a happy new year. The gift was from her. None of us would have the future we did without her. I stifled the thoughts of her contribution to how this whole mess started. It was our past. Together, we'd face our future.

Maya blushed when Mick kissed her. I'd never seen them hold hands even though we all knew they were dating. Ever and Ike . . . each of the girls was with their first love. I turned to leave the enchantment with them and walked right into Isaiah in the doorway to the kitchen.

"Happy new year, Helene," he said and kissed me on the cheek.

A surge of heat spread through me followed by the bitter guilt I associated with any relics of feeling I had for my best friend's husband, or ex-husband as they both kept insisting. The smile fell from Isaiah's lips. His reaction mirrored my own.

"I'm sorry," were the words that came out of my mouth before I could stop them, and I shook my head. I had no reason to apologize. He took a sip of his drink as his gaze wandered around the room. "Excuse me," I said and made my way to my bedroom.

As soon as I closed my door behind me, I could breath. I inhaled deeply the scent of honeysuckle as my bedroom window opened. "Don't go," I said, knowing he was leaving without even saying hello. It was as if he saw Isaiah kiss me, and that possibility wasn't without merit. I never knew exactly what Xavier saw or how long he'd been around. The isolated silence was filled with his scent and the knowledge that he was still with me. "I have a present for you."

"For me?" He openly laughed in a way he never had around me before. It was adorable.

"Yes. It's a Christmas present, but I wasn't sure how to get it to you." I turned on the light next to my bed. When I turned back toward where I thought he was, I realized I was hoping he'd show himself to me. I tilted my head and thought he was still standing by the window, but not an item was out of place on that side of the room. In the drawer of my nightstand, I found the small mesh bag with the ribbon tied tight around the top of it. The gift tag hanging from it read "Xavier."

The honeysuckle grew stronger until I knew he was standing directly in front of me. The urge to see him was hurting me. I wanted more of him than he was ever going to give me. His fingertips slid down the side of my face and soothed me.

"Here," I said and held the pouch out in front of me. He took it and the bag disappeared as soon as it left my grasp. "It's lip balm." His silence made me nervous. I shouldn't have gotten him a gift. "Since I don't know you or what you look like or what size you wear . . ." The culmination of what I didn't know was frustrating.

"Or what your favorite color is."

"It's incredibly thoughtful," he whispered.

"I just figured with all the flying, your lips probably get chapped. This winter has been bitter."

"I love it, Helene." The sweet smell of whiskey replaced the honeysuckle. The open window drew my attention. He was there but willing to leave before he'd said hello. It was as if he'd drunk texted me and then regretted it.

"Have you been celebrating?"

"Kind of." His evasiveness annoyed me.

"You could have come to our party."

"You didn't invite me."

"I wasn't sure where to send the invitation." I also wasn't sure how much time he'd give me. "I want to apologize to you."

"For what?"

"For not listening when you told me not to fly on the night of Woodstown by Candlelight." Xavier didn't argue or tell me it wasn't necessary. "And for putting you in danger of being exposed. It was selfish of me."

"Apology accepted." His voice was low and even.

"In my defense—"

"Is there a defense in this apology?" His playfulness returned.

"Yes. In my defense, I was giddy. You make me feel young, and in turn, I do stupid things that lack maturity and foresight."

"So, this is my fault."

"Thank you for seeing it that way."

Xavier laughed at me. "Of course. No trouble at all."

How can I hear you inside my head?

I don't know.

Has this ever happened with anyone else? I asked, partially afraid of his answer.

No.

My daughter can hear her boyfriend in her head. Gisel's son. She's always thought it was because he was a son of a witch.

He is that.

The quilt and mattress next to me dipped down, and I realized he'd sat on my bed. Next to me. He touched my hand, and I disappeared, too. Xavier threaded his fingers in mine and pulled me in front of him. I closed my eyes in the safety of invisibility and enjoyed the sensation of his touch. I took a deep breath and let the heat from his hand sink into every inch of me.

His breath caressed my ear as he said, "Blue."

I opened my eyes and tried to focus. "Blue?"

He kissed me. Laying me back on the mattress and climbing on top of me. "Blue is my favorite color." He kissed me again. My arms wrapped around his neck, pulling him closer to my body. It didn't make sense, but I felt safe with Xavier in my bed. I forgot about everything but the heat that coursed through my body with him on top of me. I tightened my arms around his neck and let it restore me. "Happy new year," he said as his lips dragged down the side of my neck.

Someone banged on the door, and Xavier was gone. My arms dropped to my bed, and I reappeared.

"We are not letting Ike crash in Ever's room, right?" Gisel practically yelled as she swung open the door without being invited in. She titled her head into the air as her eyes darted around the room, and she inhaled deeply. There was only a hint of honeysuckle left. I knew he was gone. "Are you alone?"

I sighed. "Yes."

Gisel's gaze raked over the room and finally landed on the open window. "Are you okay?" Her voice had an odd tone. She examined me, knowing I wasn't sharing everything with her, but to know I was hiding something meant that she wasn't sharing everything, either.

"We're not letting them in the same bedroom."

"You know she stays in his dorm."

Gisel covered her ears. "No. I don't. I'm telling them no. Just because a coven won't be born, does not mean a baby won't come."

"She's on birth control."

"I swear I was just teaching him how to brush his teeth. How did this happen?"

Gisel brought me back to the chaos of her. "I don't know." The tree outside my window caught my eye. I closed and locked the window.

"Let's get a drink," she said.

"I should just go to sleep."

"You can sleep next year." She pulled me toward the door. Right before I turned off the light, I realized the lip balm was nowhere to be found.

XIX

I KNEW IT WAS STILL dark out before I opened my eyes. It would be gray and cold and the sun would be slow to rise because this was a morning to stay in bed. My mother made every January tenth the most magical day of the year. She'd wake me with kisses and chocolate chip pancakes, and somehow the sun seemed bright like summer even if it was snowing. I'd had sixteen years of that, and every January tenth since her death seemed a little dimmer.

I brushed my teeth, found my robe hooked to the back of my door, and tiptoed down the stairs, hoping they wouldn't creak and wake everyone. I needed a few moments alone to settle into the day.

"Happy birthday," Maya said. She was beaming with pride through tired eyes as she tied a balloon's ribbon to the bottom of the banister.

"You guys shouldn't have." My eyes couldn't take in the whole first floor and everyone in it. Helium filled balloons with "Happy Birthday" and "We Love You" printed on them lay on their sides against the ceiling. A large four balloon was twisted through a zero one.

"How could we not?" Lovie said and stepped forward from the crowd of our coven and our daughters. "You only turn forty once."

Most days in this house, I still felt eighteen. I looked around and was pleasantly surprised not to find Isaiah lurking in the background.

"Happy birthday, Mom."

I gave Ever a big hug. "Thank you."

"We made your favorite. French toast."

The eight of us ate in perfect harmony. Not one mention of the Virago. It was a small glimpse of peace in the middle of a war. I carried the calm with me throughout the day. The clerk at the dollar store who checked my license when I paid with a credit card wished me a happy birthday as well. This one tiny ritual that depended on nothing but the date on the calendar made everything else seem less. We could have a broken leg, a divorce hearing tomorrow, and a terrorist attack the day before, but still someone would wish you a happy birthday.

By the time I ran out the back door with a peanut butter bagel in my hand to make it to the Project Graduation meeting on time, I'd been celebrated over and over again on my special day. Even sitting in the high school library, as I searched for a pen and piece of paper in my tote, someone wished me a happy birthday. I soaked in the walls and books surrounding me. It could have been my sixteenth birthday.

We were going to bus all the kids to the Funplex the night of graduation and keep them there until the wee hours of the morning to avoid any tragedies hitting our small town. They'd play games and ride go-carts and celebrate with the other one hundred and sixty-nine kids from their class before they left each other for the next stages of their lives. May their transitions be smother than ours had been.

"How was the Project Graduation meeting?" Lovie asked.

"Donna's in the hospital."

"Donna Holmes? The one who . . ."

"Yes. Apparently, she was walking along the side of the road and was hit by a car."

"They didn't kill her."

"But they tried." I tipped my head toward her. "And from what I heard tonight, she's so freaked out she wants to move back to the city. Mr. Frank made the announcement and passed around a sign-up sheet to take meals to her house. Only three people signed up."

"How was the Project Graduation meeting?" Sloane asked as she walked into the room with the girls following her.

"Good. I marked you all down as in attendance," I teased them.

"I think one representative per household is plenty," Sloane countered. "Besides, I took the girls and Carl to the vet."

"How is he?"

"The dog or the vet?" Sloane asked. I turned to her confused.

"She hasn't been to the vet yet," Lovie said, and everyone else in the room nodded in understanding.

"What?"

"They think he's hot," Ever finally explained.

"Not hot." Sloane corrected her. "He's handsome and . . . refreshing."

"Yeah." Ruby rolled her eyes. "That's what we're calling it."

"I went to the grocery store," Lovie said.

"You know I'd go there for you. You don't have to do all the cooking," Gisel said.

"I like it, and the meat manager is handsome, too."

"Good," Gisel responded without hesitation. She'd told me she hated to cook. At least for her family, who all liked different things.

We discussed school visitations and the idea of Sloane taking them to Vegas, me showing off Vermont, and all of us going to Hawaii. Gisel sat quietly throughout the discussion. The girls weren't interested in West Chester where she and Isaiah had graduated from, and the subject of them all leaving rendered her timid.

A day was coming where there would be no subjects that silenced one of us. Things would become "normal" with Isaiah. The girls would be settled into their campuses without any discourse to worry about. We just weren't there yet. These next few months would bring up every mistake we'd made before we were their mothers.

Helene, I heard in my head in the moment I was alone at the table while the dishes were cleared and the wineglasses were refilled. *Are you free?*

"Why are you smiling like that?" Sloane asked, having caught me wondering if Xavier was asking me on a date.

"I was just thinking how great this cake looks."

"No you weren't." She shook her head with complete certainty that she knew I was lying.

I went to the bathroom and stared at myself in the mirror. The lines around my eyes were the most telling hint of my forty years. The stories they told when I wasn't laughing.

Not right now, I thought back. *Maybe later.*

I waited to hear from him again, but there was nothing. Not a word during cake or presents. Ever gave me a hand-drawn picture of three women. It was my mother, her, and I all standing in front of the ocean. She was incredibly talented. Our faces were perfect, even my mother's, which Ever had drawn from the photograph that was framed in the living room. The three of us never had a chance to stand next to each other. My mother would have been almost sixty.

"Did you have a good birthday?"

"The best. Thank you." I stared at the picture again and realized we looked a lot more alike than I'd thought. Our chins, the shape of our lips, there were several things that looked familial if not the same. "I love it. You're gifted."

"Thanks. I'm still not taking art as a major."

"I know. Art doesn't have to be major to impact the world. Just keeping creating."

"You are such a hippie."

"Well, birthday girl," Lovie said. "I'm going to bed. Everyone has another early morning tomorrow."

"All birthdays should take place on the weekend," Gisel added. "Sleep in tomorrow. I'll drive the girls and take care of Carl. You deserve some rest."

"Are you sure? I'm fine. Really."

"Take it while you can get it," Sloane said and followed them up the stairs.

I double-checked the freezer door was closed and turned out the lights under the cabinets. I twirled around, making sure everything else was neatly put away when I saw the card propped up against the empty cake plate in the center of the table. The envelope was purple. My name was written on the front in Isaiah's handwriting. There was a Post-it note stuck to it with "He made me give this to you since we wouldn't let him come" written on it in Gisel's handwriting.

Of course he did. I opened the envelope and pulled out the card that had a black and white picture of a young woman riding a bike into the ocean on the front of it. The inside read:

Sloane and Gisel said I couldn't come over tonight. I thought they were just being hateful. Then Lovie said it wasn't a good idea, and I knew she only had your best interest in mind.

I won't push. Nothing creepy. No proclamations of love or pleas for forgiveness.

Just know it could happen. I believe anything can. You used to. You'd ride your bike into the ocean if you felt like it. Do what you feel now. If you want to go fishing naked for your birthday, I'll take you. It will be a tremendous sacrifice, but the last time we did it, we caught some good fish. We might want to wait until spring, though.

I'll still be here, and the offer will still stand.

Isaiah

I giggled a little. It was the first card he'd sent me in decades, and as always, he knew just what to say. I walked over to the trashcan to throw it away. I swung open the door under the sink, but before I dropped the card in the can, something stopped me.

The silence surrounding me gave way to a feeling that someone was near me in the kitchen. I stayed still until the back door opened and air rushed in. I ran to the door and said, "Xavier," into the night air. "Don't go."

There was nothing but darkness in our backyard. I closed and locked the door, shut off the lights in the kitchen, and climbed the stairs to my room. There should be a way I could get ahold of him. Some signal I could send that I wanted to talk to him. This was no way to begin a relationship.

The door to my room opened before I touched it. I only hesitated for a second before stepping inside.

"Surprise," he whispered and shut the door behind me. I walked over to my dresser in the darkness and put Isaiah's card on top of it. "I'm sorry. I didn't know it was your birthday."

It's okay. I switched to speaking to him in my mind. Another mystery that surrounded him.

It isn't okay. A friend would know when your birthday is.

Is that what you are? My friend? He stepped closer to me and placed both his hands on the sides of my neck, holding me as I let my head fall back and pulled a deep breath of air into my lungs.

You're angry. He kissed my chin.

Confused. His lips dragged down my neck.

I feel the same way.

I doubt it.

You shouldn't doubt me, he thought, and his lips found mine.

I forced myself to surface from the whirlwind of him. I pulled his hands down but didn't let them go. "I need to ask you something." Xavier stayed perfectly still in front of me. "Come here."

I led him to my bed, pulled back the covers, and climbed in before him. I could feel him towering over me. His hesitation wasn't daunting. I reached out, grabbed his hand, and pulled him in beside me. He slipped off his shoes as I unbuttoned his coat.

"Helene."

"Don't worry. I'm not going to take advantage of you. I just want to talk." I thought that was true. He lay down, and I cuddled in next to him. After two breaths, his arm circled my shoulder as if we'd been together in my bed a hundred times before. "Nice, right?"

"Yes." He tilted his head up until his chin rested on the top of my head. "What is your question?"

I wrapped my arm across his chest. The dress I'd worn to the Project Graduation meeting was twisted at my waist, but I didn't dare move for fear he'd leave. "How did you know where I lived?" He always seemed to know exactly what I meant, but for clarification, I said, "That first night. When you found me in the woods?"

"I was home from college for the weekend when I heard of the two witches who died in a car accident and decimated the Auburn Coven. I found you then," he said, and I rolled over and rested on top of his chest. "Something about knowing you were close to my age and out there alone made me want to meet you." I waited for the rest. I wouldn't say another word until he did. "You were heartbroken and angry and lost and beautiful . . . but you weren't alone. You had your boyfriend and your coven." He sighed. "I hope that doesn't sound creepy."

"No more than you lying beneath me in my bed even though I've never seen you and don't know your last name."

"There's more." I braced myself. "I forgot about you until I was home from college after graduation and stumbled upon your boyfriend . . . and your best friend." I pushed off him, and he pulled me back against his chest. "I waited for you to come home and followed you to the tree house. For the second time, I watched your devastation, I couldn't leave you." Mortification overcame me. "You're not the one who should be embarrassed."

"Why didn't you find me after that?"

"It wasn't that easy. I had to lurk around your friend Gisel, who I can't stand, to find out any information, and you told her none. All I had was the University of Vermont to go on."

"You should have gone there. I could have used a friend."

"I did go." I would have taken from Xavier everything Isaiah had stolen from me. I was suddenly grateful I still had my clothes on. "I should go."

"No. Finish. Please. Secrets are killers with patience." I sat up next to him and the coziness between us fell away.

"I never spoke to you because, what could I say? The only time you'd met me, you were in pain, and you couldn't see me. I had very little to offer."

"But things are different now?"

"I'm trying."

XX

THE DISHARMONY IN THE TOWN reached all the way to the sky. Property was burned to the ground. Children were taught to hate one another. A few witches moved. Vehicles were tampered with. Pets were killed. The stories were endless. The momentum of jealousy and hatred expanded as quickly as Janine Smith's friend list on Facebook. The Kingsway Coven came by every Thursday night, and we traded stories and tracked the witches on Maya's spreadsheet.

"A meeting's been called," Ruby said as she stared at her phone. She passed it around.

"What is it?" Lovie asked when it was her turn to see it.

"It's an abandoned hotel," Ruby said and snapped her lips shut.

"How do you know about it?" Sloane asked her daughter, her eyebrows raised.

"Can we just stay focused?" She flipped her hand toward the phone in Gisel's hand. "I think they're planning something. Look who has commented or liked the post so far."

Gisel passed the phone to me, but I couldn't tell anything by the names. They were "loved2u64" and "grabitifyourwantit" and, my favorite, "stopfollowingme." None of them made sense.

"You have to look them up on here. "Maya brought out her spreadsheet again and compared the screen names to her list. They matched. Every single one of them.

"What are we going to do?"

"We should go and listen." Sloane acted as if it made perfect sense.

"They'll know we're there."

"They can't feel us, remember?" Ever said.

"We don't know that for sure about *all* of them. You're talking about a big group. We still have over forty witches that just liked this post."

"I was going to go to Rowan tomorrow," Ever said. "I know it sounds unimportant in comparison. I'm just throwing it out there." She smiled weakly at us. My daughter really needed to work on her priorities. Her one overnight per month in Ike's dorm had become sacred to her. "I can go after." She broke under my scrutiny.

"Thank you," I said. I tried to tone down the sarcasm, but I'd spent the day with Sloane, which always left its mark on me.

When we woke the next morning, we still hadn't settled on a plan. Ever was throwing clothes in her backpack. For a split second, I wanted to say that she probably didn't need clothes, and then ripped it from my mind as quickly as it had landed there. I liked Ike. I loved him. It still wasn't easy to know my daughter was *with* him.

"Mom!" Maya was yelling up the stairs to Lovie.

She looked over the railing right outside my door. "What?"

"Something's happened."

I followed Lovie down the stairs. Sloane was a half-step behind me. All eight of us met in the kitchen where Maya was on the computer.

"At first, there were a bunch of posts in Janine's feed that said things like 'live each day like it's your last,' or 'Gods speed.'" I clued in on where Maya was going with this. Someone else had died. "But in the comments, after a bunch of people had asked what was going on, someone finally linked to a news story."

None of us said a word as Maya pulled it up on the computer and read the headline. "Bus Accident Kills Eleven Women from Same Town."

My mouth fell open. Ruby was getting the journal with the spreadsheet out of the drawer. Sloane leaned over Maya's shoulder and read the article. It was too much. Too much death and destruction. The tiny snowballs we had rolled down the hill had turned into boulders.

Sloane faced me and forced me to stop thinking about anything but what she was about to say. "They were on their way to New York to see the Broadway show *Wicked*."

"It's gone too far," I said.

Ruby held up the journal near the computer and crossed out the eleven names from the list.

"They started it," Sloane said. I knew she wouldn't be convinced of any other point of view. No one seemed as disturbed as I was. Not even Lovie, which was the most unhinging part.

From what we could tell, the Virago was not meeting. Too many families were involved with the arrangements that followed a death. The posts of condolences continued to dominate all the social media accounts for days. Who would celebrate a "date night!" or other meaningless moment they were "#blessed" when eleven women had been erased?

We attended the memorial service that had been coordinated for all the women. Visible and as ourselves. The list of witches who perished on the New Jersey Turnpike included the cafeteria lunch lady from the high school, the woman who worked the deli counter at the grocery store, and the secretary at our doctor's office. The entire town came out. Isaiah was meeting us there, and Ike had come home from Rowan. News trucks from the three major television stations in Philadelphia and two of the national morning programs lined the edge of the parking lot. Few details had been reported since the accident. Mechanical failure was the initial cause, and four people were in intensive care. None of the witches had survived.

There were hundreds of people in attendance. Speakers broadcast the service into the lot where many sat on lawn chairs they had in their trunks left over from the fall sports. It was painfully cold, but no one complained. Eleven women were lost to the community, it didn't matter that they were part of the Virago.

The eight of us stood in line huddled together to block the wind. Conversations flowed around us as everyone caught sight of people they knew. We had our own conversation in our head.

I feel sick, Lovie thought.

I held her hand in mine and rubbed it with my other one. We were there to pay our respects, not wallow in our guilt.

There's the new teacher everyone keeps talking about, Gisel said. I was thankful for her complete disconnect from our role in this tragedy. It was one of her gifts.

We glanced in the direction she was staring. The tall man with arms that looked disproportionately long, even in a parka, stood looking in our direction as he spoke with Principal Jeffries.

He's my modern media instructor, Ever thought. *Mr. Frank.* She didn't look away from him as she spoke to us. My daughter's eyes melded into a glare. I turned back to Mr. Frank. When I made eye contact with him, he turned away.

It's like he's watching you, Sloane thought from behind us. I hadn't realized she was paying attention.

He's always watching us. Me and Billy Roberts. Ever swallowed hard and tightened her jaw.

"Hey," Isaiah said as he walked up and joined us in the line. "It's freezing out here." His statement of the obvious opened three new conversations with the people we knew around us.

I kept my eye on Ever, who was bundled up with Ike's arms around her. I was glad she had him. Gisel nudged me forward as the line moved, and I noticed Mr. Frank still watching my daughter. My stare bore down on him until he noticed me. My eyes narrowed. My jaw clenched as I made it wordlessly clear that he wasn't the only one watching. A student approached Mr. Frank. After a few minutes of her chatter, he turned and paid attention to her.

We followed the line, past the pictures of the women at the front of the hall, and paid our condolences to their families. Gwen walked behind me, in front of her mother. She paused at each of the women's portraits and let her fingers rest on the bottom corner of the frames. She was lost in thought at the seventh one, Emily Rottingham. I touched her wrist to signal her to keep moving, but Gwen lowered her head. She was listening. I smiled at the gentleman behind us, and he nodded as tears filled his eyes. He'd assumed Gwen was in mourning.

I tugged a little harder, and Gwen followed me the rest of the way through the line and outside into the gray bitter day. None of us said a word until we were safely back in our kitchen. Our black outfits filled the room with death. Gone were the laughter and the wine. The only things left were questions and remorse.

"It does seem a little extreme, even for the Virago," Lovie said.

"I don't think it was them," Gwen chimed in from behind me. "Emily Rottingham said, 'Even lost witches are born with love.

This man was born with evil.'"

"What man?" Gisel sprung on her daughter's statements. My heart stopped in fear it was Xavier. More so, that I could be so wrong about a person. Again.

"The hunter," she said.

I T WAS MORE THAN A sense. A feeling, perhaps, that I wasn't alone. There were no tiny sounds the house usually made or evidence of the wind howling outside. Just the late February sunshine that still set too early for my taste.

My inspection continued to every window and door in the kitchen. Locked tight to the point even Xavier couldn't get in without making a sound. It was lonely in the house without Gisel, Sloane, and Lovie. Possibly without him, too. I wanted them to meet him and confirm my opinion on who or what he was.

The hint of thickness touched the tip of my nose first and burst his memory into my mind.

"Xavier."

His scent swirled around me as he moved about. "How did you know?" he asked. His voice was full of disbelief.

"I'm getting better at knowing when you're near." I tilted my head toward the corner of the room and waited for his exact location to register. I reached out to my left and touched him. Moving my hand down, I realized it was his chest. I turned and faced him with both hands moving across his shoulders and down his arms. My breaths came heavy from my body. "I miss you when you're gone."

His head lowered, and I imagined his eyes were taking me in. I reached up and found the side of his face in exactly the same position where my mind told me it'd be. "We're alone." I cradled his face in my hands and tilted it to face me. "Show yourself."

His breaths were held as still as his body. I fought through the words running through my mind to find the combination that would convince him to trust me. "I can't do that," he said and pulled my hands away by my wrists. He moved away from me, but I couldn't tell where. It took a few minutes of silence for me to sync with him.

"Why?"

"Because no one knows who—what—I am."

"I know what you are."

He was on the other side of the table as if he had to place furniture between us to protect him. "I don't have a coven like you and your family. I've always been by myself."

"You have me."

"Do I?" His voice swelled with disbelief.

"Xavier, you know so much and share nothing." He was gone. The room felt dead. Until a rush of air landed him beside me. I stood straight with my shoulders back and my arms taut at my sides. I shouldn't assume the good in Xavier.

"What will seeing me do except expose me?"

"It's more than the color of your hair or the shape of your chin." His advantage was unfair. He had my home, my family, every minute of my life to judge me if he wanted. I had a few meetings in the dark and his words. "It's the collar of the shirt you're wearing and whether your cheeks are pink from being out in the sun and the look in your eyes when you say my name." But he was right, it was so much more than that. "It's an exchange, a conversation, a moment that two people share. You're keeping it to yourself, and it belongs to me, too."

"Someone like you could never understand."

"Let me try."

He leaned down until I could hear him with only a whisper. "You know my greatest secret. Isn't that enough?"

I slipped my hand under his shirt to touch his skin. "No. I want all of you. The way you have all of me."

"Do I?" he asked.

"You certainly have enough to trust me."

"I wish it were that easy."

The back door opened, and Xavier left me alone in my kitchen.

❧

"Meet me," Isaiah's text had said. I ignored it. I shouldn't have even known that it was his number, but somehow I did.

"I know you got my text," was the voice mail he left on my phone, and I ignored that, too. The old Helene would have changed her number and flown away, but I was determined to stay in this life with my family, and Isaiah was undeniably a part of that.

The phone rang in my hand and startled me. It was Sloane calling.

"Hello," I said.

"Can you check the Virago list for a witch named, Leslie Arnolds?"

I kept the phone to my ear as I opened the drawer and pulled out Maya's journal. It's the eighth one on the list."

"You can cross her off. She was shot last night."

"What?"

"I know. It doesn't sound like the Virago."

"Neither did killing eleven witches at the same time." I counted the names that hadn't been crossed out. "We're down to thirty. Who would shoot a witch?"

"Someone without any powers."

I put a line through Leslie's name, replaced the book in the hutch, and walked upstairs. "When are you coming home? We should talk about this with Lovie and Gisel."

"I'm at the grocery store listening to everyone talk about the shooting. I'll be back soon."

"Be careful." We might have to start growing our own vegetables.

"Isaiah called me this morning," Gisel said as she walked into my bedroom and flung herself on my bed. She landed on my feet, bending them backward and not caring about what was beneath her.

I bent my knees and freed myself. I went through the appropriate responses anyone else would have to her declaration, but I couldn't force any to come out of my mouth.

"He wants to see you." Gisel was completely at ease with the subject of her husband reaching out to me.

"And that doesn't seem strange to you?"

"It's strange, but that's all."

"Gisel—"

"I'm serious. It doesn't hurt." Her eyes lit up with the declaration. It pleased her, too. "There is no betrayal. Isaiah and I are in a good place with our relationship. We love the children, and in a way we couldn't see for years, we love each other." She sat up and faced me. "But it isn't the kind of love you search a lifetime for, and *that's* what I want. Not Isaiah."

"It isn't right."

She rolled her eyes and reminded me of the thousand times she had when we were girls. "There's only one person who could be wronged, and I swear on this coven, I don't see it that way. I want us all to be happy. That's it. If that means you and Isaiah are meant to be together, then fighting it for another decade isn't going to do a thing except make you both miserable."

"What makes you think I want to be with him?" I stood and tied my robe around my waist.

Gisel waited for me to focus on her again. "Because when you two are in the same room, you look like you're in agony." Her words came slowly. She didn't want to hurt me anymore than she already had. "I think it's because you can't be near him without loving him."

I took a deep breath and left Gisel in my bed. She was happy. Every single day since she'd moved back to Auburn, Gisel had been content and fulfilled and joyful. It was because she was moving forward. Gisel had left her husband with her mistakes in her past.

My phone dinged on the kitchen counter. I unhooked it from the charger and read Isaiah's new text that said the same thing: "Meet me."

I hit the call button above his number and waited for his voice to cut through me.

"Helene?"

"Why?" One little word that had haunted us for decades. Why now? Why then? Why her?

"Because you want to," he said and reminded me that he could wound me worse than anyone. He knew me to my core. Isaiah had put me back together piece by piece after my mother died. It drew me to him and kept me away.

"Where?"

"Stoners Lane."

I laughed into the phone. Only Isaiah would suggest a location so central to our high school years. Stoners Lane was Switzerland. A clearing at the end of a wooded lane that everyone could sneak into and no one was excluded. "Do you want to chug beer with some sixteen year olds?"

"It isn't a party place anymore. The owners dropped a tree across the entrance."

"That's brilliant." The signs, threats, and police invasions never stopped us from going back there.

"It shouldn't be a problem for you. You won't be driving, and I know the new owner so I'll tell him we're going back there."

Darkness crept across the newfound light in my mind. Gisel made all of this look easy, but it would never be simple again. "Isaiah, I'm not sure what you're thinking—"

"Yes you are." His thick voice sent heat searing down the back of my neck.

"I'm not where you are . . ."

"It's okay. Just be where I am tonight. At Stoners. We'll figure this out together." He left off *the way we should have when we were eighteen.* We hung up, and I stared at the phone in my hand. If this were Sloane, I'd tell her to stay as far away from that clearing tonight as possible. If it were Lovie, I wouldn't have even let her talk to him on the phone, but it was me.

I figured we'd be sitting in his truck, which scared me. The thought of being alone with Isaiah was terrifying, but the gray skies and whipping wind felt like they surrounded us and pushed us closer together.

I was relieved to see a small fire and two chairs behind his truck.

Isaiah jumped when I showed myself. "I *hate* it when you guys do that."

"I'm sorry. I didn't mean to scare you."

He stared at me until he said, "You're terrifying." I opened my hands flat to the heat from the flames. "Are you too cold?"

"No. Just from the flight. I'll warm up in a second." I rubbed my hands together through my gloves.

Isaiah poured wine into two cups on the tailgate of his truck and handed one to me. He motioned toward the chairs. This was happening to someone else. I wasn't really going to drink wine and hang out with Isaiah at Stoners Lane as if nothing had ever happened.

The fire, the wine, and his closeness brought on what was close to a fever. I felt a little dizzy within the picturesque backdrop of the woods. Snowflakes fell on our heads, and I questioned whether Isaiah had somehow arranged it. They floated down from the sky slowly, almost lazily. When I looked away from one dancing to meet the flames, I found Isaiah staring at me.

"What?" I asked, dropping my eyes to my lap. Anything, but Isaiah.

"I'm glad you're here. What were you just thinking?"

"How unbelievable it is that I'm here."

He relaxed, taking my surprise at my own actions as a door opening in his favor. A snowflake stuck to my eyelash, and I flitted it and winked to get it off. Isaiah rested his hand on the side of my face and wiped it away with his thumb. The familiar urge to flee from him returned, and I recoiled in my chair.

Isaiah sat back and sighed.

"Thanks." My voice was soft.

"No problem." He reached into the bed of the truck and pulled out a pop up tent. He took it out of the bag and set it up in minutes. I helped him adjust the height of the poles until the roof was even above us.

The work lightened the intensity of his attention. "Impressive," I said.

"I've been setting up this tent at Ike's football games for years. Sun, rain, snow, you name it, he's played in it."

I leaned on the pole closest to me. "I don't think I ever told you how much I like him." Pride filled his gaze. "You and Gisel have done a wonderful job raising both of them."

"They're great kids." He sat back down, but I stayed on my feet.

"Did Ever play any sports when she was little?"

I laughed before I could answer. "Her father put her in every sport. Soccer, track, swimming, tee-ball, gymnastics."

"But?"

"She was too smart. Even without intent, she'd figure out a way to use her powers and win." I sat back down next to him. "How do you explain to a six-year-old to hold back on their abilities because the town might burn her at the stake?"

"Was he disappointed?"

I really didn't want to talk about Owen. "No. Ever could never disappoint him." I remembered the way he looked at her in awe when she wasn't watching. "But the lengths he went to in order to keep our secret were extraordinary. Owen protected our craft as if he'd been the one who'd grown up with the knowledge of it."

"Did he know you were a witch when he married you?" Isaiah was letting Owen join us because he was safe.

I didn't want to let my guard down with him. "I don't want to talk about my husband." I should never have come. "Or your wife."

"Ex-wife. Soon." I didn't want that for either of them. Death at one time, but never divorce. He twisted his chair in the dirt until he was almost facing me. "Gisel and I deserve something different from what we have." I had no contribution. This was their story, and I didn't want to be a part of it. "The way Ike looks at Ever reminds me of the way you used to make me feel."

He kept choosing the past as his weapon against my defenses. "Like I was going to abandon you?" I had the same arsenal.

"Like I couldn't breathe without you."

Based on the sight of him, he'd been breathing just fine. "You apparently figured it out."

He leaned across the arms of our chairs until his mouth was near my ear and said, "It took me twenty years to figure *this* out." He was crushing me and stealing my strength. Replacing it with the relics of my shattered love for him. "I'm going to get some more wood."

He walked across the clearing to the tree line. I lowered my head into my hands and swallowed down the tears rising inside me. He was breaking me. Again.

"Don't do this." Xavier's voice was low and tortured. The way I felt. It drifted with the snowflakes under the tent and through my coat.

"What are you doing here?" I stood near the fire and looked in the direction of his voice and back at my first love.

"Saving you. Again."

Isaiah walked toward me with a bundle of wood in his arms. He smiled at me until the knowledge that I was leaving registered on his face. I disappeared and flew into the night air.

"Helene," he yelled through the snow, but I was already banking south.

Xavier was with me. Whether I slowed or sped up, he stayed safely tucked in behind me. I could feel him as I dipped and dove. In the center of a field in Stow Creek, I landed and showed myself, knowing he'd never do the same. I waited. Listening to the air and peering through the dark night until the honeysuckle invaded me, and I knew he was standing in front of me. I reached up to hold his face in both my hands, but he stopped me, holding me back by each of my wrists.

Let go.

His grip loosened until my hands were free, and I touched the side of his face. I could almost make it out. His eyes and hair. Each time I touched him, he was more visible. He couldn't keep doing this. Showing up whenever he wanted but never letting me *be* with him.

"You are with me," he said, telling me more than he ever had before.

"Oh my God, you can read my mind." My hands dropped from

him, and he grabbed them and held them tight to his chest. "How long have you known my thoughts?"

"Since I've known you." His voice was low and apologetic, but I was enraged. Jagged breaths fought back the angry tears from my eyes. He came into my bedroom, my home, my mind. I'd never invited him in. "Helene." I didn't want to hear what he had to say. "You have a past. Leave it there."

"For what? A future with you?" I pushed him away. "I can't read your mind, Xavier. I can't see your expressions. You won't let me in even a little bit, and yet, you feel it fair to intrude on my life at your whim."

"My feelings for you are no whim."

"Then be here with me!" I yelled into the air.

"I can't." His voice was a whisper in contrast to my own. "I'm sorry."

"I can't, either. You're not welcome in my life anymore."

"Helene—"

"Not in my house or in my mind. This is not a relationship of any kind. It's nothing. I want you to leave me alone."

"Alone or with him?" His heat moved closer to me. His anger blocked the wind as it hit me in the face.

"That's none of your business."

"He never deserved you."

"This isn't about him."

XXII

WE HAD ALREADY CELEBRATED EVER and Ruby's birthdays over the weekend. Ruby had been born less than two weeks before I gave birth. When we'd found out we were pregnant, Sloane and I waited for Lovie to be next. Ruby was born February twenty-third, Ever March sixth, but we had to wait until August to meet our lovely Maya. None of us dared to mention Gisel. We assumed disbanding the coven and her losing her powers would exclude her from giving birth to a witch. Obviously, we were wrong.

I slipped a card in Ever's backpack when she wasn't looking. Today was her birthday, and I wanted her to know every minute that I was thinking of her and that she was loved. I waved at her as she slid through the back door and followed the rest of her coven to school.

"The way you smile whenever she's in the room is painful to watch." Sloane was hand-washing the wineglasses from the night before. We'd drank and talked and laughed like old times, but in the rare moments of quiet with these women, I missed Xavier.

"My expression of joy is now causing you distress?" There was a bitter edge to my question. More evidence of Sloane's inference.

"Is this about Mr. Invisible?" She turned off the water and silenced the last line of defense between me and her scrutiny.

I couldn't think of a reason not to tell her other than he probably wouldn't want me to, but Xavier was no longer a part of my life, and Sloane *always* would be. "I told him to leave me alone."

"Why?" She looked over every inch of my body for some sign of injury. Sloane would kill him if he hurt me. Isaiah was lucky to be alive.

I'd let my anger rule my days and mask my thoughts the last few weeks. Xavier had been reading my mind for years and never told me. He came and went when he pleased. There was no equity in a relationship with Xavier, but in Sloane's grasp, there was no denying why telling him to leave me alone hurt so much. "I wanted him more than he wanted me."

She put the empty wine bottle in the recyclable bin. Her casual movements suggested her lack of belief in the situation I described. "Please."

"It's true. I practically begged him to share parts of his life with me. He wouldn't even tell me his last name or what he does for a living. He didn't trust me with the information." I winced. He'd been in my bedroom. In my bed. I was an idiot. I didn't even know what kind of car he drove. He kept me out of the most basic details. "The color of his eyes, the shape of his hands . . . if he was smiling when I spoke. I wasn't privy to any of it." As much as I had tried since I'd left him in the field, I couldn't bring myself to stop missing him.

"Are you more bothered he wouldn't share it or that he wouldn't share it with you?"

"Why not me? I'm trustworthy. He can read my mind. He knows exactly what I'm thinking all the time."

"What?" Sloane walked over to table where I sat and pulled out the chair next to me. "What do you mean, he can read your mind?"

I let out a sigh. "Forget I said it, okay?"

"I can't do that."

"Maybe this is why he never told me?" Heat was rising behind my eyes and filling them with tears. I wouldn't cry over him again. There had been too many nights since I walked away from him that I'd cried already.

"You're a good secret keeper." Sloane broke into a huge smile that contained all the details of our teenage years when we used to sneak out and never got caught. My mood followed her. "I promise. I would trust you with any detail of my life. If I had a life, that is."

"What about Sean Watts?"

She shook her head as she inhaled. "He's great." She tapped her fingers on the table. "I've just seen how men interfere with the relationships of women, and I don't want to risk the harmony we have with the Kingsway Coven."

"Not every group of people falling in love and being friends is the crashing plane, burning inferno that is my history."

"Says you."

"Well, I like him." She walked over to the computer, pulled up Facebook, and signed in as Janine Smith. "I like how slow he's going. He's been through a lot, too, but there's no essence of desperation. He's testing the waters with you."

"That's one way to look at it."

"You're scary, too, you know."

"Thanks." Sloane scrolled through our fake newsfeed. A huge bouquet of flowers took up almost the entire screen, and in the middle of them was a card signed, "You're beautiful."

"The flowers were delivered."

"How did you do that?"

"I snuck in the flower shop and filled out an order when no one was looking. Everyone that worked there assumed someone else had taken the order."

I leaned over her shoulder and pulled up the comments. "It looks like she isn't sure who they came from."

Sloane hit the "like" button for Janine and sat back satisfied.

"You are terrible."

"What? She looks great. Lost a bunch of weight. Gina's the one who put up the bikini shot. Everyone knows that's the kiss of death when it comes to marriage."

"No one knows that."

"Bikini shot posted online with no husband and no kids in the picture . . . divorce . . . it's a six-month process."

"You're crazy."

"Andrea is going to lose it. She already thinks her husband has the hots for Gina. This is going to send her over the edge."

I took the notebook out of the hutch. I flipped to the middle and the page turned to black, making the silver writing practically glow. Andrea and Gina's names were next on the list. Every name above them had been crossed out as each of them died.

"We are leaving a trail of orphaned witches in the wake of this."

"That's one of the casualties of war." Sloane was always so confident there was a right decision. "Besides, this was your idea."

"I know. I didn't realize it'd be this easy."

Jealous, bitter women make it easy. Sloane was right, this was their problem, not ours. All we were doing was spreading love around the world. It's their problem they can't trust it.

"That's what you're telling yourself?"

"That's what I'm telling you. I don't have a problem with these witches dying. They signed their death sentence when they came near my child, our dog, and even Isaiah. He might be a idiot, but he's our idiot."

As if summoned by my saying his name, Isaiah's truck pulled in. The distinct sound of the dual exhaust could be identified four houses away. "It's as if he lives here," Sloane said with great disgust.

"Yes."

"Should we tell him to stay away?" She knew we could never do that. Not to him or his daughter. Gwen deserved to have her father welcomed whenever he showed up.

"No. He needs us."

"What am I? Mother Theresa? A therapist? He better start fixing some things around this place."

As if Isaiah could hear Sloane from the driveway, he came in carrying his toolbox. She lifted her eyebrows at me out of sight of Isaiah.

He put down the toolbox just inside the doorway, walked over to the kitchen table, and threw four tickets down near my arm.

"What's this?"

"Tickets to the Harvest Ball." I read them. Confusion mixed with excitement. "You guys haven't been to one, but it's a good time."

"I remember my parents going," I said. My mother used to get dressed up as if she were going to a wedding. My father would wait for her to come down the staircase and tell her how beautiful she looked. When he kissed her, I'd be giddier than both of them. They hadn't gone the last year she was alive. None of our mothers had. I looked to Sloane, wondering if she'd noticed it, too, but she was busy reading the tickets.

"It's this weekend," she said.

"I have full confidence in you four's ability to pull it off."

"What's it like?"

Isaiah sank into my attention. He poured himself a cup of coffee and sat at the table across from me. "It's a ball."

I laughed. "Well, I haven't been to many of those."

"What was your wedding like?" he asked and dropped his eyes to the table in regret.

"Small," I said in a quiet voice. My mother was dead. Gisel wouldn't have been a part of it. Owen and I had kept things simple. "It's okay." He winced in exaggerated pain. "Tell me about the ball, and I'll forgive you."

"There's a band. It's on a huge estate. The Reed Farm in Monroeville." He said the name as if I should recognize it, and I did. "The back patio and garden paths lead down to a giant tent lit up with lights and lanterns. There are vines everywhere and the entire county is dressed up."

"Really?" Sloane asked in disbelief.

"Well. They're all dressed. You can kind of do whatever you want, but the people we always hang out with dress as if they're going to a fancy wedding."

We. He and Gisel had gone together. More than once.

"It'll be fun," he added as if he'd notice me fall back into the past.

"We're going," Sloane said in her decisive tone. "You need a night out." She pointed at me.

I wasn't sure that was what I needed, but I was willing to let someone else make the decisions.

On the night of the ball, the girls waited at the bottom of the stairs for their four mothers to descend them. They oohed and ahhed over us and took so many pictures I had to blink away the spots dancing in my eyes. Isaiah had offered to pick us up, but Gisel turned down the offer without even talking to me about it. She'd been incredibly considerate of my feelings since she'd moved in.

The scene was enchanting. We gave our car keys to a valet and walked through the front entrance of the house. Beneath the ten-foot ceilings and the gilded moldings, I realized how small our house on the top of the hill in Auburn was. We walked through the foyer and French doors onto the patio. From there, we had a clear view of the tent and the hundreds of people already beneath it. An eight-piece band played from the corner, hors d'oeuvres were butlered throughout the crowd, and a bar encompassed the entire far side of the area.

I knew we were all scanning the attendees, looking for faces we recognized from online accounts. Gina was there, looking stunning in a backless gown. I moved closer and heard her telling the women around her about the flowers she'd received. She still had no idea who had sent them, but she spoke at length, completely gushing about it until Andrea joined the group. Her presence sucked the joy out of Gina's story. Her vexed glare sunk to the pit of my stomach. Gina was glowing from her newfound attention, but it would soon be dead from Andrea's.

Isaiah entered through the house and stepped out onto the patio. His eyes found mine, and I had to force the breath from my lungs. I hadn't seen him in a tuxedo since the prom our senior year. That night had ended with us wrapped in each other's arms, sleeping on the floor of Kate Water's shore house. My hand twitched at my side, and I pressed it against my body to control it.

"Helene, I want you to meet our vet." Lovie saved me. "This is Dr. Greer," she said as I turned to her and a man who towered over both of us. His hair was dark as was his tanned skin. Italian, Greek, or maybe Lebanese. He was enticing. I held out my hand, and the hint of honeysuckle almost dropped me to my knees.

He took my hand in both of his and braced me up in front of him. "Please, call me—"

Xavier.

XXIII

OVIE LOOKED FROM ME TO the good doctor and back again. Our silence was not lost on her. I didn't assuage her confusion. I couldn't take my eyes off him. The angle of his chin. The breadth of his shoulders beneath his suit jacket. The vulnerability in his eyes, which was hidden behind his smile.

"Would you like to dance?" he asked still holding my hand.

With a nod of my head, we left Lovie and every other person at the ball behind us. Xavier led me onto the dance floor. He turned, and the sight of him still shocked me. Xavier's hand rested on the small of my back. I concentrated on the heat his touch sent coursing through my body. He moved it up a few inches, rested it on my waist, and then pulled me closer to his body.

My right hand found his left, and I noted the small scratches on the side of his palm.

"You're a vet."

"I'm your vet," he said and pulled me closer to him.

"What are you doing?"

"Terrifying myself," he said with a gentle smile. "You've forced me into a spot I've never been before."

"Where's that?"

"The place where I want you more than I want to protect myself."

"I'll never hurt you, Xavier."

"I've seen how hard that promise is to keep." Love, intention, commitment . . . he was right. The simple was complicated as soon as love was involved.

The sweet honeysuckle mixed with a more rugged cologne. Now that I was touching him and seeing him, I realized the cologne had always been a part of my senses when it came to Xavier. I leaned against his shoulder and inhaled with my eyes closed.

I know you can hear me.

He paused in his step, but only for a second. Just long enough for me to feel his response.

I lifted my head but still shielded my eyes. They were perfectly fine fixed on his shoulders. *It means a great deal. Everything, really.* I sank into my feelings for him. The utter strength and power I felt in his arms, and the vision of him standing in front of me. It was all significant. He'd relinquished what I'd always viewed as an advantage when in fact, it was his defensive line. Xavier had given me him along with the power to hurt him.

I let my hand fall from his shoulder to his chest. The threads of his jacket formed a course cloth beneath my touch. I wanted to know what it felt like to touch his skin. I abandoned his shoulders and looked up. His lips were barely separated. His eyes were fixed on me. Deep pools of brown so dark I'd swear they were black. They beckoned me to tell him more.

I want to see you when I touch you.

Xavier stared at me until I thought he could heal me and stop me from mourning the past. "Leave with me."

I'd just gotten there. Sloane, Gisel, and Lovie had been looking forward to the four of us spending the evening together, but what I wanted more than anything was to be alone with Xavier. I stepped back from him, but I couldn't escape his dark eyes. "Lead the way."

We breezed through the house and out the front door. Past the valet to a black Tahoe parked three cars away.

"Nice parking spot."

"I told them I wasn't staying. Just picking someone up."

He helped me into the passenger seat and closed the door. I waited in Xavier's car for him to get in and drive me away.

"I'd like you to come to my house."

Each tiny gesture that every other couple would take for granted was enormous between the two of us. I'd known Xavier for twenty years and never knew he drove with his left hand on the steering wheel and his right resting on his thigh.

"Do you live alone?"

His laugh was tinged with sadness. "Yes." The nights he'd been in my home with two full covens alive around him must have been a stark contrast to his existence. Xavier held out his hand on the console between us, and I took it, twisting my fingers between his. "Except for a Turkish Kangal, a miniature Australian shepherd, and a French bulldog." Xavier, the vet.

We left Monroeville and drove toward Elmer. Just outside of town, he turned right onto a wooded lane. He stopped as a group of turkeys crossed the road in the dim moonlight. Frustrated with their slow pace, he let go of my hand and beeped the horn.

"In a rush?"

"You have no idea."

My heartbeat was strumming against my chest. I focused in

on the landscape around me to avoid thinking of Xavier or my anticipation. I wouldn't forget how he always knew my thoughts, and I never knew his.

"You know more than you realize," he said and startled me.

"This isn't fair."

"No, but you typically say what you're thinking anyway. If it were the other way around, this would be torture."

I imagined a bunch of deep yellow bananas at their peak before they're eaten.

"Testing me with fruit?"

I had too many questions to waste our time on bananas. "What have you been doing the past few weeks?"

"Thinking of you."

"I've thought a lot about you, too." It was the truth he would read in my thoughts so there was no use in hiding it.

"I know."

"I hate this."

He pulled the Tahoe into the first bay of the garage and closed the door behind us. He cut the engine and left me alone in the car as he walked around the back of it. I sighed right before he opened my door and took my hand to help me out. "I would stop it if I could."

"No you wouldn't."

The light above us in the garage turned off and left us facing each other in the dark. Xavier leaned into me until my back rested against the car. "You're right," he said and pressed against the front of me. Heat soared through my body. I tilted my head back, searching for air, but his lips near my ear stole it and made me dizzy. "I hear people's thoughts all day long. I'd silence theirs today, but I can't go on without yours." His breath was hot on my neck. His words barely made sense. "The way you think is intoxicating, Helene."

His lips found mine, and I twisted my arms around his neck to draw him even closer. I wanted to sink into the spell he had me under, but only if he sank with me.

He lifted me off the ground and into his arms. I let him cradle me there, the same way he had the first night I met him. We whisked through several rooms with varying degrees of soft light until he laid me on a bed, and the scent of honeysuckle surrounded me. I inhaled deeply the sweet divine. Moonlight dripped through the window as the clouds broke apart, and I sat up on my knees to watch him. He was everything I ever imagined.

I pushed his jacket off his shoulders and let if fall to the floor. The buttons of his shirt slipped through their holes as my fingers worked in silence to release them. Tension was knotting inside me. "I know I can't comprehend the significance of what you've given me, but thank you," I said.

Xavier threw his shirt on the floor behind him and pressed me back onto the bed. His lips found my neck and my shoulder. I could barely breathe and could only think, *don't stop.*

"I'm never going to, Helene," he said.

I surrendered to the great Xavier Greer.

Moonlight drenched the room. The sheet and blanket covering me were warm. I stuck my leg out to feel the temperature and tucked it back into the safety of the covers.

Xavier lay beneath me. His breathing was soft, measured. His shoulder was under my head. I wanted to wake him and pump him with questions about his life, his home, and his job . . . or maybe not say a word. I tilted my face toward him and inhaled the scent that had represented security since I'd first associated it with him. He'd come out of the shadows and let me have him, and for that, I'd be forever grateful, but it was more than that.

I loved him.

His chest hardened beneath me. I didn't move away. My eyelashes rubbed against his chin as I closed my eyes. *If you insist on listening, you'll hear everything.*

Xavier kissed the top of my head without saying a word.

I let my fingertips caress his chest and the top of his arm. It'd been years since I'd touched a man this way, and Xavier's olive skin was silk beneath my hand. I ran my fingers down his arm until he shivered with a chill.

"Sorry," I said.

"Don't be. Keep going."

I dragged my touch up the inside of his arm and down his side to his stomach where I spread my fingers wide. "I have to go."

"That isn't possible." He smiled with his eyes still closed. "You're trapped here forever."

"Well, I have a daughter who doesn't need to see her mother rolling in at noon in her dress from the night before."

"Don't go back at noon. Spend the day with me."

"You're crazy." I kissed him on the lips. "And a terrible influence."

"I'm equally as unimpressed with the things you make me do."

"We're doomed." I rolled on top of him and whispered in his ear, "Blissfully compelled." I kissed his cheek. "I absolutely blame you."

"I'll accept responsibility if you stay." He pulled me down until my body pressed against him, and his touch clouded my thoughts. He rolled on top of me and stared into my eyes. "What are you thinking, Helene?"

"Nothing." He was forlorn because he couldn't read me. "You stole every thought from my mind." All he left was warmth. He kissed me again, but I wouldn't be convinced. I needed to be home by the time the girls woke.

He sighed and let me crawl out from beneath him and set my feet on the floor. He rolled onto his side and watched as I found my dress and slipped it back over my head.

"Have dinner with me tonight?"

My phone dinged with a text from my purse on the chair in the corner of the room. It was Isaiah. He wanted me to know that he drove Gisel, Sloane, and Lovie home last night and fell asleep on my couch. He was wondering where I was.

"He's quite persistent." Xavier turned onto his back and stared at the ceiling.

I climbed into the bed next to him and kissed him again.

"Let me drive you home. Don't go."

"I have to." I ran my hands down the center of his chest. It was exactly as I had imagined it all these months. I faced him and said, "Pick me up at seven." I stood and straightened my dress and coat before stepping into my heels. I found my way back through Xavier's house with the morning light highlighting his lifestyle. A wood-burning fireplace with an enormous stone hearth was the focal point of the room. The kitchen had a blue tile backsplash that had an etching on each square. Three dogs sat behind the gate to the laundry room. They were all different sizes and breeds. The little bulldog's collar had "Pickles" engraved on it. Their bright eyes stood out in front of their wagging tails.

"Do you want to go see Daddy?" I asked and released the gate. The dogs sniffed and jumped up on me, but when I pointed toward Xavier's bedroom, they ran.

"Helene!" he yelled, having read my mind before they jumped into his bed. I snuck out the back door while he was pleading, "All right, get down, move over, stop licking my face."

I flew home, following Route 40 until the outskirts of Woodstown. Then I turned north, away from town and banked toward Auburn. Isaiah's truck in my driveway dashed all hope that I had about him having gone home. Through the window I saw him making himself a pot of coffee. I flew up to my window and into my room. I changed my clothes, rustled my bed sheets, and snuck into the bathroom to brush my teeth and remove my makeup. I faced myself in the mirror before descending the stairs and facing my past.

"Good morning," I said, making Isaiah jump and almost spill his fresh coffee. "Sorry."

He shook his head. "It's okay." He put the cup on the counter and examined me. "When did you get home?"

"What are you doing here?"

"I drove your drunk roommates home. Now answer my question. Where have you been all night?"

"So, you drove your wife and two of her friends home, and you think I owe you something?"

"Ex-wife, officially. And yes. Tell me, Helene."

"I was with our vet." Isaiah's brow furrowed in confusion. "Dr. Greer."

"I know who he is. Every woman in this town knows Jason Greer and half have been with him." I was thankful Isaiah couldn't read my mind.

"Half plus one now."

"You didn't!" I turned away from him and headed toward the family room. He spun me around by my arm. "Tell me you didn't."

"Let go of me, Isaiah." I stared at his hand on my arm. When he didn't move it, I bent his middle finger back until he released me and shook it in pain.

"Don't say I didn't warn you," he said.

"Of what?"

"The great doctor. He's older than us and has never been married. Why do you think that is?"

"He didn't want to marry someone he wasn't in love with and have to start over after twenty years?"

Isaiah's cheeks flushed a deep red. "Helene, please. You're not that naïve."

I shouldn't have enjoyed his discomfort so much. My lack of

empathy irked me. Torturing Isaiah was one more sign I wasn't yet completely over him. I was beginning to wonder if I would ever be. "Go home, Isaiah."

XXIV

"**W**HERE ARE YOU GOING?" ISAIAH asked as I stepped off the bottom step and into the family room.

"Why are you here? Like, all the time?"

"It's Sunday night."

"What does that mean? Are you here every Sunday?"

"I'm not talking about me. What plans do you have on a Sunday night?" Headlights flashed against the front window as Xavier pulled into the driveway. "Good night, Isaiah."

"This is insane, Helene." His eyes darted from me to the back door. "You cannot seriously be considering a relationship with him."

"I'm done talking to you about him." Isaiah moved in front of me, not heeding my anger at all. "I'm serious. Drop it."

He squared his shoulders and leaned down until our eyes met.

"Not a chance."

Xavier rapped three times on the door, and I stepped around Isaiah with the grace of a one-legged bird. "He doesn't live here. Who does he think he is?" I mumbled to myself. The sight of Xavier's face on the other side of the door soothed me. I nearly forgot about Isaiah.

"Be careful," he called from behind me, and I rolled my eyes.

"Ready?" Xavier asked when I opened the door.

"Yes." I pulled my coat off the hook near the door and stepped out of the kitchen while I slipped my arms into it. *Extremely ready.* Like, I-never-want-to-come-back-here ready. Isaiah had to find a new place to hang out. I knew he was lonely and going through some big life changes, but I didn't want to be involved. I looked back toward the house. Isaiah was standing in the kitchen and staring out the back window with his arms crossed at his chest.

There was hurt in his eyes. He wasn't joking or obnoxious. Just a silent glare of regret. It took me back to my first week at the University of Vermont when Isaiah had come to see me. He'd waited outside my classroom on the lawn to see me, but at the first glimpse of him, I disappeared. I left him standing there with the exact same look in his eyes.

I turned away from the window and was caught in a similar expression from Xavier. "I'm sorry." I didn't want him to be a part of the Helene and Isaiah nightmare. I didn't even want to be included anymore.

"You can't control your thoughts."

I shook my head. "No, but it isn't that I don't want to go."

"I know."

"I just don't want to hurt him, either. We've put each other through enough."

Xavier opened the car door for me, and I climbed inside. "Perhaps if he didn't spend so much time here." He shut the door and walked around to the driver's side.

"I think he's lonely," I said when Xavier buckled his seatbelt without taking his eyes off Isaiah inside the house.

"You can think that." He started the car and turned it around. "Unfortunately, I know *exactly* what he's thinking." I didn't ask for clarification.

He pulled onto Main Street, and I left Isaiah behind in Auburn. "Where are we going?"

Xavier smiled. He was pleased with the new topic. "Well, I wanted to take you somewhere special. I've wanted to for a while." He laughed a little. "Like a few decades." The time should have made me feel old, but sitting next to Xavier, I felt alive. "But I can't."

"Why?"

"I need to have you all to myself. I don't want to hear another person's thoughts except yours." I leaned over the console between us and watched him as he drove. "Even if they're painful."

"I never want to hurt you, Xavier."

He reached out his hand and laid it flat between us. I slipped mine in his, and we drove the rest of the way in silence. My mind wouldn't keep quiet. I sat beside Xavier and fretted about him and his feelings and how I could protect him and disentangle myself from Isaiah. The thought of him sent my mind back to the look in Isaiah's eyes when we pulled out of the driveway. It was time to move. I didn't want to leave Auburn, but I at least needed another roof over my head. Things were so perfect between the four of us and our girls. Why did Isaiah have to ruin it? I wondered if he felt the same way about my return.

Xavier turned onto Broad Street, and the new landscape stole my attention. He appeared sick behind the wheel. I caused that with my musings.

He turned and stared at me, confirming my assumptions.

"I'm sorry. I don't know what to do."

"It's okay."

"How can that be?"

"Because I hear your thoughts about me, too." I blushed. The way I'd thought of him in the shower earlier flew through my mind, and I closed my eyes. When I opened them, he was glancing over at me with a huge grin and wide eyes.

"How far away can you hear them?"

"Your thoughts?"

"Yes. When you're not with me, do you know what I'm thinking?"

"No." He paused as if he were thinking through the details. "Typically, I would have to be in your presence. Or at least in your house while you're in the shower to know what you're thinking. Somewhere close by."

"Typically?"

"Last night when I was driving to the Harvest Ball, I was alone in my car, at least five miles away, and I thought I knew what you were thinking. That's never happened to me before."

I searched my mind for what I was thinking about before I was introduced to Xavier.

"Most of it was details about the location. You take in points of interest others miss, Helene." The deep brown of the hanging lanterns I thought was the color of tree bark. "Exactly. The beveled edge of the dance floor, the lack of bees flying around the flowers, the darkness surrounding the tent." He squeezed my hand. "You had not one thought about another woman's dress or hair. You were frantically trying to place everyone so you didn't hurt anyone's feelings by not recognizing them or not remembering their name."

It was fascinating. We should test it out. An experiment to determine how far away he could be.

"When I heard your thoughts right before I stepped onto the back patio at the ball, I almost turned around and left." I had been thinking about prom.

"We have a past."

"From what I've seen, it's a horrible one."

"I know, and I don't want to talk about Isaiah with you or anyone else these days, but I can't deny there were four great years before we split up. Two of which we were friends. Like laugh until we cried, snuck out and lied, best friends, and two when we were in love." Xavier's gaze stayed fixed on the road. "I keep denying it, and he keeps reminding me, as if I truly forgot. He thinks that if I'd just recall the way things used to be, they could return to that." Xavier's grip tightened on the steering wheel. "But, we're both wrong. I should stop trying to forget, and he should stop hoping things can ever be the same again."

"Are you sure they can't be?"

"Yes." The word was a hundred percent truth. "We were completely different people back then, and I'm honestly grateful he was a part of my life. When my mom died, I needed him. More than air, I needed him, but we both grew up, and he raised a family with Gisel. I don't want to be any more a part of that than I am right now."

"What if he hadn't married her? If they'd never had children?"

I tried to imagine what coming home would have been like if Gisel had married Kevin Flitcraft and Isaiah was single. Then I scoffed. He never could stand the thought of being alone. I figured that was a large part of his pursuing me again. With Gisel gone, this was the first time he was going to be completely alone. It was also his greatest fear when I was going to leave him and move to Vermont.

"Never mind," Xavier said, already having read all my thoughts.

"Relationships must be rather painful for you."

"Never as much as this one," he said but smiled slightly to soften the blow.

I took in the edge of his cheekbones and his tanned skin. Already, and it wasn't even April yet. "How come you're so tan?"

"I went skiing last weekend."

"You ski?"

"When I can. Yes. Do you?"

"I did in Vermont, but I think it's required if you live there." The trees on each side of the road caught my eye and reminded me of what I wanted to try. "Can you pull over?"

He glanced at me, and without question, he turned on his signal and pulled to the side of the road.

"I'm going to get out here. I want you to drive away. Say ten miles, turn around, and come back toward me. Keep an eye on the mileage and note when you first hear my thoughts. I want to know how far away you can still read my mind."

"It's already dark." He looked through the front windshield and in the rearview mirror.

"I'm not afraid of the dark."

"I know."

I opened the car door, and Xavier tilted his head, taking in all the sounds and scents of the woods nearby. "Tell me when you're coming back, and I'll start thinking about something fun. When you know what it is, check your odometer."

"Okay." He shook his head, acknowledging that he had no say in whatever we were going to do.

Xavier drove away while I took in the silent darkness around me. *I miss you. This is a terrible idea.*

It will take ten minutes, and then we'll know. This might be useful.

So would already being at my house. I couldn't keep the smile from my face. Three deer walked near the edge of the woods behind me. A mother and her fawn. She stopped and stared, but her gaze was fixed behind me. I turned to find nothing but the empty road to look at. When I looked back, the deer ran off.

After a few more minutes, Xavier thought back, *Okay. I'm ten miles away, resetting the trip mileage, and I'm coming back toward you.*

I'll start thinking.

I moved away from the side of the road and leaned against a tree. I wanted to have a clear train of thought for Xavier to clue in on. I thought of his dogs. The little one, Pickles, who could melt a girl's heart. The tiny little guy that—

Pickles is a girl.

You should have started from farther away.

A wind gust flew by my face. I pulled my coat up around my neck and looked down the road for Xavier's car. The wind came toward me again . . . and then—

"Helene, wake up," My head hurt. I thought I was going to throw up. The light was squeezing my head in its vice-like beam. I couldn't bare it.

"Turn off the lights," I said and tried to raise my arm to cover my face, but I couldn't lift it.

"Helene!" Xavier sounded desperate. His voice was scaring me. "Move your fingers." His lips were near my ear. I couldn't open my eyes, though, the light hurt too much. He moved his hand under mine until my fingers rested over his. I squeezed them together. "That's good."

"Can you turn off the light now?"

"We need to go." He lifted me off the ground placed me in the passenger seat of his car before buckling the seatbelt.

I let my head slump to the door after he closed it. Holding it up was exhausting.

"Helene, don't fall asleep."

"Xavier, what happened?"

"I don't know, but your head is bleeding."

It seemed like an hour later we were pulling into his veterinary office. "I've never actually been here."

"I know. Lovie or Sloane always bring Carl in."

"Did you know he was Ever's dog?"

"Yes. That was the first time I'd met her. When the dog was hurt at Marlton Park."

"Was I hit by a car?" I reached up and touched my head as blood dripped down my cheek and onto my coat.

"I don't know. I should have never left you on the side of the road like that. What was I thinking?"

"Did you see any cars?"

He jumped out, unlocked the front door of the clinic, and came to my side of the car. He unbuckled my seatbelt and reached under me to carry me out, but my head was less groggy.

"I can walk."

Relief covered his face. He supported me with his arm around my waist and his other holding my hand. Xavier didn't say another word. He sat me on a chair in one of the examination rooms and went to work gently cleaning my wound.

I kept my eyes closed. It was less debilitating, but I still didn't like the light.

"You need a few stitches, Helene. I can take you to the hospital."

"No. Just do them here."

"Are you sure?"

"Yes. I trust you."

He moved the chair over to the sink and motioned for me to sit in it. "Let's get the blood out of your hair first." He covered the wound with several gauze pads and then placed my hand on top of them. "Can you hold these while I wash out your hair?"

I nodded, and it felt good to move my head without a wave of nausea. "What? No magic?"

"Some things I like to do the old fashioned way." He kissed me gently. It felt good to close my eyes.

I opened them to the light and the pain in my head reminded me why I was sitting in a veterinary examination room. "If you didn't see a car, what hit me? Did a tree fall?"

"I don't know. Nothing was out of place when I got to you. You were thinking about Pickles and then your thoughts just cut off." He shook his head in disgust. "There was nothing. Losing your thoughts like that—" He gently brushed my hair back into the running water. "Helene."

"What?"

He turned off the water and helped me sit back up. "A section of your hair is missing." I stared at him, but couldn't understand what he meant. "I think someone has cut it out." I reached up to the back of my head and felt the jagged ends, a handful of hair that was at least five inches shorter than the rest of my head."

Tears crawled up the back of my throat. "Who would . . ." And then the anger set in. "Alone and on the side of the road." I shook my head and dropped the pads from my wound.

Xavier returned my hand to my head. "Let's get you fixed up."

"And then I need to go."

"You're not going anywhere for a few days. You've had a traumatic head injury. You probably have a concussion, if not worse. If you're not going to a proper hospital, you're staying home and getting some rest."

I exhaled and didn't waste my time arguing. When Xavier finished sewing my head back together, he cleaned the room, took off his gloves, and stared at me.

"What?" I asked.

"Is there any chance of you staying at my house tonight?"

"You know I can't do that."

He leaned down, resting a hand on each side of my chair. "The only thing I know for sure is that I'm not letting you out of my sight ever again." He kissed me on the lips.

"It's going to be hard to get any work done if you're always looking at me."

"It's been a challenge since you moved home."

"I need to go home and tell Lovie and Sloane and the girls. No one should be out alone, and we'll have to figure out what we're going to do next."

"You don't remember anything."

I thought back to the side of the road. The smell of the crisp air . . . the gust of wind.

I looked up at Xavier. The significance of my thoughts that he'd read wasn't lost on him.

"I'm going to have a word with them."

"The Virago?"

"They can't touch you or hurt you or be waiting to attack every time you leave Auburn."

"How is it you know so much about Auburn?"

He reached up and extended his hand to me. I took it and stood on unsteady feet as my heartbeat pulsed through my skull. Xavier went to the receptionist desk in the hallway and came back with three Advil and a cup of water. "Here, take these. You're going to be in pain for a while."

He drove me home in silence. This was supposed to be a first date. A lovely evening in which we had dinner together and could finally talk like two normal people. The same night was happening all over the world and no one was being attacked and left on the side of the road to rot. Hopefully, anyway.

Isaiah's truck was still in the driveway when we pulled in. Of course it was. Why would it ever occur to Isaiah to be anywhere but my house at ten o'clock on a Sunday night?

"My thoughts exactly."

"I'm sorry about tonight. When will I see you again?"

"I'm coming in with you."

Isaiah walked across the kitchen in front of the window. "That isn't necessary. I'm feeling a lot better."

"I think he has some things to say to me."

Because you can hear his thoughts, too. I leaned back in my seat.

"Yes. And until he says whatever he needs to say, this is going to be a problem for him. Unless you've changed your mind and you'd like to live with me and never see him again." A small laugh escaped my lips. Even after everything that happened tonight and the prospect of seeing Isaiah with Xavier, the idea of moving in with him was impossible.

Xavier came around to my side of the car and opened the door. When we walked into the kitchen, Sloane and Lovie were waiting for us. They stood in silence as their eyes examined every part of my body from the bruised and bloody stitched area near my hairline to my arm that creeped up to the back of my head and held out the shortened section. Sloane gasped with hardened eyes. Lovie's hands covered her mouth.

"I know." I looked horrible.

Isaiah walked into the kitchen and stopped short next to Lovie. "What the hell happened to you?" He turned on Xavier, and his eyes narrowed "What did you do?"

"Nothing," Xavier answered with a cooler head.

"Well, I sure as hell never brought her home like this." Isaiah cut the distance between us with large strides. He touched my arms, ran his hands up my shoulders, and cupped my face. His eyes focused on the sutures.

"No, but you've left her worse off."

Isaiah's hands tightened and then dropped to his sides. "You know nothing about us."

"I know more than you think. Mostly that it's over."

"Why don't you go save a cat or something?"

"Why don't you get a cat and maybe spend some time at your

own house. Leave the woman alone for another couple of decades, because I'm tired of witnessing the carnage from a relationship with you."

Isaiah's eyes darted to me for an explanation, but I had none to give him. I wasn't ever going to share Xavier's secret, and I didn't owe Isaiah any information even if I was. He stormed out of the kitchen. His truck door slammed shut before he careened down our hill.

"I'm going to go." Xavier walked over to me, took my hand in his, and kissed me on the cheek. "I'll check in with you later," he said so only I could hear.

I took in the curve of his mouth and the concern in his eyes before he turned his back on me. He paused and tilted his chin toward the stairs. He was listening.

Gisel entered the room with wet hair and her robe collar pulled up around her neck. "What's going on?" she asked before she got a good look at me. "What happened?" She took my hair in her hand as she examined my face. She was concentrating on every inch of me until she stopped and stared at the floor. She inhaled deeply and turned on Xavier.

"You. It's you. What are you doing here?" Gisel put herself between me and Xavier, shielding me from him. "What did you do to her?"

"Nothing." Why would she think he'd ever hurt me?

"Helene, he is evil." My mouth fell open. I shook my head without speaking. "Listen to me. He is a scary dude. What did he do to you?"

"He saved me. The same way he always does." I turned to Xavier, seeking his forgiveness. I was opening up his past and his present to Gisel without permission. Whatever she was putting together in her head wasn't the reality of Xavier Greer.

He was gone. I held my hand up to halt Gisel's next statements and felt for him still with us, but there was nothing. Not even a hint of his scent. The lights of his car exited our driveway, too.

"Who is he?" Gisel demanded.

"Our vet!" Lovie finally joined in the madness. "What do you mean he's evil? He saved Carl's life."

"And he's beautiful," Sloane added, only half kidding.

"He has been hunting you for years, Helene." My thoughts clung to the word hunting. The warnings of the hunter. "He came to me when you three were gone and asked all kinds of questions about you. He's been waiting twenty years to find you, and I don't trust him." Gisel could have been talking about Xavier or her husband.

"What did he ask?" Gisel was in motion. She sat on the couch, straightened the cushions, moved the glass away from her on the coffee table, and turned off the television. She stood again in an uneasy stance. "Gisel. What did he ask?"

She froze in front of me. For a woman who never considered the consequences, Gisel looked worried. "He wanted to know where you were. I didn't tell him. I didn't even know." My heart broke a little more for our past. "And on what I now know was Ever's birthday, he came to me and said something had happened to you, but he didn't know what. Something significant. I guess he thought it might have been important enough that you'd share it with me." I took a deep breath. "He taunts me, though. He's no friend."

"So, he came to see you looking for me and then again to make sure I was okay. That seems like he was concerned, Gisel. Have you seen him since?"

"I never saw him. Until tonight."

Her eyes fixed on the pillow in her hand. "He can read your mind. He knew my thoughts." I wasn't sure how to respond. "What did he do to you? What happened to your head?"

"It wasn't him. It couldn't have been."

"Why not?" Sloane asked.

"He wasn't even with me. I had him drive away. I wanted to see how far he could be and still hear my thoughts." I left off that I knew in my heart, he could never hurt me.

"We have to be careful, Helene."

"He's a good person."

"What else is he?" Sloane asked. I stood in front of her without an answer. "Right. You need to be more careful."

I held out the back of my hair to Gisel's disgust. "Does this look like something a man would do?"

"No, but it does look like something a man would do if he wanted you to think it was a woman."

"Did he try to convince you to go home with him?" Gisel asked.

"This is crazy. He would never hurt me." I left off that I love him because I couldn't witness the doubt and suspicion that would be in their eyes if I were to say it. "I'm going to bed." My head pounded against the sides of my skull. One massive blow and too many confrontations for one night.

"Just call if you need anything," Lovie said and rubbed my back as I walked toward the stairs. The three of them would stay up and discuss Xavier until they were sure they'd thought through every detail enough to sleep.

I opened the door to my room and was engulfed by the honey-suckle scent. I stayed still until I felt him lying on my bed. I could almost make out the length from his head to his toes. Peace filled me just having him nearby. They couldn't be right. I hung my blood-stained coat over the back of my chair and took off my watch and earrings. The dress I'd worn for our first official date followed. Then I kicked off my shoes, nudged them under the bed, and crawled under the covers until I met him in the middle. My fingers played with the buttons of his shirt, and he rested his hand on top of mine.

"How's your head?" he asked.

"The least of my problems it would seem."

His chest rose beneath my head as he inhaled. "I wasn't sure whether to come."

"I'm glad you did."

"Sometimes I don't think you even know what you're thinking. Not just when it comes to me." His answer was unfair. He shouldn't be able to hear what I was thinking. "Don't leave me because of it." There was a fragility to his voice I'd never heard before.

"I feel like I should be telling you the same thing. The inside of my head is a tormented place."

He pulled the covers up and over my shoulders. I slept curled against Xavier's body until the morning light woke me. When I opened my eyes, I was alone, but there was a note on my nightstand. I rolled onto my back and let my eyes focus on his handwriting.

My dogs needed me. I'm sorry I left. Call me when you wake up. I want to know how your head is, and I want to hear your voice.

X

"WE'RE NOT JUST GOING TO let this one slide. They beat you upside the head and cut your hair." I reached to the back of my hair for the hundredth time. I might never get used to the new length. "I don't want you here alone," Sloane said.

"I know, but someone needs to stay and take care of Carl. Gisel's never been to Las Vegas, and Lovie really needs to get out of here. I'm the best choice."

"The way you make it sound, you are the only choice." I kept moving around the kitchen, not letting her attention engulf me, but I knew she was watching me and wondering why I wasn't more interested in touring UNLV with Ever and the rest of my household.

"I don't think Ever will go there."

"Me neither. Where do you think she'll choose?"

"I'm still hoping for Vermont, but she got an acceptance letter from USC, and her excitement surprised me."

Sloane slumped into a seat at the kitchen table. "This is really going to happen. They're going to leave us."

The four of them had just returned from the senior trip to Florida, and they were all ready to get back on a plane and go on another adventure. "And they're excited." My own college visitations and the way Isaiah had complained about my moving came back. "We should have been, too." The dark clouds of fear and anger that doused our college excitement with drama would forever be stuck in my mind.

Gisel walked into the room, yawned, and poured herself a cup of coffee. Her presence ended my and Sloane's conversation. At least the part of it that had to do with our emotional state back then.

"What's going on?" she asked.

"We're talking about going to Las Vegas for the girls to tour UNLV."

"Gwen cannot stop talking about it. Do you think she has a gambling problem? She always loved those claw games at the arcades."

"She's fine."

"She scares me, but I guess now that she has her powers that claw game's never going to get the best of her again." Gisel drank her coffee like it was medicine and she was dying.

Sloane turned to me. "I'm worried about you staying here alone."

I touched the back of my head out of habit. "I'll be fine."

"How do I know that?"

"I'll stay in Auburn." I wasn't sure how much else to share. "And I'll invite Xavier to stay with me." Sloane's eyebrows rose higher than I'd ever seen. "What? He's good."

"I believe that you think that."

"That's different from you believing he's good."

"I know," Sloane said. "I'm trying to keep an open mind, but it's hard to get the image of your head broken open and your hair missing from my mind. Forgive me."

"He didn't do this."

"You don't know who did it."

"I don't trust him," Gisel chimed in. She'd been listening to Sloane and me without a word of input, which in and of itself was odd. "I never have. Why couldn't he have come to me as a normal person all those years ago and ask if I knew where you were? He didn't have to scare me the way he did. Break into my house in the middle of the night like some criminal who was going to murder my family.

"Okay, that's a little dramatic, don't you think?" I asked.

"Is it?" Sloane joined in, and I felt ganged up on. "What do we really know about him?"

"He doesn't know anything. He was adopted."

"What is he even?" Gisel waved her hands in the air as if we couldn't rule out alien or terrorist. Anything was still a possibility when it came to Xavier, but it was all evil.

"He knows his birth mother's name was Sickler. Other than that—"

"Did you say Sickler?" Gisel asked.

"Yes. Why?"

She stared down at her hands for a moment before looking back at me. "I know about him. His mother was a fire witch from Upper Pittsgrove."

"What?"

"Uncle Stump. When he was here for Momma's funeral, he told me about the Upper Pittsgrove Coven and how they all died. The Virago was torturing them." She looked at me but didn't say a word about the similarities. "One of them escaped. She left town, and the rumor was that she was pregnant. Uncle Stump never knew what became of her, but the baby would have been born about four years before us."

I studied every syllable that came from her mouth. Xavier's erased history tortured him. "He's four years older than me."

The three of us sat around our kitchen table and stared at one another.

"What else did Uncle Stump say?"

Gisel shook her head. "He didn't know much. He said our mothers' coven went to Upper Pittsgrove and cast a spell to make their land sacred ground like Auburn, but the two witches were found dead on the Elmer Lake outside the Upper Pittsgrove line. He didn't know what happened to the last witch."

"She must have been terrified." A witch, possibly pregnant, returning home to have had her entire coven murdered by the Virago.

"I can't imagine," Sloane said.

"I never asked him what happened. He only has her maiden name to go on, but I have to tell him all of this."

"Just because he was born to a coven of witches doesn't make him good," Sloane said and confirmed that she was on Gisel's side when it came to Xavier.

"And just because we don't understand his history . . . or what he is, doesn't make him bad. Ike can hear Ever, does that make him evil?" I was done defending Xavier because it felt like I was defending my judgment as much as his character.

Sloane softened, and Gisel stayed quiet, deferring to her.

"You have to trust me."

"We will, but if the choice is ever between this coven and him . . ."

"It never will be."

No man would ever come between us again.

"Would you like something to drink?" Carl ran around in Xavier's yard with Pickles and Rex and Olive. They were as diverse as an international classroom but played as if they'd known each other their whole lives.

The moments Xavier and I were together seemed fake, as if I hadn't earned them because I'd only known his identity or the most basic details about his life for a short while. Our history was based on a feeling, a connection neither of us understood. We were going to build something real and alive in the present, and the significance of what everyone else in the world takes for granted everyday hit me.

"We're real," he said, having reduced my mental rambles to one statement.

"What are you having?"

"Bourbon."

"Whatever the doctor orders," I said and tilted my head toward him.

Xavier stared at me until the need to hear his thoughts cut me. "A drink would not be my first order of you, but I'm trying to actually slow down and possibly let you eat something."

My stomach growled. "I appreciate it."

When Xavier delivered a glass of bourbon to the arm of the Adirondack chair I was resting in, I was lost trying to figure out what, how, or whether I should tell him of Gisel's knowledge of his past. I smiled as soon as he paused in front of me and forced myself to just start talking. I wanted to actually tell him instead of having him overhear it in my mind.

"I hope you don't mind, but my coven and I were discussing your past."

His eyebrows rose. "What about my past?" Xavier's voice deepened slightly with a hint of defense.

"About your birth parents. I'm sorry if it's intruding, but my roomies are not what I would call a trusting bunch. I want them to know you the way I do, but they don't share our history."

"Of course." He sat in the seat next to me. "What did Gisel say?" There was a twinge of exhaustion in his voice.

"Do you not like Gisel?"

"No." He answered too fast. "I mean, Gisel is fine. She's just not my cup of tea, and I'm having trouble forgiving her for what she did."

"If I can forgive her, you can."

"I'm much more capable of holding a grudge."

"Even if the slight wasn't against you?"

"What she did was wrong. In every way."

I rested my hands in my lap. "I don't want to talk about that."

"Yes. My family. What did Gisel say?" Xavier took a long sip of his drink.

I did the same. "Her uncle remembers a coven from Upper Pittsgrove. Three of the witches were killed by the Virago. One, their fire witch, escaped the area. The story is that she was pregnant and unwed." Xavier was attentive but not intrigued. He would dismiss any information that came through Gisel. "The only other thing he remembered about the witch was that her last name was Sickler."

He sat still in the chair beside me. Rex ran up with a stick. Xavier stood, waited for Rex to drop it at his feet, and threw the stick toward the back of the property. All four of the dogs ran back to Xavier realizing he was standing and willing to play with them. They waited for his attention, sitting perfectly still and behaved. I followed their lead.

"That was my mother."

"What happened to her?"

"According to my adoptive mother, she was a waitress at the shore that summer. She met a med student, and they fell in love. The only way she could describe the relationship was that it verged on obsession. It was physical and emotional and beyond either of their grasps at such a young age. My biological mother and father had a two-month-long love affair that resulted in me."

I waited, letting him take his time.

"What my mother didn't know that summer was that my father was engaged to another woman. Another med student, who was studying abroad. His life was on the track he'd always dreamed it would be on, and it didn't include a farmer's daughter from Upper Pittsgrove."

"What difference would that have made?"

"Things were different back then."

"Not that different." I stood in front of Xavier, wrapped my arms around his waist, and rested my head on his chest. If we'd had the summer he described, nothing could come between us.

"You of all people should understand how fleeting that summer was." I stepped back and examined him. He wasn't trying to hurt me, but he had. He pulled me back against his chest in apology. "He left her and never looked back. I don't think he even knew about me."

"So her family sent her away?"

"Yes. And she had me. I was given to my adoptive parents. They never had any children of their own."

"That's why you've been alone this whole time."

"Yes. Who could I tell about this?"

I pulled Xavier's face down to mine and kissed his cheek. He leaned over and rested his head on my shoulder. I wanted to be there for him all those years ago.

"You never told anyone?"

"I tried to tell my mother once, when I was little, and she told me never to speak of it again. I didn't until she finally told me the story of my mother and her coven. She made me promise to never use witchcraft or tell anyone. She said I'd die if anyone knew."

I wasn't sure she was wrong. Even now, if the Virago knew who

Xavier was, their history might dictate he should be killed as well.

"I have no problem with the Virago." I started to take a step back at his suggested alliance with our enemy, but he held me close. "Except for their actions against your coven." He held my face in his hands as his eyes bore into mine. I didn't know if he was reading my thoughts or trying to implant one in my head.

"Do you know who they are?"

"Yes. At least the ones who still attend meetings."

"Meetings?"

"They're a group of bitter, misguided, lonely women who are seeking some order in their life to replace what they've lost, or for some, what's been taken from them."

"Where do they meet?"

"They have a few locations throughout the county. Sometimes, if attendance is expected to be small, they meet at a member's house."

It was all so fascinating. He spoke of them like a disgruntled group of the ladies auxiliary or the PTO. I referred to them as a hellish group of heartless killers. To hear Xavier talk, they were exchanging crock-pot recipes and hair dye tips.

"Not quite," he said. "They're a dangerous bunch. They killed my birth mother the day after she returned to town."

"I'm sorry."

"There was a tremendous amount of fighting for territory back then. Although now, it's starting to feel the same."

I sighed. "I know."

"Do you? Because I know you've been plotting against them in your own way."

I smiled coyly at him. There was no point in lying, and I didn't want to be anything but truthful with Xavier. "I don't know what you mean," I said and laughed.

His eyes widened. "No? Well, there have been several accidents, fights, and deaths within the ranks of your enemy. I suspect . . ." He tilted his chin down and raised his eyebrows. "That you and your cohorts have something to do with all of it."

"Why, Dr. Greer. I am insulted. I would never. Besides, a witch cannot kill another witch." He stared straight at me. "Not an honorable one, at least."

We ate on the patio with Pickles, Rex, Olive, and Carl at our feet. Ever texted me twice. Once to send me a picture of the four of them in front of the fountains at the Bellagio Hotel on the strip, and once to request a picture of Carl.

Xavier served me baked salmon and string beans he'd sautéed in olive oil and crushed red pepper. It felt like a real date, which was probably something he'd done a hundred times. I glanced up to see him smirking at me.

"I'm just not used to"—I waved my hands in the air—"dating and all of this."

"And you assume I am?"

"From what I've heard, you're quite active socially."

The smile drained from his face. "And you heard that from Isaiah?"

I sighed. It wasn't fair to anyone, his access to the inside of my mind.

"I can't stop hearing your thoughts."

"I know." I did. I lowered my eyes and moved the last string bean around on my plate.

"Are you finished? Would you like some more?"

I dropped the fork. "I'm done."

I followed Xavier into the kitchen with my dishes. "Have you ever told someone that you love them?"

"I've told many women that I love them."

It wasn't exactly the answer I was hoping for. "Were you lying when you told them?"

"No. I always find something to love about them."

My blood boiled in my veins. He was cruel with his advantage. "But nothing about me?"

He faced me as if he'd never been invisible. The intensity of his feelings was naked in his stare. It was what I'd spent months longing for. "What I feel for you is twenty-years deep." His chest rose with his breath, but his eyes never left me. "It is built on a whisper. It cuts me and delights me." He moved closer, and I stopped breathing. "But most of all it terrifies me." His lips brushed against mine. "Is that love?"

DECEPTION

Helene

"ARE YOU NERVOUS?" I ASKED him. He was unusually quiet. Lost in his thoughts that I could not hear. "Should I be?"

"Well, I am. It's the first time I've ever introduced a man to my daughter. This is new territory for both of us. We've never even discussed my dating someone."

"She's eighteen. She knows you're in love with me without you telling her."

"How do you know that? Did she think it?"

"Not around me, but she isn't obtuse, Helene. Ever sees and hears more than you think."

"She's been so distant lately. Barely eats, never talks, and appears to be in a constant state of worry. No matter how many different ways I ask her what's going on, she never gives me a straight answer."

"She'll talk to you when she's ready."

"You know something!"

"No. I don't. I'm rarely around her. I swear. I know nothing."

"Would you tell me if you did?"

"I don't know. The relationship between a mother and daughter seems like one I should stay out of." The idea of him somehow between us made me laugh. "I've never had any sisters, or daughters that I know of." I rolled my eyes. "But all of you are a bit terrifying."

We pulled into my driveway and relief flowed through me at the absence of Isaiah's truck. This would be too much to handle with him there, too.

The aroma from freshly baked pound cake wafted through the kitchen and met us at the back door. The pan was cooling on the top of the stove. A tablecloth covered the kitchen table and nine chairs were squeezed around the outside of it. I turned back to Xavier and remembered how overwhelmed Owen always was when Sloane and Lovie came to visit. Xavier would have to face two full covens, one of which included my daughter.

"There you are," Lovie said and waved us farther into the house. "Come in." Thank God for Lovie. She would somehow make this work. "The girls helped me cook dinner." She dipped her head, lowered her voice, and added, "I think they want everything to be perfect tonight."

I inhaled deeply as I looked around the room. It was the right time to bring Xavier home. I spun around to see him standing stiff near the doorway, but there was a smile on his face as he followed along with my thoughts. He was tall and broad shouldered. Rugged, yet elegant. Unlike Isaiah, who took up the entire room, Xavier left space for the rest of us. The kitchen filled with the women of my home. Chatting and laughing, they moved through the kitchen until they were between us and around us and folded us into their energy.

"Come. Sit down," Lovie said through the chaos, and we all moved toward the table.

I gestured to the chair beside me. Xavier stood behind it until Ever sat in the one next to him and the rest of us took our seats. Then he sat. Isaiah was family and acted as such. Xavier was our first male visitor. Maybe ever.

"We're going to start with the salad the girls made." Lovie passed the bowl to the left, and then followed it with the bread basket and the butter. Everything was running smoothly.

"So what made you become a veterinarian?" Sloane asked.

"Yeah. Why don't you tell us a little bit about yourself?" Gisel chimed in. Xavier only looked at her kindly before returning his attention to Sloane.

"I'd always been good at anatomy."

"I'll bet," Sloane said, and the heat rose to my cheeks. I should have had him meet my coven before our daughters.

"And I love animals. It was a natural choice."

"The salad is delicious, girls." I stayed focused on Ever. She wasn't being critical of Xavier. In fact, she looked to barely be paying attention as Sloane continued to drill him.

"And you went to Woodstown, right? What year did you graduate?"

"I was just a few years ahead of you four. I graduated high school the year you graduated from eighth grade."

"Cradle robber," Giselle said before I shot her the glare of death. Her comments and continued resentment of Xavier were unwarranted. He'd visited her and asked her where I was. What was the big deal?

Gisel, please. I needed her help tonight. I'd certainly done plenty over the last few months to make her life easier.

Sorry. I'll stop. The corners of her mouth turned up so slightly I was the only one who could even detect the hint of a smile. *I promise I won't say another word.*

"So, you must have known Rerun and the Kerns."

"Yes. Of course."

"They were a few years ahead of us. I don't remember the name Greer, though. It's unusual."

"I was adopted," Xavier said, and the commotion around the table ceased.

"I was raised by women other than my mother, too." Lovie said. "My mother died giving birth to me. These girls' grandmothers took on the responsibility of my upbringing. They filled in for my mother and relieved my father of having to figure out how to raise a witch." Lovie covered the entire table with her love. "Please stop me if I'm making you uncomfortable, but were you aware of your birth mother's identity?"

"I have very little information about her or her family. I was grateful to the Greer's for their love and kindness. I didn't want for a thing as a child."

"Are they still living?" Sloane asked.

Xavier's hands paused over his salad for a second before he said, "Thankfully, yes." He gently placed the fork on the edge of his plate. Xavier had lived a lifetime of not making a sound. He turned to Ever beside him, but before he spoke, he silently observed her. He was listening, and I was terrified of what he heard. "Ever, have you decided where you'll go to school?"

The question was discussed more often than any other at this table. What would these girls do? Ever looked at Ruby, who nodded. My eyes shot to Sloane, Lovie, and Gisel confirming they'd all just seen what I had.

"Well, I have a few great choices, but I *have* made a decision."

"Where have you looked?" Xavier asked.

"All over. NYU. Rutgers. The University of Vermont. Penn. University of Delaware, UNLV." She smiled at me. "I really do feel like we've explored a wide range of options."

The suspense was killing me.

"Well?" Sloane asked to put us all out of our misery. Gwen snickered on the other end of the table. "Have you *all* decided?" Sloane's question was directed only toward her daughter.

"I'm going to St. Mary's," Ever said. She beamed with pride or excitement or possibly the thrill of having the decision made.

"As am I," Maya said. Lovie gasped. The thought of the two of them together filled my heart. It swelled as I floated into their love for one another.

"And me," Ruby said, raising her fork in the air for a second before she continued eating.

I closed my eyes, realizing what they were doing. My hands pressed together against my lips. We all turned to Gwen, waiting for her decision.

"And me, of course." The tears spilled over my eyelids.

"Oh," Gisel practically wailed the only sentiment that came close to what we were thinking. The four of them were amazing.

"Why St. Mary's?" Xavier asked. He was the only person at the table capable of forming a question.

"They have a great chemistry department," Ever said. "And it's close. Just a short flight across the Chesapeake Bay and the Delaware River home."

Close to Rowan University. I should be happy she wasn't enrolling there just to be with Ike.

"It's on the water. We can join the sailing team," Maya said.

"And study theater," Gwen added.

"And English," Ruby chimed in.

They all seemed so grown up. They were women. I'd brought my boyfriend home to meet my little girl, and she'd surprised me by telling me her plan for her future. I studied each of them as they rattled off points of interest about St. Mary's. They were as beautiful as they were smart, and they were together.

Gisel sobbed at the end of the table. "I know. I know." She waved her hand in front of her face to cool herself and halt our concerns. "It's just. I've been so anxious about this time because of . . ." She sobbed again. Lovie stood behind her and rubbed her shoulders. Gisel rested her hand on top of Lovie's. "I just love you guys, and I'm thrilled the four of you have chosen to go away together."

"Are you sure?" Sloane asked what I was thinking.

"Certain," Ever and Ruby answered at the same time. They looked to their counterparts around the table with love.

Maya and Gwen cleared the salad dishes and served each of us lasagna tableside. St. Mary's College was the topic of choice for the rest of the meal. The girls were genuinely excited about their selection, and I had to admit, I was thrilled with it, too. St. Mary's was close. I'd wanted Ever to go to Vermont because of the safety of the region. The Virago was nonexistent in that part of the country, but I let her make her own decision. It was her first adult choice to make without me.

"You guys took forever. Ike thought about it for two weeks, took a tour of the school, and met with the football coach before choosing Rowan."

At the mention of Ike, Ever put her fork down and lowered her hands to her lap. The rest of the table kept talking, but I watched my daughter. Something was going on between her and Ike. The idea that they were breaking up was unimaginable, at least by the way he looked at her when he'd been home the last time, but there was something, and she wasn't telling me.

Xavier tilted his head toward Ever and turned to me. I couldn't decipher what he was thinking, either. His expression was mixed with frustration and pity. The look in his eyes terrified me.

It's okay, he thought.

I warmed at his words. I closed my eyes and lowered my head.

Sorry. I keep forgetting you can hear me.

Never apologize for that.

I touched the side of his leg under the table. Sloane cleared her throat as she eyed me. I returned my hand to my lap even though I didn't want to.

We finished the meal with pound cake and wine. Gwen poured herself half a glass.

"Uncle Stump," Gisel said and rolled her eyes. She quieted as if the memory had brought on others that consumed her.

"I'd better get home. I have three dogs waiting for me," Xavier said and stood from the table.

"Already?" Lovie would have let him spend the night.

"I think so." He watched Gisel as he spoke. "I can't thank you enough for dinner, though. It's been a long time since I've been at a family meal such as this one." He poked Gisel with the words. To remind her this was new for her, too. Gisel glared at him. "And congratulations on all your college choices. St. Mary's sounds wonderful," he told the girls.

"I'll walk you out."

The night air hit me as soon as we cleared the back door. I pulled the sides of my sweater across my chest and held it tightly wrapped around me. Xavier pulled me close to his side and under his arm as we walked to his car.

"I wish you could come home with me," he said. I did, too, but I didn't respond. He knew this without my thinking it. "I still like to hear your voice." He kissed the top of my head.

"Can't you hear it inside your head?" I stopped walking next to his car door.

"Yes."

"Could you tell what Ever was thinking during dinner?" Xavier paused. I knew he didn't want to get in the middle of it, but I had to at least ask. "I'm just worried about her, and she isn't talking. I know it's something about Ike."

"I would tell you. Even though I shouldn't." He kissed me lightly on the lips and leaned back until I could see his eyes in the moonlight. "But I don't know. I couldn't hear her."

"What?"

"I agree, she had a lot she was thinking about, but I couldn't decipher what those things were."

"How?"

"Only chemistry."

"What?"

"She was like a low hum mixed with chemical formulas."

"Formulas for what?"

Xavier laughed a little even though none of this was funny. "Gold, hydrogen, copper. The list goes on. She's smart to study chemistry in college. She obviously loves the subject."

"Has this ever happened before?"

"Never. Does she know I can read her mind?"

"Yes. Gisel told all of them during one of her rants."

"Well, either she was withholding her thoughts on purpose, or there is something different about your daughter that makes it so I can't read her."

"Are you calling my daughter weird?"

"Of course not." He pulled me close to his chest and dropped a kiss to the top of my head. "It is unusual, though." Chemistry. What was she thinking? "I'll call you later."

"Call me?"

"Yes. Tonight was special. I like being a normal couple with you."

"Who says you get to say what normal is?" Xavier froze at my words. He took one step back. "What? What did I say?" I thought back over every word, trying to figure out why they'd upset him.

He shook his head. "Nothing. I'll talk to you later."

He drove away and left me in the driveway staring at the moon in the sky. When I thought he must be at least ten miles away, I let myself think of Owen. I wondered if he'd be happy I was with someone. If he'd be excited about St. Mary's, and most of all, if he forgave me. Because he should have been sitting next to me when Ever told us what college she had chosen, but when I married him, I knew he wouldn't be. I shed a tear in the moonlight for my late husband.

"Mom," Ever said. I didn't know how long she'd been there. "What are you still doing out here?"

"I was just thinking of your dad." I let that statement sink in and gave her time to run from it. "He would be so proud of you, Ever."

"Mom, you didn't kill him."

"It wasn't fair to him."

"When you guys got pregnant, you were still hoping to find a way out of the curse. You didn't know for sure what would happen."

I wanted to agree. To tell my daughter that I was as innocent as she was, but the first thing that appealed to me about her father was his strength, and that wasn't by accident. Even if it was subconsciously, I was choosing a warrior to go into battle with me. One he had no knowledge about.

"Did you ever think about telling him?"

"No. What would I say, and what good would it have done?"

"Gwen says he isn't mad. None of them are."

"Oh yeah? Well, Gwen sees things in a positive light."

"No. She's talked to them."

I froze. Gwen was a bridge. *Our* bridge.

Ever turned to walk away but then looked back and said, "I like him, Mom."

I knew she was no longer talking about her father. She wholly loved that man. "You do?"

"Yes." She came and took me by the hand to lead me back to the house with her. "It's weird, but he's calm and quiet. There's a real power to that, and I love it around you."

"He is. He's very guarded. It took a long time for him to trust me, and I think coming to dinner tonight was a significant step for him as much as it was for us."

"Well, you should bring him back. As long as Mr. Kennedy isn't here."

"Maybe it's time we looked for our own place?"

Ever stopped walking. "In a few months there will be four less residents, and the thought of you alone after having all of this . . ." Through the kitchen window we could see Lovie and Gisel laughing as Ruby threw dish suds at Gwen. "Scares me."

"You're right. I couldn't leave this without you."

Ever

I LANDED WITH MY BACKPACK behind Ike's dorm at nine in the morning. The campus was quiet. Few students were up. The days were longer now and the parties were endless in the warm weather. The hint of summer's approach had everyone in a good mood.

Two students lay on their backs on the lawn. The tops of their heads were touching. Both had bent knees and arms crossed over their chests. It appeared they were just watching the clouds go by. I waited to hear what they'd say. What their observations were, but neither said a word. From what I'd seen, college students had odd experiences.

Birds chirped, the cars on Route 322 motored by, and a guy on a bike whizzed past me on my left. His backpack was bright orange and the only detail I could make out about him as he soared past the dorm while standing up on his pedals.

I stayed hidden while the door opened and slipped through it after two girls in their clothes from the night before exited. I ignored the nagging jealousy of all the girls who got to see Ike more than I did. Only one goal consumed my mind: climbing into bed with him for the next thirty hours. I should have brought food with me to sustain us. I didn't think I was going to let him out this weekend at all. His roommate had been forced home because of a cousin's wedding, so we had whole room to ourselves for the entire night.

Ike, I thought. I could have shown myself and knocked on his dorm like a normal person, but we weren't normal, so I didn't. *Ike, I'm here. Heading toward your door.*

When I reached it, it was open and he was standing behind it on the other side. His hair was growing and billowing out from the sides of his head. He had on pajama pants and no shirt. The light coming through the window shone on his chest as if he were a Greek god to be admired.

I inhaled my duty to the gods. "Good morning," I said.

Ike pulled me to him without a word. He kissed me, taking my breath away and making me forget about every other girl on campus. He took my backpack off my shoulders and dropped it to the floor without ever releasing me from his navy eyes.

"I love you," he said before lifting me and tossing me on his bed. He climbed in after, and the seriousness of the morning was replaced by my playful boyfriend stealing me from my life without him.

"What are you thinking about?"

My mind had been dodging around a hundred different subjects since I'd rolled off him and slid in next to him under the covers. "I'm not sure."

"Tell me, Ever." I knew he was smiling even though I couldn't see his face. I could feel his emotions.

"This dorm, you, your body."

"Sounds good."

"The end of school. Summer. Your body." He laughed and ran the tips of his fingers up my arm. When I shivered, he pulled the covers over my shoulders. I exhaled on top of him. "College. Leaving . . . and my father."

Ike leaned up to see my face. "What about him?"

"I've been dreaming about him."

"I thought witches didn't dream."

"I know." I wasn't sure what was going on, either, but sleep had become my torture. "I dream about him and you and losing you both."

"It's completely different. I'm not going anywhere. We're going to talk all the time and see each other as often as possible, and *none* of this will last forever. Except us."

"He'd hate the fact that I was nervous. My father would tell me to 'Get in there and give 'em hell.' One time, a boy had taken the basketball away from me at recess and refused to give it back." Stinky McBride was what I used to call him, but only in my head. My mother would have killed me for calling another child names. "I didn't even bother to tell my mother because she would have told me to ignore him and get another ball."

"What did your dad say?"

"He told me to, 'rip that ball out of the kid's hands, bounce it off his head, and go play basketball if that was what you want to do.'"

"Sound fatherly advice."

"He always used to tell me that sometimes you have to show the crazy people that you're crazier."

"I would have loved your father."

"He would have loved you, too." I ran my hand across his chest and kissed him there. "Not all of this, but you, yes."

It physically hurt me to leave him Sunday, but I did. Ike had to study. I felt less pressure academically since a decision had been made about next year, but I spent the week completing projects and studying for quizzes. I wanted to finish the year where I'd started—near the top of the class. My father would have expected it.

In a few months, Ike and I would both be living away from home. We'd go in two different directions and hope to stay connected in between. I could feel our mothers' nervousness as graduation and the date when we would leave approached. Without knowing the details, I knew the adults in our lives were on edge about a lot of things recently.

Ike spoke to me after his last final. He was going out. I told him I loved him and to be careful. That was eleven hours ago, and I hadn't heard from him since. I couldn't remember a day we went eleven hours without speaking. He could have been drunk or hungover, but on those rare occasions, he spoke to me more than ever. He was emotional and loving and told me the last remaining sentiments he was too reserved to say on a sober afternoon.

Ike, I thought again in my head as I strummed my nails on the kitchen table.

"Something wrong?" Ruby asked.

"I don't know. I can't get ahold of Ike."

"Have you tried the phone like the rest of us do when we need to talk to him?"

I huffed, picked up my phone, and pressed Ike's number into the screen. It went straight to voice mail. I held it up between us for Ruby to hear his recorded message.

"Weird," she said. "How long's it been?"

"Since after his final yesterday."

"Maybe he's passed out."

I relaxed my fingers. "Maybe." I couldn't rid myself of the sinking feeling, though.

I ran errands with my mother all morning. I half-listened as she spoke of Maryland and St. Mary's.

"What's Ike say about St. Mary's?" she asked. I wrung my hands at the mention of his name. "Ever, what's going on?"

"I don't know." Tears filled my eyes. I couldn't suppress them. My weakness made me feel like a child. "He hasn't spoken to me since yesterday afternoon."

"Well, I'm sure he's busy. It's finals time. This is totally different from high school."

"I know, Mom, but he had finals at the end of the fall semester. We made it through football and midterms at the same time. Something is different today. He isn't just busy. He's silent."

My mother stared at me while we sat at the red light at the entrance to the mall in Delaware. When it turned green, she accelerated through the parking lot and back onto the highway.

"Where are we going?"

"Home. We need to see if Gisel or Gwen have talked to him. Do you know his dad's cell phone number?"

"Yes."

"Call him and see if he's talked to Ike." I thought I'd feel better if someone else understood the significance of Ike's silence, but my mother was terrifying me.

I dialed Mr. Kennedy, and when he answered, my mother pulled the phone out of my hand while she drove with the other.

"Have you talked to Ike?" Her voice was near hysterics. "It's Helene."

I could hear him tell her he knew who it was and that he hadn't talked to him.

"Meet us in Auburn." She was silent for a beat. "No. I don't know that anything's wrong. Ever and I just feel like something is."

She sped home. Her reaction to my concern overtook me. I practically ripped the car door off when we pulled into our driveway.

Mr. Kennedy's truck was parked behind Gisel's. He walked outside and met my mother by the minivan we'd been in.

"What is going on?"

"I don't' know. Ever hasn't talked to Ike. It's probably nothing, but I'm . . ." She lowered her voice until I could barely hear her say, "Scared."

Mr. Kennedy took my mother by the hand and walked her into the kitchen with me following.

"Ever!" Gisel called. "How long has it been since you've heard from him?"

"Almost twenty-four hours." It would have sounded ridiculous, except everyone in the room knew I had unlimited access to Ike's words. "He isn't saying anything. I can't tell if he hears me calling out to him."

"I called his roommate, Jeremy. He hasn't seen him since yesterday afternoon," Gwen said, and horror overtook the room.

"I'm calling the police," Mr. Kennedy said and walked over to the phone on the wall.

Something on the floor caught my eye, but there was nothing there. It was a sense of movement. The same as a fly buzzing through a sunbeam or a creak in the wooden second story floor that could only be made when a foot steps upon it. My sight circled around to the wall, the ceiling, and finally the center of the kitchen table.

The piece of paper seemed to appear out of nowhere. It slipped a few inches to the side as the air from movement pushed against it. My heart stopped with my breath. We weren't alone. I pointed at the paper.

"Close the windows and doors," Sloane yelled. "They're in here."

We sprung into motion. Maya, Gwen, Ruby, and I flew up the stairs and sealed off every entry to the house in the attic. Whoever had just left the paper was still inside with us, and they knew where

Ike was. No one said a word aloud.

Stay upstairs, girls. Lovie and Gisel have the second floor.

We waited in silence. We'd stand all night by the house's windows and doors to find out where Ike was.

A crashing sound was followed by yelling on the first floor. We raced down and saw my mother and Sloane flying out the broken window. They disappeared as they exited the house. I moved in a circle in the center of the kitchen, listening for sounds of someone still with us. I inhaled deeply. There was a slight hint of Parmesan cheese, but no evidence of where it came from.

The paper still lay near the middle of the table. I took a deep breath and unfolded it.

If you want him, come and get him, or he'll be dead by Monday. We'll be in touch tomorrow.

The paper slipped through my fingers onto the kitchen floor. Anger seared through me until my whole body shook. I closed my eyes, unable to see the world around me when Ike had been taken. One by one, the plates displayed on the top shelves of the hutch burst into shattered pieces.

"Ever!"

I heard my mother's voice, but it couldn't cut through my horror. I opened my eyes and found Gwen staring at me. My Earth witch who loved Ike as much as I did. Her lightness was cemented to the ground with the anger in her eyes. Her glare bore into me until every door in the house swung open with a gale force wind behind them.

Ruby grabbed me by the upper arms. "Stop." She turned back to Gwen. "Both of you. We'll get him back." I inhaled her control and let her hands on my arms settle me. "I'll go up to his dorm and see if I can find anything else."

"I'll go with you," Gwen said. I didn't offer. I knew nothing was there.

"We're going to get him back."

"Do you remember what they did to Carl?" I don't know why I asked. None of us could ever forget.

Ruby didn't say another word.

"What did they do to the dog?" Ike's dad asked, but my mother and Sloane's return dropped the question.

XXVIII

Helene

OUR KITCHEN TABLE HAD NEVER felt so small. The eight of us sat around it. My daughter sat at the head with her leg resting over the chair arm. Ever's eyes were swollen from crying and lying awake the entire night before. Not one of us had the answer of who exactly had Ike or where he was. The list of witches who were members of the Virago was still long. Maya had the journal and spreadsheet in front of her.

"I usually speak to him so many times in my head. His silence is making me insane," Ever said. Her voice broke a little on the last syllable.

"Maybe we should try to talk to them?" Lovie said. "This has gone on long enough. There's no reason why we can't all just get along."

"You mean, besides the fact that they're crazy witches?" Sloane was disgusted. She'd depleted her patience with the Virago a year ago.

"If there wasn't a reason, there is now. I will kill every single one of them that has anything to do with taking my son."

"It probably wasn't many of them. From what Xavier has told me, they're not that organized. At least not enough to form a solid enemy attack. This is probably the work of a smaller group within the Virago."

"We can't know that for sure," Sloane said.

"No. We can't."

"Focusing on only a few at a time has been working." Maya counted the names on the list and handed it to Ever. "They're down to twenty-eight, but even if the Kingsway Coven fights with us, we're outnumbered. They'll mow us down."

"How did they get in here? What is happening that Auburn is not sacred?" Gisel asked. We'd been asking the same question since Maya's dress was destroyed the year before. She pulled her hair off her neck in one rough motion. The frustration and anxiety of not having her son was wearing on her. Gisel would begin to make bad decisions if we weren't careful with her.

"If only we could talk to them." Lovie believed anything could be solved without violence.

I stood from the table. The two covens of my home stopped talking and stared at me standing above them.

"We should talk to them. Settle this like grown women like we should have done in the first place. I'm going to ask for a meeting with the Virago tonight."

"For who?"

"Just me. They've already attacked me once, but they left me alive. There is a reason for that." I touched the back of my hair. "I'll go alone while you guys look for Ike. Those who have him will think it's a trick. The witches who weren't involved with taking him will want to hear what I have to say."

Sloane stood across the table from me. "They also want to kill witches."

"And they love to brag," I said. "Maybe they'll tell me something that will help us."

"Or murder you as soon as you walk through the door."

"I don't think they will. Where are the theatrics in that?" I tried to sound more confident than I was. The idea of reasoning with these crazy witches seemed a stretch. "If nothing else, it will keep a large part of the Virago occupied and out of the way."

"I'm going with you," Sloane said. I loved her. Since we could walk, she'd had my back.

"I need you to be where Ever is."

Sloane didn't argue. She understood. They all did. If anything happened to me, I'd want the rest of my coven to make sure Ever was safe.

"We should call Maryann. They need to know what's going on, and they hate the Virago as much as we do." We all nodded and Sloane grabbed her phone and started texting.

"How are you going to arrange it?"

"Xavier can do it. He knows—" I stopped myself from saying, "a great deal about them."

Sloane was the first to catch my pause. "How do you know you can trust Xavier?"

"I feel it in my heart."

"No offense, but you've felt that before," Ever said. She brought up the lasting weakness of Gisel and Isaiah's love affair. "And this is Ike we're talking about. I can't trust his or your safety to Xavier Greer, a guy we don't even really know."

"He isn't a risk."

"He's also not a part of this family or anyone else's. I've always had a bad feeling about him," Gisel said. Her coolness to Xavier had never been a secret, but she was portraying him as evil when he'd never done anything wrong. Keeping a secret to protect himself wasn't wrong. We did it every single day of our lives. "You said yourself he wasn't forthcoming."

"Not being forthcoming does not mean he would sabotage a plan to save your son."

Gisel stood. "I don't want him to know about any of this."

"Why does he have to know?" Ever asked. She and Gisel would unite to bring Ike home.

"Because I trust him, and I'm going to ask him to arrange the meeting. He knows the Virago, and he knows how to get ahold of them."

"I think that's reason enough not to tell him the truth," Lovie said. Hers was the final word because her statements always came from the right place.

"Fine." I turned toward my daughter. "Ever, I'm going to need your help keeping something from him." She looked up at me confused. "You're the only person who's been able to hide their thoughts. He said you mask the things you're thinking in chemistry formulas." She winced. "You'll have to show me how to do it."

"And this should be the last part of any plans you're aware of." Sloane was asking me to leave.

"But—"

"But nothing. You've never kept anything from him before. If you fail, or if Xavier is not the person you think he is, we can still operate safely executing the rest of the plan."

"He wouldn't betray us." I kept pleading Xavier's case. I felt like that was all I ever did with these women. For women who were supposed to be full of love and light, they were so quick to rally against him simply because they didn't understand him. Would they rather me fall back in love with Isaiah? Was he the only "safe" man left on Earth? He'd nearly destroyed me twenty years ago, and they acted as if he was the best choice. He wasn't a choice at all anymore.

"Xavier can read our minds," Lovie started out calmly. "We've never met anyone like that." That shouldn't mean that we can't trust him. "For all we know, there are others like him who will be at the meeting with you." My shoulders sank in defeat. "You have to admit it. We don't know exactly what powers these women still have or even what they were born with. If Xavier can do it, a member of the Virago might also. You can't know the details if you're putting yourself within their grasp."

Our debate was put on hold as Tara Jane walked through the back door with her coven following. Tara Jane was in a wet swimsuit, and Maryann's hair was full of foils. She still wore the hairdresser's cape. Sloane stared at her without saying a word.

"The text had three Xs at the end." She held one hand up as she professed the obvious. "That's the code. I came. What's going on? I don't want my hair to fall out."

"They took Ike. Gisel's son," Lovie said.

"Who did?"

No one answered. We didn't have to.

Maryann took a deep breath. "I'll call Michael and have him get the kids." She pointed to Riley, her water witch. "Can you wash out my hair?" To the rest of us she said, "We'll get him back."

"Helene is going to meet with the Virago tonight. We were hoping you could go with her. Without being seen," Lovie said.

"As a backup," I added.

"Where?" Tara Jane asked.

"I'm not sure yet?"

The four of them looked to each other. I knew they were speaking in their minds. We didn't have to give them privacy.

"We know it's a lot to ask."

"It's nothing since they came into my home," Maryann said. The ever-present joking smile drained from her face, leaving me wondering what else they'd said in their minds.

"You'll need to stay back. My escort can read your thoughts, and he doesn't know about Ike's kidnapping or the real reason I'm going."

Tara Jane's eyes narrowed as she concentrated on every syllable that left my mouth. She stood straight and finally asked, "How do you know he isn't one of them?"

Lovie was the only one who looked at me with sympathy.

"I have to go." I stood and left the room. Tara Jane and everyone else were right to be suspicious, but betraying Xavier was wrong in every way. I flew up the stairs to the second floor and dropped down on my bed.

Ever followed me in. She was exhausted. Twenty-four hours of not hearing from Ike was killing her not so slowly. Dark circles surrounded her eyes. Her skin was pale with worry, and her lips appeared carved in stone, as if they wouldn't shift into a smile ever again.

"I'm scared."

"I know. We all are. It's making us say and do crazy things."

"What do they want? Why take Ike?"

"They want us to leave."

"I don't know what I'll do if they've hurt him," she said as her gaze stared off through the window next to my bed. My daughter was lost in a situation that was too painful for her to reflect upon.

"Let's just take it one step at a time. We're going to get him back, and then we're going to carry on like the proper witches that we are. Now, tell me how you keep Xavier from reading your mind."

"I wasn't doing it on purpose. Well, not to him at least. I feel like you've always known what I'm thinking, even when I don't say a word aloud. I think I started hiding my thoughts when I was little. I didn't want to cause you more pain after Dad died, so I'd ramble on about other things in my mind to throw you off."

"How? What other things?"

"Like, say I didn't want you to know I was sneaking out and seeing Ike last year." My attention was caught. I tilted my head to her. How could I not have known this? "Really, Mom. Focus." Ever's voice was flat as she pushed on. "Whenever I came near you, I'd start running through chemistry formulas in my head. I have them memorized, so it's somewhat thoughtless, but I have to concentrate to remember all the atomic numbers and abbreviations."

"That's all you do?"

"Yes, but I do it over and over again. I'm guessing you don't know all the atomic numbers and abbreviations for the elements of the periodic table."

"No." I suddenly wished I did. Ever's approach to hiding her thoughts was perfectly simple. "What if I used some other subject? Something I could easily reflect on without expansive knowledge. Like a recipe or Carl?"

"That will work, but it's going to seem purposeful if you're not careful. Make it something surrounding you. It will jumble your thoughts, and Xavier will probably wonder at first if there is something wrong with him. Isn't that what he thought the night we had dinner together? When I hid my thoughts from him?"

"Yes. What were you hiding that night?"

"I don't remember." Ever's face dulled. She was still looking at me, but her gaze drifted away.

"Are you running chemistry formulas?"

"Yes. You're catching on."

"I'm afraid he will, too. He's been listening to people's thoughts his entire life, and mine for a long time."

"You're going to be meeting with the Virago. You'll be more nervous than you've ever been around him. A frantic mind will be justifiable."

"I hope you're right."

"I'm going downstairs to help them come up with a plan for how we're going to get Ike back."

"I think I can be involved in that. I won't let anyone find out."

"But if you're not involved, we know for sure that no one will find out."

I didn't take offense. If I were in their position, I would be doing the same thing. It just hurt that they didn't trust me or my judgment enough to let me and Xavier in on the plan.

I stared out the window at the gray sky. Not a hint of blue to be found. Billows of varying shades of charcoal floated across the gloomy day. I picked up my cell phone and entered Xavier's number.

"Hey," he said when he answered. His voice calmed me enough to talk to him. Ever was right. This wasn't going to be easy, and I'd had no time to practice.

"Are you busy? I need your help." I barely paid attention to my own words. I focused on the one gray cloud that was bigger than all the others. If I assigned an outline to it at least, which I did. I gave it edges that, in reality, were invisible as the cloud's border melded into all the others surrounding it.

"Never for you."

"We've been talking over here." I noted how close the treetops seemed to the sky today. It wasn't just cloudy, it was closing in on us. "I want to meet with the Virago and discuss our shared existence. A peace summit, if you will."

"I don't think that's a good idea."

I concentrated on trying to read his thoughts instead of my own. "Why is that? Peace is what all of us want."

"It isn't. Peace is what you want. They want you gone."

"Well, they want us to leave, and we're not going anywhere. We can discuss how our coven and the rest of the witches who have not joined them can live safely and without fear."

"I think they'd let you speak." Doors opened and footsteps

could be heard through the phone. A final sound and then there was nothing but silence on the other end of the line. Bothering him at work was another cause for suspicion. Blue clouds. Two birds. I stared at the tree outside. "You're assuming you could hold up your end of that bargain."

"Why couldn't I?" I'd never go near them if they hadn't—

I focused on a cloud in the distance that was the shape of the papasan chair Ever used to have in her room in Vermont.

"Helene, are you all right?"

"Fine. I'm just trying to understand."

"In order to keep a peace deal like that with the Virago, you'd have to mind your own business, and you've already made it painfully clear that you'd have to step in if faced with certain circumstances." He was talking about my anger with him for not helping when they attacked Isaiah.

"Well, I just can't sit back and watch them hurt an innocent person."

"Exactly. They're not going to just hear what you have to say and behave. Some sort of arrangement might be worked out in regard to witches, but you'd have to turn a blind eye to the rest of the residents."

"That's crazy."

"That's them."

"I still want to meet with them. Would you mind arranging it? For tonight?"

"Why so soon?"

The unformed circular edges of the clouds gave way to a darker band without any definition. "I don't know." I assumed it was raining beneath them. "I'm just ready."

"Are you sure you're okay?" he asked.

"Fine. I just want this to be over."

"I'll see what I can do and get back to you."

"Thank you." He was my only hope. I caught myself wandering back and added, "I love you."

Xavier hung up. I pressed end on my phone and fell back onto my bed. Everyone else was in the kitchen planning an attack on the Virago that I wasn't privy to. I would serve as a decoy as I deceived the man I had fallen in love with and convinced to trust me. I would lie to him to save Ike.

Isaiah came in and lay on my bed next to me without a word. He wasn't in on the plan, either. He was only in pain.

My feet reached to his shin. His arm touched mine. His son was missing, and I couldn't face his blank stare, which was locked on the ceiling.

I rolled over and wrapped my arm around him the way he did to me when my mother died. Isaiah didn't move.

"We'll get him back. I promise."

Ever

WE WAITED. MY MOTHER WORKED her end with the Virago leadership through Xavier. Lovie was baking brownie cupcakes with an Oreo as the bottom of each one. This would have excited me if I weren't desperately worried about Ike. The silence was so heavy, so consuming, that not even hunger could break it.

A knock at the door startled us. Ruby stood and pushed in her chair but kept her hands on the top rung of the wood, preparing to use it as a weapon if needed.

Sloane answered the door, and a little girl walked in with her mother in tow handing out flyers advertising pool memberships at the Chestnut Run Pool in Woodstown. Lovie chatted with the woman as Gwen spoke to the little girl. I stayed silent on the opposite side of the room from Sloane and focused solely on the woman.

She didn't seem anything but genuinely interested in what the girl had to say. When they left, the seven of us exhaled. Lovie went to get the mail and brought back several catalogs, two bills, and a letter with no writing on the outside of the envelope.

She laid it on the center of the table.

Ike, if you can hear me, say something. I love you, Ike.

Gisel tore open the envelope. Her eyes shifted back and forth as she devoured the message inside.

"They want Ever to go alone."

"That's never going to happen," Sloane said.

"They said if any of us are with her, they'll kill him instantly."

"She isn't going in there alone, and her mother doesn't have to be in the room to tell us that."

"I can go alone."

Gisel's glare left Sloane and found me. "Sloane's right. That isn't an option."

"What is then? What did they say?"

"They want you to go to a house on Harney Street at eight tonight."

"It's a trick of some kind. That's the street Billy Roberts lives on. It's residential. Right on the other side of the Woodstown Lake. That's just where they'll capture us. Which house do they want me to go to?"

Gisel glanced back at the letter. "Number nine."

"That isn't Billy's house."

"Maybe Billy's part of the Virago. His mother was a witch," Ruby said. "And he can disappear. He has some powers."

"What do you mean *some* powers?" Lovie placed her bowl of batter on the table.

"Like Ike, he isn't a witch, but he's . . . something."

"Well, you either are or you aren't," Gisel said.

"Right. Like only women can be witches. We should ask Xavier about that."

"What else can Billy Roberts do?" Sloane asked.

"Repulse me." There was no time for Ruby's flippancy. She pursed her lips and thought before adding, "We're not sure if he can fly, but he doesn't seem to be able to move things or talk to anyone inside his head."

"Although, according to his mother's diary, there wouldn't be anyone to talk to. She was the last living member of her coven."

"Why do they want you to come alone?" Ruby took out the journal and spreadsheet from the drawer.

"I don't know. It has to be part of the mind game."

She walked over to the computer and checked Instagram and each of the remaining witches' Facebook pages. "This used to take much more time."

"They're numbers are dwindling." Gwen said. "They're getting desperate."

We flew as a large group over Harney Street, being careful not to get too close to the house or Billy's toward the end of the street. Both were completely void of life. Not a window was opened or a car in the driveway.

Ike, say something if you can hear me. Ike, please.

I circled back behind the rest of my coven and flew lower to the house. *Ike! I'm here. Say something so I know you're okay.*

Stay away. I dove low to the ground without breathing. He was alive. Somewhere.

Ike! Where are you?

I floated above the row of homes and waited in silence as the seconds ticked in my mind.

They want you, Ever. Stay away. His words were slurred. I flew away from Harney Street with the sense he wasn't there. He wasn't in the house. I couldn't be sure, but I didn't think Ike was being held on Harney.

I don't think he's in there. Fly around with me and keep calling his name. He might hear one of you, I thought. We flew in pairs around the town until it was clear we weren't going to find anything, and Ike wasn't going to say another word.

"He talked to me," I said as soon as we landed in the backyard. I pulled Gisel's arm back to keep her from walking into the kitchen. My mother couldn't hear anything about this if she was going to be safe when she met with the Virago. "He said they wanted me and not to go there."

"Where?" Ruby was behind me, practically on top of me, and listening to every word.

"He didn't say. Just to stay away, and I was who they wanted." Gisel looked out at the tree line. "Something is wrong with him. He was slurring his words."

Rage turned the skin near Gisel's collarbone purple and rushed up to her cheeks. "I will *kill* them," she said. I let her go on. She was voicing the limited emotions I was still feeling. Why wouldn't he answer me again? Where was he? Every attack I'd heard of flew through my mind with Ike as the victim. They were hurting him, and I couldn't save him. I knelt down on the ground with my head in my hands.

Ike.

My mother left the house at seven. She hugged each one of us, saving me for last. She held me tight against her. For the first time in my life, she seemed small. I was eclipsing her in power and strength, and yet, I was sending her into a lion's den.

"Come back," she said as she stared me in the eyes. The Kingsway Coven was lined up behind her.

"I will if you will," I said. "Where are you meeting Xavier?"

"At his house. We're going to fly there together." She glanced back at our allies. "They're going to follow from a distance."

"I'm sorry you couldn't—"

"Don't mention it. For real. Like, never mention it again. This is all going to work out, just bring back our guy, and we'll figure out what we're going to do from there." It was the first inkling of the horrors we were about to set into motion. Tonight would be the first battle of a new war. My mother turned to face our covens. "We'll meet back here?" she asked.

"It's the only safe place left," Maya said and triggered a thought in my mind.

"Is it?" I asked. "Whoever had Ike was in our house when they left the note."

"Maybe they had someone else leave the note—"

"I need to go," my mother said. She couldn't be privy to any more conversations tonight. Not before meeting with the Virago. "Do whatever you have to do to bring Ike home."

"Honor is only honor when it's tested," Lovie said, and Gisel's face hardened.

"If it were your son—" Gisel began to say.

"We can't spend the next few hours like this." Lovie touched Gisel's arm, as if she could physically convince her with a gentle touch. Gisel's neck straightened. She wouldn't be so easily controlled. "We need to be together. That's the only way to defeat them. It's our only power they can't figure out how to harness."

"She's right," my mother said and walked out the back door with Tara Jane, Maryann, Jennifer, and Riley following close behind her.

Whoever had Ike knew us. They knew what he meant to all of us, where he was, and the best time to take him. He was supposed to go out that night. I wouldn't have been alarmed by not hearing from him until the morning. Curious, yes, but not frantic with worry. He was in college. Once in a while, he did go out and not check in when he got back.

"They know us and that there is no way I'll show up alone."

"They don't even have to know us to figure that out. Why would anyone let you go alone?"

"Anything that they are expecting should not be done."

"Ever—"

"Hear me out." The six of them stared at me. "They're setting a trap for all of us. They'll corral us and somehow stop us from using our powers long enough pick us off. If they're expecting us to come as a battalion, we can't go in that way."

"How do you expect us to go in?"

"They say they want me, but I have nothing for them. It's all part of the trap. I should go alone."

"Stop talking," Sloane said. "We might let it look like you're alone, but you never will be."

Ruby and Maya lounged on the couches in the family room. The television was not on. They weren't talking. Nothing. My mother had been gone for a half hour, and she took with her everyone else's ability to communicate. Even without having to keep things from her, we were locked in silence.

"I want us to cast a spell," I said.

"For what?"

"To even the playing field. We may be outnumbered. If we go in, we won't be able to see them, and they'll bum rush us and kill us before we've even said hello."

Gisel sighed. We all knew it was true. "There are more of them, but they can't speak to each other in their heads." I hoped. We weren't really sure of what they could do, but at least the two I'd run into in Upper Pittsgrove didn't seem to have the ability to sense our presence or communicate with each other silently. "And they're not stronger than us when we're all together. Think of our increased power with Gisel and Gwen back in the fold."

Sloane leaned forward on the couch. "So, what are you suggesting?"

"My coven will cast a spell that whenever we're visible and someone comes within fifteen feet of us, they become visible, too." Our mothers concentrated on each word as I said them. "It's changing things, but it still has balance. We'll be visible, too."

"What about us?" Lovie asked.

"I think you guys should remain the same. They'll expect us to come as a unified front, but the three of you will be able to remain invisible and still see them if they're close to us."

"It can't be undone. A witch's spell," Gisel said.

"I know." I'd thought a lot about it. It was naïve to believe there was no downside, but we'd sacrifice the impact on the future for the advantage today.

"I'm in," Ruby said. Gwen and Maya agreed as well, and we moved into position. The four of us holding hands in a circle. Gwen was across from me. Ruby and Maya on each side.

"I've got it," Ruby said, and we all closed our eyes to accept the spell she'd written. At once, the four of us inhaled our power and began to recite it.

In the air or on the ground
The fifteen feet that surrounds
Clear sight of those who see me
Shall reveal the enemy

Helene

"I'M JUST NERVOUS."

"Your mind is like scrambled eggs." Xavier stared at me from three feet away. I focused on the thoughts swarming through my mind. The weather. What I would say. Whether we should fly or drive. Between those thoughts, I turned my mind to the clouds swirling around us. I stared up at them and cemented their existence in my mind. Dark edges with a steel-gray interior puffed out. "Are you sure you're okay?"

"Yes. There's just a lot riding on this."

"I think we should fly."

"I'm good with that. Where exactly is this?"

"They meet in the abandoned hotel down by the bridge. It's become a bit of an art show." He laughed a little.

"What is that supposed to mean?"

"You'll have to see it for yourself." He closed the distance between us, touched his hand to my face, and kissed me. "I'm going to be right next to you the whole time."

"I know." I let my head rest in his hand. I couldn't wait until tonight was over. My gaze darted back to the sky. The wind was picking up.

"Just be yourself and don't let your guard down. I'll keep an eye out behind you, but if things turn, they'll attack without warning."

I nodded and disappeared in his arms. I flew next to Xavier toward the Delaware River. Just before the end of the turnpike, we veered south and landed in the parking lot of an old hotel. I'd forgotten it was even back there.

I was still holding his hand as we walked through the missing front doors. Small pieces of broken sky-blue glass covered the floor and crunched beneath our shoes. Xavier flew above it and took me up with him. I floated on my own next to him and above the battered floor. Wires, panels, and tubing hung from the ceiling. A housekeeping cart had been abandoned near the front door. The name "Rosa" was written in black marker on the front, depicting who it belonged to when it was used to clean the rooms.

Drawers, fast food debris, and papers were strewn throughout the deserted lobby. The stand that used to hold the television hung empty from the top corner of the wall, and in the breakfast nook area, every drawer of the buffet was opened and emptied. Darkness fell on the space, and I wished there weren't boards covering the windows and blocking the light.

We approached a woman sitting at the abandoned reception desk, which still had the green tile inlaid in the brown veneer exterior design. Room key cards, rental agreements, and an old Rolodex sat on the counter. A box on the floor held pencils, pens, and a large knife. I squeezed Xavier's hand at the sight of it.

The woman began singing as we came near. Her hair hung down

her back in two braids of light brown mixed with blond.

"Hello," Xavier said. The woman seemed not to sense him until he spoke, which answered the question of whether they still had that power.

"Who are you?" she asked without a hint of alarm. She wasn't afraid, because she'd easily kill us if she had to. If that became an issue, she could sound the alarm to the hotel room full of witches behind us.

"It's Xavier."

"Well, hello, old friend. It's been a while."

"You look well."

"And who knows how you look, but you sound great." I relaxed at the camaraderie between them.

"I've brought a member of the Auburn Coven with me." The witch stepped back and tilted her head to the side as she engaged all her senses. "Her name is Helene."

"How very brave of you."

"They are expecting her."

"I'll bet they are." Xavier pulled me closer to his side.

The witch motioned to the dark hallway behind her. Xavier led me away from the safety of the outside light. We passed the old staircase. The railing had been ripped off and a few stairs were missing. Down the dark hall, voices could be heard from every corner of the hotel, but nothing moved in front of us. More glass. The door to the outside had the Roman numeral seven painted on it in red. The paint had dripped before drying and now looked like blood trickling from the wound. It was the same as the doors in Maryann's house.

We stepped into the bright and shining atrium that used to house an indoor pool, a large bar, and a party space between the two. Floor-to-ceiling windows extended to the arched roof and were covered in plywood. The room was surprisingly bright and deadly silent even though I could feel the crowd surrounding us.

"Good evening," Xavier said, as if he were a formal friend of the group or the guest speaker for their monthly meeting.

"Well hello, Xavier." The woman's voice was familiar, but I couldn't place it among the other sights and sounds my mind was attempting to take in. Toilet seats were hung as a crude art installation from the ceiling over the drained and graffiti-covered pool. There were at least thirty that were staggered in height and design and swayed gently without a breeze. In front of the bar, five witches appeared. All dressed in white and sitting behind a conference table with a torn table cover and a banner that read: Welcome Class of 1991.

What a freak show.

Be respectful, Xavier thought.

Of course.

As we walked deeper into the room, our feet stuck to the floor, giving away our location. Xavier fell in behind me. The witches at the table sat straight and stopped chatting. The air around us pressed closer, and I knew we were surrounded.

"Welcome, Helene. You can show yourself. We all know what you look like." I thought it would be a concession of goodwill. I stood in front of Xavier and showed myself to the enemy in the room. "Your hair is growing back nicely."

My hands fisted at my sides.

Easy.

"What brings you by?"

"I'd like to discuss a truce." Two witches on the panel were visibly shocked. "We've all come from the same place . . . a similar history. South Jersey is a sufficiently large area to house us all. There is no need for our current—" I searched my mind for the word. "Discourse."

"A barn was burned to the ground last year. There's a reason," the witch on the end said. I recognized her as one of the witches who lived on the farm we burned.

"Someone had destroyed our daughter's dress. It was in our house in Auburn."

"Well, we didn't go into Auburn. It has been cast as sacred ground."

"As has Upper Pittsgrove." I reached up to the back of my head. "And you were certainly there."

A witch leaned forward on the table and looked across at her counterparts. They whispered and nodded in debate before she faced me. "You're confused, Helene. Upper Pittsgrove is no longer protected."

"But my mother's coven cast it."

More silence as they looked at each other. "About a year ago, we began to notice changes. Things returned to a time before your mother's coven cast their spells. At least the spells we were aware of. We never knew why, just that it had allowed us greater freedoms." She tilted her head and laughed a little at me. "I'm surprised you didn't know." My eyes wandered to the toilet seats above us to avoid making eye contact with her. The destruction we caused applied only to Clara's curse. At least that was the extent to which we knew. What else had we destroyed or unleashed that day?

"It wasn't our understanding that a witch's spell could be un-done." She hammered away at my stance. "Let alone, every spell." The reasons Clara's curse was cast, overturned, and apparently demolished every other spell in the history of a coven was my family's secret to keep.

They're telling the truth, Xavier communicated having read their minds.

"My mother's coven had special circumstances surrounding it."

"We're aware of some. It's nice to see you're all back together."

My lips pursed. I was getting nowhere. I would remind them of our common ground. "Do you have a bridge among you?"

The women at the center of the table showed recognition on their faces before they were able to mask their responses. "It's none of your business who resides in our ranks."

The air shifted. Bodies moved about the room. Xavier's heat pressed closer to my back.

"We've received messaged from the departed." I'd give them this much, but never Gw—gray skies, blue clouds, lightning. I took a deep breath. "It's our belief we share a common enemy. Have you ever heard of a man known as the hunter?"

"My grandmother told stories of families who raised their sons to hunt witches," the last witch seated at the table said. I recognized her as one of the Salem witches we'd assumed weren't part of the Virago. We'd put them on a watch list. I would have to move them when I got home, which would bring the number back to thirty. "I'm not sure. It's only a story."

"At the memorial, Emily Rottingham mentioned the hunter."

"And how do we know you're not making up this hunter to hide the crimes you've committed?"

"We have honor. A witch cannot kill another witch." Our only crime was exposing a bitter witch's weaknesses.

I needed more time. Xavier stepped closer until he was practically touching the back of my body. The toilet seats in the ceiling were similar to the clouds in the sky. Mixed with varying colors of white and gray. Swirling and chaotic.

Why do you keep thinking of the sky? Are you okay?

Instead of responding to Xavier, I addressed the panel again. "Surely, there are those among you who still believe in the honor of our craft."

"You question our honor?"

I stepped forward and felt the air move in closer behind me. "You were all born into a coven. Most of you, for years, resided there.

There must be things you miss about it." The woman directly in front of me yawned and sat back in her seat, but the witch on her side was listening with great intensity. "Just because there's been a rift in your family doesn't mean you have to be alone."

"We're not alone. We have each other."

"What I'm suggesting is a life that's as rich and loving as the one you used to live."

"What you're suggesting is impossible. We've given away the dreams of our old life in exchange for some of our powers back. There are certain requirements. As you know, these gifts don't come for free. Whether bestowed by the universe or reinstated by the Virago, there is a debt to be paid."

"I'd like to invite any witch here." I paused and looked around the silent room. "To join my family. For holidays and Sunday dinners. We play cards and share in the stories of our children's lives. We support one another. We are friends, and we are sisters. There would be no hesitation in giving up our powers to maintain the bond we share."

"Someday you might have to," the witch in the center said.

I focused on the two women to her left. "There are other options of community. Other messages of hope. You can choose to believe the singular doctrine of this committee, or you can open your mind to the other voices in the world."

"Oh, please stop. My lunch is coming up in my mouth. Why don't you run back to Auburn and guard your home?"

It was another subject that needed to be addressed. The lines of Auburn were not to be breached. "The sacred ground of Auburn was established by a coven other than my mother's. The security should stand."

"And it does. We have not been there."

My thoughts scattered with my racing heartbeat. "Then who?"

"Is it so hard to believe you're not hated by someone other than us? Perhaps it's your made-up enemy." She rolled her eyes.

"The hunter."

They hadn't been to Auburn or our home.

Sloane! I screamed in my mind. *It isn't them.* To my entire house, I screamed inside my head, *They weren't there. Come home!*

What are you doing? Xavier pleaded with me to let him in.

"We're not interested in peace, and we don't believe that's why you're really here."

"How long has it been since you've believed in sisterhood?"

The air around us whirled. And before I could take my next breath, I was tackled to my knees, gathered into a ball, and thrown back into the air. I closed my eyes and inhaled the honeysuckle scent. We careened through the room, down the dingy hall, and out the broken entrance of the hotel.

"I'm out," I yelled into the parking lot.

Trees were ripped from the ground and stacked in front of the hotel's entrance.

What's going on? Xavier thought. He eased up and turned slightly back so he could see, too.

Over his shoulder, I watched the trees burst into flames. Black smoke billowed into the air as the plywood covering the windows flew behind it. The parking lot surrounding the hotel filled with witches who were escaping the building, only to be trapped in an invisible hold at the edge of the flame.

Tara Jane's coven would exact their revenge on the Virago. Xavier turned and took off again, flying northeast toward Auburn. I hid my face in his chest. I held my breath until he landed with me still in his arms in my backyard. When he set me down, I rested my hands on my knees and gasped for air as if I'd been the one flying.

The house was empty.

Sloane. Gisel. Lovie. I called out in my mind. *Ever.* It was practically a cry. They were walking into an ambush they knew nothing about. This wasn't an enemy we'd ever faced before.

XXXI

Ever

Three hours earlier . . .

GWEN LAY UNDER MY COVERS with Carl curled up next to her. We were waiting for eight o'clock. The minutes dragged by with the silence in my mind.

I slipped in next to the two of them. "What are you doing in my bed?"

"Listening." My heart seized in my chest. If Ike was talking to her, that meant he was gone. "To your father, I think."

The breaths returned as jagged exhales. I covered my eyes with my arm. I needed Ike back. I couldn't properly function without him. I peeked out and examined Gwen. "My father?"

"Yes." She turned on her side to face me. "He said he's sorry."

"But my father has nothing to be sorry for." Except for leaving me, but it wasn't as if he did that by choice. "Your mother was different. He couldn't do it, and then there was you." Gwen spoke with absolute certainty.

"Gwen, are you sure you're talking to the right person. None of what you're saying makes sense."

"He's worried about tonight. Everyone is. The voices of all the covens before us are running rampant through my mind with concern." The Virago could even stir up fear from the dead. Gwen closed her eyes. She was tortured by the voices. "He said to give him hell."

Tears filled my eyes. "Give 'em hell, you mean."

"No." Gwen's voice leveled off. "He said 'him.'"

I held still on my bed and let the information sink in from the heavens above. If that was in fact where my father was speaking from.

"Gwen, you're sure."

She sat up and took my hand. Voices filled my mind. Crazy, constant, chaotic calls of warning and concern. "Stop," Gwen said. She inhaled deeply, and I heard, "Give him hell, Ever." It was his voice. From my childhood. The one that said, "Good night" and "I love you." I squeezed Gwen's hand tight, needing to hear more, but his voice never came.

"They'll let me think now." Gwen wrung her hands together as she spoke. Her fear was infectious.

"It's a man," I said.

Gwen's forehead scrunched. She didn't agree.

"We can't rule out there's someone doing this other than the Virago. Auburn is only sacred against their membership. Someone acting alone is something else entirely."

"The hunter," Gwen said. "Rebecca Callahan said to fear the hunter as well as the hunted."

"What if the Virago are now the hunted?" I asked, but my thoughts were already wandering to the eleven witches killed on the bus.

"I think it was the Virago," Gwen said. "It's too close to the attack on my dad."

"Or." I wasn't sure which enemy was more terrifying. "Someone who wants us to think it's the Virago." My father had told me everything I needed to know. "It's a man. Not the Virago." My mind was racing. The army we'd been facing didn't have Ike.

Gwen held her pointer finger in the air as she tilted her chin to the side. Her brow furrowed, and then she spoke with an unsure cadence. "How the evil of mankind is planted, cultivated, and spread through the world."

My mouth fell open as I fought for air. My mind chased the oxygen until it landed on the memory of the words Mr. Frank had said at the beginning of the school year. I opened the window and launched into the sky. Gwen's voice calling my name behind me disappeared as I did.

I searched every place in a fifty-mile radius that Ike and I had ever been—Dead Field, bonfires, every house around the lake, his tree house. I landed on the balcony and listened for him. If he was in the woods, I would somehow know it. I'd feel him nearby.

My mind kept spinning, though. The way Mr. Frank watched Billy and me in class. His seeming fascination with our relationship or lack thereof. *You'll lose someone, the way my mother was taken from me.* Billy's threat from the beginning of the school year emerged from my nightmares to the light of day. He'd left me alone for months. Barely looked in my direction.

Billy and Mr. Frank were in this together.

I flew back toward the school. The side door near the cafeteria was opened a crack. Through the window, I could see Mr. Frank. He had a backpack sitting on the table next to him with a gun on top of it. He was sorting through a stack of papers.

He examined the gun and put it in his bag. I stayed perfectly still until he returned to reviewing whatever was in front of him. Ike was not there. Mr. Frank would never hold someone at the school. Billy was with Ike. I could feel it in my bones. I launched again, flew across town, and over Wawa. I went by the church, the firehouse, and the football stadium. I checked the concession stand and then flew to Marlton Park and searched every building and shed for any signs Billy or Ike had been there.

Ty and his family were in Denver for his brother's graduation from the Air Force Academy. The shop in the backyard was secluded and locked. I peered in through the window and could see Ike tied to a chair. His head was bowed, and his legs were outstretched. I leaned on the wall for support as I watched Ike's body for movement. His chest rose. He was alive, and I could breathe again with the knowledge of it.

Ike, I'm right outside. I know you're at Ty's. If you can hear me, say something.

I waited. His head rolled to the left.

Ike. It's me. Talk to me.

Go away, Ever. Don't come in here. He's insane.

He . . .

Is it Billy? Alone?

Go away, Ever. He knows what you are. What my mother and my sister are. He wants to expose all of you.

I was sure that was what Billy had told him, but he didn't want to expose us as much as he wanted to *be* us. I wasn't certain of the limits to his powers, but I knew there was no limit to his cruelty.

I searched every inch of the exterior of the building. It was concrete block. Ike's head turned again, his eye flitted shut.

Is he there with you? I asked Ike.

I don't know, he weakly thought back.

Sneaking in was out of the question. I held the door handle in my hand. It had been over a year since the first time Ike had brought me to this work shed. There were secrets between us then, nothing would stand between us ever again. The locks on the other side turned and clicked into position for me to open the door. I turned the knob and pushed the door in.

I appeared, walking into the center of the room without a word. Ike lifted his head. His left eye was swollen shut. His lip was cut and bleeding. Purple bruises covered his forehead. My stomach churned at the sight of his tortured body.

"I'm here, Billy," I said loud enough for anyone close to hear. "Why don't you show yourself so we can talk?"

The stagnant air in the room moved first. It rushed toward me, and as it passed, Billy came into view running in my direction with his hand fisted near my head. I threw him against the wall, and he disappeared again, having left the fifteen feet of visibility surrounding me.

"You little witch!" he spewed from the corner of the room.

"I could say the same about you." I sensed his movement. He was leaving the corner and approaching Ike. I closed in on them, and he appeared with a knife poised at Ike's neck. His arm jerked and lodged the knife in his own thigh. Billy lay on the floor, pulled the knife from his flesh, and covered the gash in his jeans with his hand. Anger burned in his eyes as I flicked my hand, sending the knife skittering under the workbench.

I flew around the room without disappearing. Every corner, from floor to ceiling, and back again. I flew diagonally through the center and confirmed we were alone as I untied the roped around Ike's wrists with my mind.

"You can fly," Billy said with great amazement. "And you can move things with your mind."

"But you can only disappear." I landed next to him. He gritted his teeth in frustration. "Except for now." He stared at me until I thought he could kill me with his eyes.

"What time is it?" he asked.

"It's after eight."

"He'll be here soon. If none of your family shows up on Harney Street, he'll kill Ike." He snorted a little. "He'll probably kill him anyway. After the house on Harney blows up from the tragic gas leak." He shook his head in a tisk-tisk fashion.

"Mr. Frank?" Shock registered on his face. "You should be ashamed of yourself. Working with a witch hunter after what happened to your mother."

"He'll kill me, too, but who he really wants is you."

"He's never going to hurt any of us." I practically spat the words at Billy. His detached boastfulness was grating on me, and the sight of Ike was making me want to kill Billy.

"They're dead witches." His face froze into an expressionless void. He tilted it to the side and said, *"Kaboom."*

"Please. You forget that I can talk to them in my head." Billy's eyes widened. "Or maybe you never knew that since your mother never had anyone to speak to."

Ruby, don't go in the house on Harney.

Where are you?

Don't go in the house. It's set to explode. Stay out of the house.

Ever, what's going on? Where are you? We're leaving now.

"Even if they don't die today, he's going to kill all of you."

I turned back to Billy, who was watching me as if I were an experiment we were working on in lab. "That's your only power, but you know of the others because of your mother's journal."

"Don't mention her."

"She loves you."

Billy's anger melted away as he pushed himself to his feet. It was replaced with a kind, serenity that surrounded him. The hair on the back of my neck stood on end.

"Here, kitty, kitty," he said and ran toward me at full speed. I didn't have time to shift or launch into the air. He hit me hard in the midsection, and when I fell back, he landed on top of me.

Kill him, Ever.

"It didn't have to be like this," he said as his hands circled my neck.

"What else can you do?" I croaked out as his fingers lifted off my neck one by one and bent backward.

"Argh," he cried out in pain as his body lifted off me, and I threw him against the wall.

He disappeared again, and I flew to Ike. "Can you walk?"

He only shook his head, so I rested my hand on his shoulder and searched everywhere around the room using my sight, hearing, and every other sense he'd ignited. Billy couldn't come near us without being seen, but I knew he wouldn't give up.

A gun cocked from the other side of the room. My chest tightened at its warning. I squeezed Ike's shoulder and zeroed in on the distance and location of the gun's sound. My breath held in my chest. I listened for the signs of Billy's life. He'd brought a weapon he didn't have to be close to me to use.

"Billy don't do this."

I concentrated on the space between me and the origin of the gun's sound. I wouldn't be able to see the bullet to move it with my mind. The air came first. I closed my eyes and moved every particle, including the bullet, to the wall above the workbench.

I kept everything moving as another shot was fired.

"I'll kill him, and we can be together. With our powers, we can rule the world."

"I don't want to rule the world, Billy." He was always misguided. He'd been born into a family that murdered its only heart. He stepped closer to Ike and me. He couldn't beat me with the bullet from farther away, but he couldn't stay invisible if he were this close, either. Billy stepped back and forth in and out of invisibility until he calculated the limitations of the spell.

"This is new," he said. "It isn't a power. You've cast a spell. You and your galère."

"That's what you've always wanted, isn't it? A place to belong."

Billy's laugh was void of any jovial feelings. "Oh, Ever, you will never understand. How could you? Being born to a mother and father who love you?"

"Tell me, then. I'll share your pain, Billy."

"You already share more than you realize. Disappearing is not my only power. I could read the words in my mother's books."

A book came flying through the air and became visible in enough time for me to catch it before it hit my face. I didn't open it. I had to keep my focus on Billy and whatever else he fired my way.

"Open it," he demanded.

"Why don't you just tell me what it says?" I put a few feet between Ike and myself. I wanted Billy to come into view, for the gun to be vulnerable.

"My mother knew your father." He lied again. He'd taken my only living weakness to this workshop and beat him, and was trying to use my dead father against me. "He wasn't just a marine. He was a witch hunter, exposing witches had been a profession in his family since before the Civil War. He was good at it, too. Until he met your mother."

"Billy, this is pathetic."

"Read the book, Ever."

"Give me the gun, and I'll read it."

He laughed. "Instead of killing your mother the way he had mine, he fell in love with her, and then you came along."

Billy stepped into view and just as quickly fell back and invisible. I focused on the area he'd just been standing in.

"This is where the story turns tragic. So, the witch hunter falls in love with a witch and has a daughter, but the one witch who turned him was the one cursed to kill him. Your father died because he didn't kill your mother first."

"It's like fiction is your calling."

"Read the book," he roared from the corner behind me.

I spun around. "If he killed your mother before he met mine, how is it even in the book?"

"My mother was a special kind of witch. She was a bridge. It was written when the four of you were born. When your grandmothers couldn't witness your lives from heaven any longer, but it wasn't until you moved home that it appeared in my house. I think my mother thought I'd help you, and you'd save me." Billy had an ironic smile. He shrugged as if he were talking about a television show episode from the night before. "The departed tried to warn my mother about him. She wrote it all down, but she couldn't protect herself alone, and then she left me here with a monster."

I faltered a step. I grabbed the chair in front of me. *Give him hell.*

Billy stepped into view with the gun pointed at Ike's head. I ripped it from his hand and held him in the air. The gun dropped as he hovered above Ike.

"You'll never get out of here alive with him," Billy said.

A shot rang out. Billy's body fell to the floor of the shop.

Ike was holding the gun in his free hand. His eyes were fixed on me. "A witch can't kill another witch, but I can."

Billy lay lifeless on the floor next to Ike's feet that were still tied to the chair legs. "What?" My mind fought to take it all in. Ike killed Billy. Billy was dead.

"I was just keeping my promise." I ripped my sight from Billy's open and empty eyes and faced the love of my life. Ike's stare bore into me. Horror, either at the situation or what he'd done, settled onto his bruised face. His breaths were shallow.

"To who?"

"To him." He glanced down at Billy in disgust. "I told him a year ago if he ever touched you again, I'd kill him."

Everything I knew about honor slipped away as I beheld the man who would take a life for me. "Ike." I kissed the side of his face and his forehead. He winced. "What's hurt?" I ran my hand down his arm and over his thigh. I leaned back and looked at his feet.

Ever, I need you to say something, Ruby thought with a desperate voice.

I rested my head on Ike's shoulder to touch him in as many places as I could. *I have Ike. He's alive. Billy is not.*

Oh . . . Thank God. What is Mr. Frank doing here?

He's the hunter, and he has the house set to explode once you're in there, I said.

An eerie pause filled my mind followed by the knowledge of the closure Ruby was capable of providing. *Say the word, and he'll never hunt again.* It was an offer only Ruby could make. She wanted to kill him, but because Ike had been taken from me, she'd let me decide his fate.

May God forgive me. *Keep him inside,* I told my fire witch.

"Sorry." I focused back on Ike. "What hurts?" I ran my hand down his arms and legs, gently feeling for any wounds. Ike could barely hold his head up.

"If I had to guess, I have some cracked ribs and a concussion." He swallowed hard.

I touched his swollen and bloodied lips. "Ike, not hearing your voice almost killed me. You can never stop speaking to me again."

He rested his hand on my back.

"Why didn't you answer me?"

"I told you. I didn't want you anywhere near Billy Roberts."

"You're impossible."

"I love you." The statement hit me the same way it did every time he'd ever said it before.

"You're a lover." I kissed his bruised forehead.

Wow, Ruby thought. *Explode it did. Where are you?*

The shop behind Ty's house. I could use some help over here.

We're on our way.

"I can't wait to get you out of here." I looked around the shop, hoping the solution on how to move him was somewhere nearby.

By the way, my mother is going to kill you for going alone.

I lowered my head almost to his lap.

"What?" he asked. "What's wrong?"

"Nothing now."

"Ike!" his mother screamed as she flew into the room.

"Oh, good," Ike said. His sarcasm was beautiful evidence he was still exactly the same as the last time I'd seen him, but his voice was weakening.

She practically tripped over Billy's body as she made her way to her only son.

"None of this is good." She kissed him on the cheek and then turned his head with the tip of her finger to see his injured eye. "I'm going to kill someone."

"I already did," Ike said. His voice was soft and low. Gisel looked at Billy, who was lying on the floor in a pool of blood.

"We have to get you to the hospital and get this place cleaned up. Where is Ty?"

"They're gone through the weekend."

"Where's that horrible motorcycle of yours?"

"The last I saw it, it was at Rowan."

"We're going to need it."

Ruby appeared as we were helping Ike out of the chair he'd been tied to for days. She didn't say a word, only looked from Ike to me with sympathy. She stepped behind us and spat on Billy's face.

"Do you know how to ride a motorcycle?"

"Are *you* asking? Or my mom?"

"I am," Gisel said.

"I can get it. Where's the key?"

"In my dorm. The top drawer of my desk."

"Do you need help?" I asked, knowing I wouldn't be able to leave Ike's side if she did.

"No. I've got it. I'll be back in a few."

"Hurry. I want to get him to the hospital as soon as possible."

"Mom, I'm fine." Ike rolled his good eye.

Helene

*W*E HAVE HIM. HE'S OKAY. *Come to Ty's house on Stewart Road when you can. Bring the minivan. The Virago are all worked up tonight.*

Xavier was still standing behind me in the backyard, waiting for me to look him in the eyes, but I couldn't.

"You can't face me unless you're lying to me."

I turned. "I'm sorry." He deserved so much more, but today was the one day I couldn't give it to him.

"We could have been killed. I took you there thinking I knew what was going on. They're not going to let this go." He wasn't afraid of the Virago. He was irate with me. "What have you done? Why?"

"Someone took Ike. Ever and the rest of my house went to find him. We thought it was the Virago, and we wanted to make sure the majority of them were not available when they went.

"You used me." His glare bore into me.

"I had no choice. They wouldn't meet with me unless you arranged it."

"That isn't what I'm talking about. Why couldn't you tell me the truth, even if you kept it from them?"

My mind betrayed me and the look on Sloane's face when she said I shouldn't trust him came back to me. It was followed by Gisel's warnings and the final decision to exclude Xavier from the plan. I couldn't have kept it from him forever, but I didn't want to hurt him.

He walked over until he was in front of me. His height and power were on full display. I leaned back on my heels. My muscles tightened.

"My God, Helene. I would *never* hurt you." He was appalled by my reaction to him.

"I know." I closed my eyes, trying to regain my sanity. "It's this day. It's playing with my mind."

"How have you kept this from me?" He tilted his head, putting the pieces together.

"I asked Ever to teach me how to hide my thoughts."

"The sky . . ." He closed his eyes and shook his head in disgust. "I've been a fool."

I reached up and grabbed his face, forcing him to look at me. "No you haven't. I love you."

"Obviously not, Helene, or maybe you've forgotten what it means to love someone."

"You can't understand because you've never had a child. She was in danger. Gisel's son was missing. I couldn't take any chances with them."

"You shouldn't have viewed me as a chance. I would have protected Ever as my own, because she is yours."

"I know that! I'm sorry. We didn't have a lot of time, and there were more than my feelings to consider."

"There always are with your coven." He turned to walk away. "Did *he* know?"

"Ike is his son." I wouldn't lie again and tell him Isaiah had been excluded. "Xavier, please don't go."

"Why don't you focus on the sky some more?" He disappeared and left me standing by the fire pit in my backyard. I wasn't sure if he'd taken off or how far he'd flown, only that the world was an empty place without him.

I wanted to throw up, and I would have if I allowed myself even a second more to think about what Xavier's leaving meant. Later. I would try to fix this later. Instead of wallowing, I went to Ty's house and helped removed any evidence that we'd ever been there. Billy's body was taken by Sloane and Lovie, never to be seen again. Once I was positive there wasn't even a hint that something had happened in the room, I flew home and waited for Ever to return. They were at the hospital with Ike, waiting for him to be treated for the injuries he'd sustained in his motorcycle accident. I should have gone, too, but there were enough worried souls desperate for his release.

My mother's coven's spells had been overturned.

I flipped on the basement light and descended the stairs as if I was entering the kingdom of the dead. The last remaining remnants of my mother's coven's spells were preserved in a coffee can on the shelf in the basement. It held a small notebook and a votive candle. I pulled out the sheets of paper, which seemingly held a recipe for banana bread and a bulk of blank pages. I stared at it until it transformed in my mind to a list of spells.

"What are you doing down here?" Sloane asked.

"When we overturned the curse, every spell our mothers' coven cast was reversed as well.

"What?"

"I'm afraid you heard me." I focused on the list in front of me.

The first line read: Reinforce structure of Borough Hall.

The historic building in the center of Woodstown had partially collapsed during the storm that ensued when we overturned the curse. The list of other spells was four pages long.

The second line read: Stop the voices in Evan's head.

"I'm going to throw up." I ran upstairs and heaved into the kitchen trashcan.

Ever

I WATCHED HIM SLEEP. COUNTED every breath Ike took. Memorized the shape of his lips and the movements of his closed eyes. I clung to him. I could have lost him. If it weren't for my father's warning . . .

Ike's arm twitched. I ran my hand up it and kissed his shoulder. We were sleeping in his mom's bed until he healed. No one even blinked an eye when I moved my blanket and pillow in there with him. They'd let me stay home from school for two days, but tomorrow, I'd have to return. Somehow, I'd leave him in the capable hands of both his parents and the rest of our family. The thought of walking out the door tore at me. I couldn't spend eight hours in the Woodstown High School when the place I belonged was right next to Ike.

The prom was the following weekend. I wasn't going without

him, which meant I wasn't going at all. I hadn't told anyone because I knew there would be arguments from everyone, including Ike. It was perfectly clear in my mind. I was going to be where Ike was. Not at a dance I couldn't care less about. We could sell my dress online for all I cared.

I had just finalized my resolve when my mother stuck her head in the room. She saw Ike was sleeping and closed the door again without a sound. I slipped out from under the covers and followed her down the hall and into her room.

"He's getting stronger every day," she said.

"He's doing great." I fell onto her bed. "How are you doing?" Rebecca Callahan's journals were stacked on top of each other on her nightstand.

"I'm not sure. I think I might be numb. I'm afraid to let myself feel anything."

"He loved us. He said he was sorry." My father's role in Rebecca's death and the murders of six other witches had been detailed in the journal. My mother would have been number eight.

"So much about his family, his father in particular, makes sense now."

"Grandpop asked me once if I thought I could fly."

"He did?" She sat on her bed with me. "When?"

"When we went to the lake with them over summer break. I was standing on the end of the dock and looking at the sky."

"You were six that summer."

"I know, and I could fly."

"What did you tell him?"

"I told him only witches could fly."

"Oh Ever, your father would have killed you."

"Apparently, for real. I wonder what Grandpop would have done if he'd found out. Do you think he'd kill his own blood?"

She picked up the top journal and flipped through the pages. "I honestly don't know. Based on the way your father hid our powers, maybe."

"That's so sick." I never felt that warm "Pop Pop" thing with my grandfather, so him being a hunter explained my natural aversion to him. "Mr. Frank wanted to avenge Dad's death?"

"I suppose he knew that he would get the whole coven if he could get to you."

"Are there others out there?" What I was really asking was would I ever be able to sleep again and know Ike was okay. That he'd come home from work and love me the way he had when he'd left in the morning. If my children would be safe. Witch hunters were a new enemy. One I wanted no part of.

"I don't know." She dropped the book and hugged me. "We're trying to find out as much as we can about them. We can't be the first coven to survive a meeting with a hunter." She let me go and shook her head in disgust. "How could I not have seen it?" She exhaled loudly. "I am terrible at choosing men."

"Have you talked to Xavier?"

"He won't speak to me, and I don't blame him."

"Well, you didn't choose him. If I have the story right, he found you. A couple of times."

"He feels betrayed. By me. I did this."

"Didn't you tell me that he'd never fight the Virago? That they coexisted because they stayed out of each other's way?"

"Yes."

"So, you didn't ask him to fight. The Kingsway Coven feel the same way we do, and they were willing to kill the Virago if they had to."

"I thought they were going to trap them in that hotel and let them burn to death."

"The way Mr. Frank died in his explosion?" I asked.

"That's different. He wasn't a witch." In my mind, neither were the Virago.

"Well, Maryann let them out."

"Thank, God. From what Tara Jane said, not a moment too soon."

"She made her point." And Ruby made hers.

"We need you downstairs." Sloane came in to get my mother. "We're working on a master list of spells." It was disturbing. The life's work of our ancestors erased because of us.

"I gave you guys all that I knew. It's Clara's list that we have no idea about."

"Lovie found notes from her mother in the box that held her jewelry. We need to compare everything we have archived."

"I'm coming," my mother said. She labored to get off the bed as if movement of any kind was the enemy. She was pale. I'd neglected her and everyone else around us with my obsession with Ike's progress.

"Are you okay, Mom?"

"I'm exhausted." I waited for her to say more. I thought she was going to, but she took a step toward the door.

"He'll forgive you."

"I'm not sure that he will." She stepped into the hallway and then stuck her head back in. "I haven't forgotten the prom is this weekend."

I sat up, ready to argue. "You should. I'm not going."

"I wouldn't either if I were you."

"Go see Xavier."

"Maybe this weekend."

XXXIV

Helene

I FLEW TO HIS HOUSE. He wouldn't answer my calls, not in my head or on the phone. I knew how he felt. I'd been betrayed before, and I spent the next twenty years trying not to accept anything that might lead to an apology about it. I didn't want to let go of the hurt and anger, because it meant letting go of the rest of it, and that would have crushed me more than the pain.

He was in the backyard throwing balls for the dogs to fetch and bring back to him. He pried one from Pickle's mouth and tossed it toward the trees at the back of his property. His head tilted toward the sky as I hovered above him. He turned and took a step toward the house, causing my chest to tighten.

"Xavier, wait." I showed myself and landed in front of him. "Please. Hear me out, and then if you don't want to see me again, I'll leave and never come back."

"Helene, there's nothing to be said."

"I'm only asking for a few minutes." I slipped my fingertips into his half-clenched palm and pulled him toward the chairs on the patio, but Xavier didn't sit. "I always trusted you." He practically swallowed me with his eyes. I just wanted him to love me again. To feel his warmth instead of the emptiness he'd left me with when he'd abandoned me in my yard.

At the hearing of my thoughts, Xavier's head hung, and he focused on a spot on the pavers between us. "Helene, I've never believed in anyone before. No one except the woman who raised me. Telling you my whole identity was a tremendous risk. Territory I wasn't prepared or equipped to navigate, but I did it because I wanted you more than I wanted to keep my secret safe."

"I know. You deserved better." I took a step closer to him, and he held his hand up between us. "Xavier, I know you've heard my thoughts. You can read my mind right now. There's nothing but pain for how this turned out. Hurting you or betraying you was never my intention."

"You knew that's exactly what you were doing, though."

"I had to."

"You didn't."

"I couldn't take that chance. This wasn't about you and me or your secret. It was about keeping Ever safe, and that never depends on the cost to me."

He huffed a little. "Which I will never understand because I've never had a child." He was so incredibly alone and willing to stay that way to never be vulnerable again.

I'd come to tell him the truth, and I'd let it speak now. I pushed his hand away and stepped closer to him. I looked up into his tortured eyes.

I love you. I thought. He stood unwavering before me. He'd let me go and live his life without me to protect himself, but he didn't have that luxury anymore. History was a hellion, and in this case, I'd take it.

I thought the only other truth I needed him to hear: *I'm pregnant*.

The Spells of Clara's Coven

THE DEAD FIELD SPELL

At the age of thirty-five.

"WHO IS TAKING HELENE TO homecoming?" Poppy asked as she licked the batter off the spatula. It was so much easier this year. Now that the girls were sophomores, they knew everyone in Woodstown High School. It was their school. Helene, Lovie, Gisel, and Sloane loved it as much as we had.

"Dan Furfari." Although I was surprised it wasn't Isaiah Kennedy. I could tell by the way that boy looked at my daughter it was only a matter of time.

"Tony Furfari's kid?"

"Barely a kid any more. They're all turning sixteen this year, but yes. Tony and Mary Lou's youngest.

"How many did she have?"

"Three boys. Poor woman." We watched as our four girls ran around, exchanging earrings. Sloane was putting the finishing touches on Gisel's hair when Clara walked in with a scowl on her face.

"What's wrong?" Poppy asked.

"Nothing now. I'm glad to be over here. My mother is driving me crazy." She inhaled deeply the aroma of the cake baking in the oven. "And I don't want Lovie to ever hear me complaining about my mother because she never even knew hers."

There were mornings I woke up still ready to tell her something. Sixteen years and I could almost feel her next to me during the moments of quiet. Sometimes, I thought she was with me when I was flying alone. Her death made the least sense of every unknown in this world. "I still miss Bonnie every day."

"Every single day," Poppy said.

"I know you guys think I'm crazy, but I swear she spoke to me this morning. Told me to have Lovie wear her brooch if she wanted to," Clara said.

I longed to hear Bonnie's voice or be near her warmth that could penetrate everything cold in this world. The fact that she'd died bringing her little witch into the world she helped brighten was especially cruel. We helped Lovie's father pick her name. It honored Bonnie's spirit better than any other. He'd also given us Bonnie's jewelry at the time of her death to keep safe for Lovie. I think even back then, he'd known we'd outlast him. "Do you have it?"

"I do, but do you think it's going to make her sad? She's waiting for her homecoming date. Do I have to bring up her dead mother?"

"Go see if it matches her dress," Poppy said and watched a sedan pull up to the curb in front of the house. "They're here."

Dan Furfari, who was followed by his parents and the families of three other dates, came through the front door like a parade from our past with the bright and beautiful floats of our present. Each boy held a corsage and a nervous smile.

Clara took over our beloved Bonnie's role with the jewelry and the snacks. She offered drinks and cookies as pictures were taken. It would be weeks before we got around to having them developed, but none of us minded. We should have invested in one of those new video cameras.

"So, Helene tells me you're building a new house?"

Mary Lou rolled her eyes. "We're trying. Been trying for years it seems like."

"Has the process been difficult?" Poppy asked. "I hear it's a huge undertaking."

"The house is a lot of work, and we've never done it before. You know. No one ever needs a new house around here. The real problem has been the land."

"But both your families have plenty of land out there," I said, not understanding.

"We chose one parcel because it never held a good crop, but the soil tests came back and said there's too much arsenic in the ground to build." I cringed. "At least we know why nothing grows there."

"I've never heard of that."

"Now that it's happened to us, I'm hearing of it more. We went around and around about it and finally broke ground down the road from the original spot. Every time I drive by there, it makes me sad, though. I call it Dead Field."

"Mary Lou, are you still complaining about that field?"

"Be quiet, Tony!" Mary Lou laughed at her husband. She straightened Dan's tie one last time before the kids dispersed into cars to be driven to the dance.

"We'll pick the girls up," I said. Helene shot me a look. I'd already promised all four of them that they could fly home. I winked at her. I couldn't very well tell Mary Lou they were flying.

When the house was quiet and my cake was out of the oven, Poppy, Clara, and I decided to take a flight of our own. We flew over the high school and out of town toward Upper Pittsgrove until we landed near the construction site of Tony and Mary Lou's new home. Just down the road was Dead Field.

We flew over it. I inhaled deeply, trying to detect the arsenic Mary Lou spoke of, but I'd only heard about it in spy novels. There was nothing there but barren ground under our feet when we landed.

"I can see how this would drive her crazy. A perfectly good piece of ground taunting her every day that she lives nearby."

Let's change it, Poppy thought.

Clara opened her mouth to argue. I only smiled at Poppy to let her know I was on her side.

Just to let something grow. We won't get involved in the future of the field. It can still be dead, just with a little life in it. Poppy waited for Clara to roll her eyes and agree.

We closed our eyes and stood in a circle holding hands. Every time we did this, Bonnie's absence tore my heart into another tiny piece. *Bonnie would have loved this.*

She would have, Clara thought and squeezed my hand.

Dead field, arsenic abound
Spare the flowers in her ground
Overcome what man has done
Growing more, rise to the sun

EVAN'S VOICES IN
HIS HEAD SPELL

At the age of sixteen.

BONNIE BROUGHT EVAN INTO MY bedroom. No one would be home at my house until after dark. If my mother or father had come home early, he'd have to jump out the window because I was not getting in trouble for having a boy in my room for Evan. I wasn't even in love with him.

"I hear them all the time," he said, and I felt guilty. I wouldn't make him jump. He needed us, and although I wasn't in love with him, I did love him. He was one of only seven kids that went from Oldmans Middle School to Woodstown High School as a sending district, which made us all part of an extremely small club of outsiders. "Even when I know it isn't real, I listen."

"What do they say?" Poppy asked. She had an old psychology book on her lap and was leafing through the pages. The headings that caught my eye were schizophrenia and bipolar disorder. She stopped on a summary page and listened.

"They tell me I'm a star in a Broadway show. They say I'm being watched and listened to by the Soviet Union. They know I hate my father, and sometimes they tell me that I hate myself."

"Oh, Evan." Bonnie rubbed his back.

"Yesterday, when you found me sitting by the crick, they said that I should kill myself."

"No." Came flying out of my mouth. "You can't listen to those voices." I wanted to scream, "They're crazy," but I was afraid he would connect the dots that the voices were only a part of him. It was all in his head.

"I know." He nodded and stared at his hands, which were propped up on his knees. "I know it's all fake. My mother tells me every morning not to listen, but they won't stop. I get so tired. By the end of the day, I start to believe them."

"We're going to try something," Poppy said. "Just stay sitting right where you are. Don't move. Okay?"

With Evan not saying a word, we sat in a circle around him on my floor. We held hands and closed our eyes. We could stop the hate in the voices of Evan's mind. We could make them be kind, the same way he had always been to us.

We chanted:

Stop the hate, the horror, the fear
Hear God's words that strum in your ear
Never again, the awful words spoken
Mute your mind to thoughts that are broken

We said the verses three times, not sure if their results were enough to save Evan. We'd never known anyone like him. The voices in our heads were only each other's. The doctors couldn't help Evan, and he almost died yesterday. Tomorrow, he'd try again. We were sure of it. Unless the words of our spell could change the conversation in his mind.

Evan graduated. He went on to become a doctor, specializing in the brain and the disorders that affect it. He was a psychiatrist and practiced out of the University of Pennsylvania hospital, but he kept his home in Pilesgrove. He married and gave birth to a son he named Evan junior. Evan Jr. married a woman from Alloway named Nicole, and they had three daughters. The middle girl would be named Chrissy and become a cheerleader at Woodstown High School.

THE CRACK AT
BOROUGH HALL SPELL

At the age of eleven.

CLARA'S FATHER COMPLAINED EVERY MINUTE of every day. It was worse when he drank, which was only on Fridays and Sundays after two o'clock. The other days it was his normal lamenting about everything that was wrong with the world. It was so ingrained in her life, Clara barely seemed to notice his spewing or her mother's arguing with him. We only spent a few minutes at Clara's when we went to get her. More if her mother had baked cinnamon rolls, but mainly, we hopped between Bonnie's and Poppy's and my houses, spending most of our time outdoors if the weather allowed.

"That building is going to kill someone. Damn crack has been there for six months now. It's right across the foundation. I'm telling you, Edna . . ." He shook his head and sneered with his top lip almost touching his nose. "That building's going to fall one day. Mark my words, and just pray I'm not in it."

"Oh, I'm praying," Clara's mom said and laughed. I wasn't quite sure what was funny.

"They won't stop," Clara said as we walked out the door. "He goes on and on about this crack in the foundation. That building has been around forever. It's going to fall down from age, not some crack."

"Maybe he's right," Bonnie said. "Let's go see it."

"No." Poppy put the kickstand up on her bike. "We have much better things to do."

"We'll do all of them, but first, let's go see the crack that's driving Clara's dad crazy. It must really be something," Bonnie wasn't relenting, and she rarely had a strong opinion on where we went or what we did, so we went.

We rode our bikes out of Auburn and into the town of Woodstown. It felt like we were going five miles an hour. We probably were, but compared to soaring through the air, it was a snail's pace. Poppy was very patient and didn't complain the entire ride. After all, complaining is what had brought us there in the first place.

We parked our bikes behind the building and walked all the way around, looking for a crack in the foundation. Bonnie was the only one of us who even knew what a foundation was. Instead of looking down, I stepped back from the building and eyed the copper weathervane sticking out from the cupola on the roof. It pointed west. I tipped my chin toward the sky and felt for the air.

"Is that it?" Clara asked.

I was afraid it was a crack you could only see from inside the basement, but then, behind the bushes on the back corner, I saw it. It was a black line that thickened and thinned as it crawled up diagonally from the ground to the brick above it.

"It is," I said.

"That's it?" Poppy stood next to the wall and held her hand out flat toward the crack. "This is what your father has been spouting off about for months?" We all just stared at the crack. "Your poor mother."

"I know. The woman is a saint."

From the top of the building, to as far as I could see in every direction, we were alone. "Let's fix it," I said.

"I didn't realize you were an eleven-year-old engineer." Poppy refuted my plan without even knowing the details.

"Well, something is causing the foundation to crack. Let's halt that from happening. Shifting earth, settling ground. We'll cover a few of the obvious reasons and maybe it will stop the damage."

"It's certainly not going to hurt anyone," Bonnie said and took Clara's and my hands. We waited for Poppy to join the circle. "We need a spell." Poppy usually wrote them. She was rhyming before she was speaking in whole sentences. They came easy to her.

She rolled her eyes. "I'm not some carnival show, you know."

"Just give us a spell," I said. My voice was gentle and light, reminding her it was summer and merely a crack in the wall. There'd been enough complaining about it already.

Shifting earth, settling the ground
Where you are may never be found
Stay solid, lifted, and strong
Absent cracks, here for so long

We recited it in our heads. Over and over until we all stopped. We could feel the spell in place.

Borough Hall held strong through decades of hurricanes, tropical storms, and even a few tornadoes. Hurricane's Floyd and Sandy did nothing to topple the building, but the storm last May, caused the entire side to crumble. It fell right to the ground as if the foundation were made of cookies stacked one on top of the other.

THE GETTYSBURG SPELL

At the age of ten.

CLARA AND BONNIE SAT IN the seat in front of us. Clara almost always sat with Bonnie. She was patient with Clara and would play with her hair when she got upset. Even back in second grade, Bonnie knew just how to soothe Clara, making sure she caught her on the first sight of a lip quiver. Usually, it was Clark Mattson who took the brunt of it. If he butted in line for kickball or threw sand at her, Clara's reaction was always swift.

Poppy leaned down in her seat and pulled me down by my pigtails. "I am in love with Jimmy Turner."

"No you are not," I whispered.

"I am. I can tell. I've been reading the books my mother keeps by her bed, and I feel the same way about Jimmy as Audrey Lawrence felt about Oliver Pritchett in *The Last Song*."

"I don't know who any of those people are, but I know they are fictional. I'm not sure you should take love advice from books written specifically about love."

"That makes no sense," Poppy said.

Hector Villafane leaned over into our seat from his across the aisle. "Do you guys want some mango slices?" he asked. Poppy peered over the seat top. "No one can see us. They're dried."

I had never had dried fruit before. Neither had Poppy. I'd been privy to every piece of food that ever entered the girl's mouth. Corn on the cob was her favorite.

"Thank you, Hector," I said and took a slice of mango. It didn't taste like real fruit. It was drier. Less juicy.

"What are you doing? You're not allowed to eat on the bus."

"Relax, Clara. Don't get all worked up. We're tired from touring Gettysburg, and we're enjoying a slice of dried fruit," Poppy said. She wasn't sweet like Bonnie, but who was. "We're not back here smoking cigarettes and cussin'."

"Yet," Hector said, and Clara's cheeks turned red.

Bonnie's head popped up over the seat as the teacher at the front of the bus yelled, "Everyone sit down. There's a lot of traffic and we need everyone in their seats for a safe ride home."

Clara rolled her eyes.

Bonnie winked at me. She had just mastered the skill, and she winked at each of us at least once a day.

The bus tires screeched as they locked up against the pavement beneath us. The bus turned, traveled down the highway sideways, and rolled over again and again before coming to rest in the grassy median between the north and south lanes of Interstate 95.

My face was on my left hand on the seat Poppy and I had been sitting in. She was under my legs and against the window that was pressed into the ground. There was less life on the bus than a moment before.

Bonnie screamed out, "No!"

The other children's voices followed in the wake of her despair. There were sobs and questions and names of our classmates. We'd come all the way from Auburn to tour the battlefields of Gettysburg and had almost made it home.

A dried piece of mango rested on the window beside Poppy's head.

"Are you okay?" I asked, but my voice was weak. My stomach hurt, and both my shoulders throbbed.

Poppy nodded and attempted to get her legs under her. I searched for which way was up and flew just inches away. My body would always know the way to the sky.

Bonnie was crouched near the window with her hands covering her head.

"It okay. We're okay." I pulled her hand away from her head and kissed her forehead the way my mother would have done if she were there. "Bonnie, where's Clara? Do you see her?"

The doors had opened in the back of the bus, and the front sliding one was bent in half on the grass between us and the highway. Several windows were broken. Glass and jagged edges covered the surfaces of the bus. I flew forward, letting my feet touch the edges of the seats, and found the driver with his seatbelt still buckled. Nothing about him seemed alive. I searched for our teacher, but Mr. Tessmer was nowhere to be found.

A man I'd never seen before pulled himself up the side of the bus and stuck his head in the doorway with the missing door.

"Hi," he said. His voice was gentle. "Are you hurt?" I stared at him. "My name is Mr. Madden. I'm going to help you guys, okay?" I nodded. "It's a bunch of little kids!" he yelled back over his shoulder. "Can you move back so I can climb in with you?" I did as he asked and gave him room.

I flew, still touching all the seats with my feet and searched for Clara. She had crawled over next to Bonnie and was lying with her head on her lap. "Clara." Her head was bleeding. She held out her hand to me, and I took it. "We're all okay. The four of us. We need to help the others."

"Their voices," Clara whispered. "They won't stop crying in

my head."

I moved in closer to Clara. The pain in her eyes was hurting me. "Who?" I whispered back.

"Frank and Linda and Angel and Jeannie. I can hear them, but only in my head. The bus driver's voice keeps coming through, but I can't understand what he's saying." She clasped her hands over her ears and shook her head. "And Brian and Diana. They all keep talking to me."

"What are they saying?"

A tear rolled down Clara's cheek. "Goodbye."

Mr. Madden awkwardly moved through the mangled bus until he was next to me. "Where was your teacher sitting?"

I held Clara tight against my body and faced Mr. Madden. "He was up front with the driver, but I haven't found him."

Mr. Madden took in the whole bus with his eyes. He looked from one corner to the next and listened to the children crying around us. When he looked at me again, his eyes widened with the details of the disaster now trapped inside his head.

"There were twenty-one of us on the bus," Poppy said. "We are Mr. Tessmer's fourth grade class from Oldmans Elementary School in Pedricktown, New Jersey."

"That's good," he said, but he didn't look at Poppy when he spoke. He was staring at Linda in the seat next to us. She hadn't moved since the crash. "Twenty-one not including Mr. Tessmer and the bus driver."

"Okay." He was coming around, regaining his bearings. "I'm going to help you climb off the bus to the people who are waiting outside."

"Why don't you take the others first?" Clara said. "We'll be fine as long as we're together."

"I'm going to go see which of our friends needs the most help." I stood and climbed over Mr. Madden. He followed me as we made our way over the seat tops.

"If you can walk, move toward the back of the bus. There are adults there that are going to help you off."

"What about my backpack? It has my snacks," Adam asked.

"Leave it," Mr. Madden said before I had the chance to yell at Adam.

We watched Mr. Madden lift the other kids out of the bus. Sirens descended on us. Other adults came in. They carried boxes with handles like small suitcases, but they were white with reflective stickers on them like the decals on my bike. The boxes opened like a tackle box, and inside them was every type of Band-Aid in existence. Of the children who could walk, Poppy, Clara, Bonnie, and I were the last to be taken off the bus. We helped a policeman write down each of our names on a piece of paper and identify all the kids who were still inside being helped by the paramedics. Everyone was accounted for but Mr. Tessmer and Hector Villafane.

"He was sitting right next to us," Bonnie said.

"We'll find him," Mr. Madden said and was taken away by a policeman to answer questions. "Sit right there. Don't let anyone wander away, okay?" he called back over his shoulder, but we had to find Hector.

I could go. Fly around and look for him, Poppy thought.

My leg hurts. I think it's broken. Clara hadn't even mentioned it on the bus, but she was gritting her teeth as she spoke. The pain must have been horrible. Clara was trying hard not to cry.

"This is the teacher!" a man yelled out from the ditch on the other side of the road.

"Any sign of the boy?"

He didn't call back, only shook his head and kept walking the grass near the highway as the paramedics rushed to Mr. Tessmer.

Women from every car we could see were suddenly tending to us. Their attention made it impossible for any of us to fly. We needed to find Hector.

We'll do a spell.

We'll have to think it without speaking.

When the women had moved on to the rest of the children in our line, we held hands. One woman elbowed another, having her look at us as if we were enchanting in some way, but we just huddled closer as if we were comforting each other.

Seeking Hector to be found

Zero sightings, not a sound

May the sunbeam guide us there

Fast enough, his life to spare

Poppy said it in our heads. We kept silently repeating it until the clouds broke open and a sliver of light shined through unbelievably far down the road from us.

"Check down there." Bonnie pointed toward the light.

No one paid attention but Mr. Madden. We'd been in this together since the beginning. He'd go look just to keep us calm. He was our ally because he found us first. Mr. Madden paused and stared at us. I listened hard in case he was trying to tell me something inside his head, but none of his words came to mind. He walked at a brisk pace toward the light, stepping over debris we couldn't see before disappearing into the tall grass.

"Over here. Send the ambulance over here."

Men ran toward him, circling around. The paramedics were the last to get there, but Hector was loaded into the first ambulance to leave the side of the road.

Poppy's mom and mine took the four of us to see Hector in the hospital. He said the doctor told him he could have died if they hadn't found him when they did. Mr. Madden was there. He'd driven up from Virginia Beach, which was where he lived, to check on Hector.

"Well, there are my little heroes," he said when he saw us. "The four of you were so brave." I introduced him to my mother and Poppy. "I'm afraid I never got your name," he leaned down and said to me.

I liked Mr. Madden. He was helpful without being controlling, and he only asked the right questions, not the ones that made us quiet about our powers. Because of all this, I told him, "My name is Elizabeth, but you can call me Eliza."

BONUS MATERIAL

The Witches of Auburn

Ever	Helene	Eliza
Ruby	Sloane	Poppy
Maya	Lovie	Bonnie
Gwen	Gisel	Clara

The Kingsway Coven

Jennifer
Maryann
Riley
Tara Jane

Acknowledgements

THE TREMENDOUS NUMBER OF HOURS that have gone into these witches did not belong only to me. As with the first book, there are many people to thank.

Beth Rey, for sharing Rowan University with me and her memories of the undergraduate world. It was a pleasure to bask in that time with you.

Darian and Becca for their keen scene location scouting.

The dozens of people who tolerated random questions about their work, schools, and daily life. Thanks especially to Gabrielle Hastings for enduring more than the rest.

Jill, for your poetic gifts and unending patience.

Kate, for your creative eye and gift with words.

And Maryann. Please don't block my contact. Although, I won't promise to change my ways. I have interrupted your vacations, happy hours, and family time for your opinions on the witches' lives, and as always, you were generous with your brilliance. Also, thanks for letting me hang out with the Kingsway Coven. *Always* a good time.

Ashley Williams. Your love of witches almost equals your gift for editing. Thank you, thank you, thank you.

And finally, to John, my #hotaccountant. You are so much more than that.

HAZEL BLACK

HAZEL BLACK GRADUATED FROM RUTGERS University and returned to her hometown in rural South Jersey. Her mother encouraged her to take some time and find herself. After three months of searching, she began to bounce checks, her neighbors began to talk, and her mother told her to find a job.

She settled into corporate America, learning systems and practices and the bureaucracy that slows them. Hazel quickly discovered her creativity and gift for story telling as a corporate trainer and spent years perfecting her presentation skills and studying diversity. It was during this time she became an avid observer of the characters she met and the heartaches they endured. Her years of study taught her that laughter, even the completely inappropriate kind, was the key to survival.